Kiss & Tell

ALAIN DE BOTTON was born in 1969, educated at Cambridge and lives in London. He is the author of *Essays in Love* (1993) and *The Romantic Movement* (1994). His work is translated into fourteen languages.

Also by Alain de Botton

Essays in Love

The Romantic Movement

ALAIN DE BOTTON

Kiss & Tell

PICADOR

First published 1995 by Macmillan

This edition published 1996 by Picador
an imprint of Macmillan General Books
25 Eccleston Place, London SW1W 9NF
and Basingstoke

Associated companies throughout the world

ISBN 0 330 34759 4

3 5 7 9 8 6 4 2

A CIP catalogue record for this book is available from
the British Library.

Typeset by CentraCet Limited, Cambridge
Printed and bound in Great Britain by
Mackays of Chatham plc, Chatham, Kent

To my father

It is perhaps as difficult
to write a good life as to live one.

Lytton Strachey

CONTENTS

PREFACE *1*

I. THE EARLY YEARS *11*

II. THE EARLY DATES *28*

III. FAMILY TREES *46*

IV. KITCHEN BIOGRAPHY *75*

V. MEMORY *89*

VI. THE PRIVATE *106*

VII. THE WORLD THROUGH
ANOTHER'S EYES *142*

VIII. MEN AND WOMEN *163*

IX. PSYCHOLOGY *175*

X. IN SEARCH OF AN ENDING *218*

XI. AFTERWORD *237*

INDEX *247*

PREFACE

Whatever one's experience of this globe and its inhabitants, however impartial one's judgement and varied one's acquaintance, it would be no surprise if the most enchanting person one had yet encountered, someone whose tastes in love and literature, religion and recreation, dirty jokes and household hygiene all lay beyond reproach, whose setbacks were capable of eliciting inexhaustible concern and pity, whose dawn halitosis was the grounds for no quiet shudder and whose view of humanity seemed neither cruel nor naïve – one might without presumption suggest this person to be none other than oneself.

However gloomy the thought may strike those of ethical disposition, there is a difference between letting it bubble discreetly in one's mind while squeezing an orange or skimming through the channels of late-night television and hearing it confirmed in the fury of another's accusation, along with a couple of vases sent crashing to the ground to emphasize the point.

The charm of self-inflicted insults comes in knowing how far to dig the knife and, with a surgeon's precision, how to avoid the rawest nerves. It is as harmless a sport as trying to tickle oneself. When Elton John sang a beautiful love song in which he lamented to his beloved, in the well-worn tradition of singers and moist-eyed poets, that he only wished his art could do justice to his ardour ['Your

1

Song', 1969], we would be foolish to suppose that he doubted his talent for even a moment. The ability to deprecate his musical skill was premissed on an apparently humble but profoundly arrogant belief that he had in fact written something of a gem. As Dr Johnson remarked of these self-administered insults, they are a pleasant sport for they allow a man [aphorisms appear to find no room for women until at least the middle of the twentieth century] 'to show how much he can spare'. What musical confidence it must take to sing melodiously one has not a jot of it. What greater assurance could one attain than casually to spare the thought one is a self-centred churl? Johnsonian deprecation appears as a branch of the cocksure, 'Look, Mum, no hands' cycling boast, in which the need to keep a firm grip on the handlebars of self-respect can temporarily be relaxed, so one can freewheel down the hill shouting merrily, 'I'm such a lousy singer,' and 'Oh, what a brat I am.'

But as soon as it floats out of another's mouth, a previously cute deprecation develops sharper claws.

'It took me a long time to figure you out,' began a letter from a woman who had shared six months of my life, then decided she would have preferred to see me dead, 'to understand how someone could have been so un-self-aware and at the same time so self-obsessed. You said you loved me, but a narcissist can't love anyone but himself. I know most men have little clue of how to communicate, but your incapacities were tediously extraordinary. You had no respect for anything I gave a damn about, you approached everything with the same high-handed, self-righteous manner. I wasted too long with an egoist incapable of listening to my needs, someone who would have had trouble empathizing with anything further than his own ear-lobe . . .'

The reader may be spared the range of accusations; in the polite language of human dynamics, it suffices to say that Divina and I were not well matched.

The tenor of her charges made an impression nevertheless. They now sparked doubts when at gatherings guests politely excused themselves to fetch another drink but never returned, leaving me alone with the peanuts and a more tenuous hold on the honey jar of self-love. The ear-lobe stuck particularly in mind.

I was browsing in a London bookshop some weeks later; it was a Saturday morning and Mozart's clarinet concerto was being piped through the speakers in a self-conscious attempt to add the elusive classical quality ascribed to music written before nineteen hundred. On passing a table above which the word biography had been stencilled in gold, I clumsily brushed against a swollen tome which slid from its pile and fell onto the burgundy carpet, coughing a trace of dust and raising the attention of an angelic-looking assistant working on a crossword at the counter opposite.

Noticing a small tear I had inflicted on the book's jacket, I feigned momentary interest in the contents, hoping that the assistant would lose her interest [officiously administrative, alas] in me. The work was an account of the life of Ludwig Wittgenstein, comprising two chronologies, a bibliography, forty pages of notes and three sections of photographs showing the philosopher in his bathing trunks and in his nurse's arms, but apparently less concerned with illuminating the reader on the one issue about which the deceased subject would have shown an interest.

But what did thought matter when the work promised to locate the linen of the author of the *Tractatus*, and moreover, included hitherto undiscovered material concerning Ludwig's relation with his brothers?

The shop assistant having returned to her crossword, I prepared to replace the damaged book unobtrusively on its pile when, in a context other than ear-lobes and my incapacity for it, my eye was caught by the word 'empathize' which stood out in the centre of its corrupted dust jacket.

'One person can rarely have taken such interest in another,' judged a critic, 'rarely has a biographer empathized so much with a subject. The author has examined every aspect of Wittgenstein's life, psychological, sexual and social, and in the process recreated the inner life of the century's most complicated thinker.'

In a phenomenon beloved of those who search for patterns amidst the chaos, one may sometimes focus on a particular word, then mysteriously hear or read of it in several different places within a short period. Either the word has always been there, and is noticeable simply because one's senses have been alerted or, more mystically, bits of language appear to be trailing like signs from above. Whatever the explanation for this literary *déjà vu*, the empathy of which I had been said to have had so little had now resurfaced in the context of a biographer positively overflowing with the substance – and the disparity led me to a childish burst of jealousy at the virtue of the Wittgensteinian sleuth, this in the middle of a sober literary bookshop, under the searching eyes of security cameras and angelic assistants.

It served as a reminder of my role in the baneful but

prevalent disregard with which most humans contemplated their fellows, ignoring their chronologies and earliest snaps, their letters and diaries, the locations of their youth and maturity, their school bench and wedding parties. Bursts of selflessness aside, stubbing a toe on the edge of a steel table was always enough to divert attention away from communal matters in the name of an immediate concern with our lightly bruised hoof.

A few months before, I had watched my grandfather succumb to cancer and die on the eve of his eightieth birthday. He had been forced to spend his last weeks in a busy ward of a London hospital and there had befriended a nurse from his native village in Norfolk, to whom he had begun to relate episodes of his life when she had moments to spare. When I visited him after work one evening, he mentioned in a restrained, self-mocking voice that senile grandpas shouldn't bore such busy staff. He had been talking to his nursing friend that afternoon about fighting Rommel in the desert in the North African campaign; how he had joined up shortly after war had broken out, had trained in a special base and then travelled through the U-boat infested Mediterranean to Alexandria. There followed stories of tank battles, terrible thirst and a brief period of internment in a camp, but when he had looked up at the height of his tale, he saw that his listener had had to leave and was now standing with a doctor and a sister at the entrance of the ward.

'You see, they run them off their feet here,' he explained, though one could detect the hurt beneath his old man's pride. One minute, there had been a kindly woman listening as he hurried into the back room to fetch his memories, and the next, as he was unwrapping them before her, she was gone. I imagined the wound he must have felt at seeing how stories so central to who he was should have required an act of charity from a young nurse to be heard. He had no biographer to pick up his words, to chart his movements, to arrange his memories, he was leaking his biography into a host of different vessels who would listen for a moment, then pat him on the shoulder and move back to their own lives. The empathy of others was limited by the demands of the working day and so he died leaving fragments of himself haphazardly scattered amongst a box of fading letters, unlabelled photos gathered in family albums and anecdotes told to his two sons and a handful of friends who made an appearance at his funeral in wheelchairs.

One might of course rejoin that never before have so many people devoted so much time to the minutiae of others. The lives of poets and astronauts, generals and ministers, mountaineers and manufacturers all lie before us on the tables of elegant bookshops. They herald the mythic age prophesied by Andy Warhol where everyone would be famous [that is, biographed] for fifteen minutes.

Yet there has always been some complexity in the fulfilment of this noble Warholian wish. Purely on a numerical basis, with the earth's population staggering past the five and a half billion mark in the last decade of the twentieth century, it would take no less than 1,711 centuries to give all those currently breathing fifteen minutes of attention.

And whatever the practical difficulties, in a sombre though unplanned Warholian parallel, the philosopher

Cioran once wrote of the impossibility of one person being truly interested in another for longer than quarter of an hour [don't scoff, try it and see]. And even Freud, who one might have expected to cherish hopes for human understanding and communication, told an interviewer at the end of his life that he really had nothing to complain about: 'I have lived over seventy years. I had enough to eat. I enjoyed many things. Once or twice I met a human being who almost understood me. What more can I ask?'

Once or twice in a lifetime. What a solitary sum, though what haunting paucity, provoking us to doubt the depth of our relations with those we sentimentally call our friends. One can imagine the wry smile Freud would have reserved for the arrogance of biographers who followed him beyond the grave and reported from jacket covers that they were the first to have grasped the nature of his identity.

Despite the claims, despite the obstacles, something about the biographer's mission tempted my imagination; the idea of understanding a human being as fully as one person could hope to understand another, submerging myself in a life other than my own, seeing the world through new eyes, following someone through their child-hood and their dreams, tracking the range of their tastes from the pre-Raphaelites to fruit-flavoured sorbets. Why not attempt a biography myself? It would be but a small penance to pay for the years I had failed truly to listen to others, the times I had silently yawned and wondered what I had planned for the next day while portions of mini-biographies were unfolded to me over a final cup of coffee.

But, given the ethical value of the biographical impulse, my search for a suitable subject surprised me with how narrowly practitioners had traditionally hunted out their targets amongst the billions of souls who were or had once been on the planet. If, as Warhol had implied, there was going to be a traffic jam of 1,711 centuries simply to accommodate everyone then living, there was something selfish in the way certain characters had persistently hogged the biographical field: Hitler, Buddy Holly, Napoleon, Verdi, Jesus, Stalin, Stendhal, Churchill, Balzac, Goethe, Marilyn Monroe, Caesar, W. H. Auden. It wasn't hard to see why, for these figures had exercised enormous power, artistic or political, beneficial or not, over their fellow men and women. Their lives were what might lazily have been called larger than life, they expressed the outer limits of human possibility, something one might gasp at and be thrilled by on the morning commuter train.

However, on closer look, it appeared that biographers were not primarily concerned with highlighting the *difference* between the great and mortals consigned to using public transport, but rather were keen to show how their charges had [despite conquering Russia, subduing the Indians, writing *La Traviata* and inventing the steam engine] been much the same as you and me. The pleasure of reading biographies arose in part from a reminder of flesh and blood in creatures one imagined to have been fashioned of sterner stuff; personality was of interest, the humanity which arose from a telling detail and history had airbrushed from its solemn portrait.

There was a thrill in learning that Napoleon [invincible Bonaparte whose body lay in glory beneath ten feet of marble in the gilded Invalides] had a fondness for grilled chicken and jacket potatoes. With his love of this humble fare, what we might pick up at the supermarket on a weekday evening, he could become a tangible human being, a figure with whom one could identify. He came alive in the degree to which he partook in everyday activities, in so far as he wept and had messy affairs, bit his nails and was jealous of his friends, liked honey but reviled marmalade – anything to melt the stony heroism of the official statue.

Paradoxically, the imposing curricula vitae of biographical subjects might have concealed a more general and baser curiosity as to the activities of others. The voyeurism of biographies was excused by the fame of their subjects, when what underlay their consumption could have been a desire to snoop and see someone negotiating the business of life. Learning of Napoleon's sexual tastes was fascinating not only or even primarily because the man was famous, but because there was general delight in discussing bedroom orientations. Austerlitz and Waterloo might have been fig-leaves for a process bearing similarities to a group of fishwives gossiping over the garden fence.

Nevertheless, an assumption remained that only the great were fit fodder for biographies.

A couple of centuries before, a dissenting voice had briefly shattered this puzzling unanimity, only then to be ignored amidst the growing mountain of biographies amassing over its owner's grave. The voice had belonged to Dr Johnson, and it had mused that, 'There has rarely passed a life of which a judicious and faithful narrative would not be useful. For, not only has every man great numbers in the same condition with himself, to whom his mistakes and miscarriages, escapes and expedients, would be of immediate and apparent use; but there is such a uniformity in the state of man, considered apart from decorations and disguises, that there is scarce any possibility of good or ill, but is common to human kind.'

The idea seemed momentous, a Copernican revolution in the field. What biography disguised, in its concern for unusual lives, was the extraordinariness of any life, a singularity which led Johnson to boast both of the worth and his ability to complete a spirited account of the life of a broomstick.

In dwelling on the actions of those we can never share drinks with, biographies shield us from our universal involvement, explicit or not, in biographical projects. Every acquaintance requires us to understand a life, a process in which the conventions of biography play a privileged role. Its narrative traditions govern the course of the stories we may tell ourselves about those we meet, it shapes our perceptions of their anecdotes, the criteria according to which we arrange their divorces and holidays, the way we select, as if the choice were natural, certain of their memories but not others.

Such concerns rarely appear in the questions asked of their profession by self-reflective biographers; whether to rely on the letters or diaries, interview the maid or gardener, believe the poet laureate, his deceased wife or their newsagent. But it suggested that there was no reason why the next person to walk into my life should warrant less than the empathetic effort one could expect from the most banal of biographers. It seemed that unusual value might lie in exploring the hidden role of biographical convention in our most ubiquitous but complex pastime – understanding other people.

I

THE EARLY YEARS

When historians come to narrate the second half of the twentieth century, it is unlikely that they will pause for long to consider the arrival in the world of a blood-clotted four and half pound infant bearing the name of Isabel Jane Rogers, daughter of Lavinia and Christopher Rogers, shortly after midnight on the 24th of January 1968 in University College Hospital, London.

They are even less likely to note her mother's awkward grimace at the sight of this red-faced creature who had dared tumble into existence and now began gazing so expectantly at her. The father, who held the warm bundle as if it were a grenade, melted on noticing how tiny Isabel had exactly his eyes and her mouth tapered at its edges in the way he recognized from his father and grandfather – though for the mother, such inheritance merely served as a reminder of how the child had prevented her from marrying the only man she had ever loved, a French artist with almond eyes and a sunlit studio, and had instead forced her together with a Classics graduate recently employed in the accounts department of a multinational food conglomerate.

In later years, though her imagination would recoil from conceiving the mishap, the intellect informed Isabel that her appearance on earth was proof that Lavinia and Christopher had once shared the act of coitus.

The moment had fallen on an April day in a field ordinarily used for grazing sheep outside the village of Madingley, a few minutes' drive from the University of Cambridge. It was a sad paradox that Lavinia should have granted Christopher such intimacy, when it was his close friend, artistic and continental Jacques, whom she desired. Then again, it was not so paradoxical [but as sad] when one realized how few signs of interest Jacques had shown in this freckled language student and former head girl of a Scottish boarding school. Lavinia had hence turned her attention to Christopher in the hope of igniting a spark of jealousy which she had learnt [most recently from Stendhal] to be the catalytic ingredient of many Gallic passions.

She had started by suggesting a drive through the countryside within ear-shot of Christopher's desired friend, but though nature did its best to charm, the trip was marred by Lavinia's frustration at Jacques's evident reluctance to display any objection to it. Some of this resentment found its way onto Christopher's shoulders. At the end of a pub lunch, she teasingly remarked how she had read that men passed the peak of their sexual performance at the age of nineteen, information she followed with a gratingly prolonged giggle. It might have explained Christopher's forceful attempt to draw Lavinia into an adjacent field, and there into a cuddle which assumed a frenetic rhythm. Behind Christopher's eagerness lay a desire to prove he had reached his twenties libidinously, behind Lavinia's failure to prevent him doing so lay the thought of how the incident might be related to her insultingly indifferent Gallic lover in days to come.

However, by the time Jacques was informed of and shrugged his shoulders at the coupling, 250 million sperm had swum an initial lap, a few hundred had reached an egg high in the Fallopian tube and a lucky one had gnawed its way inside. It was an age when such luck was not corrected in polite society, so Lavinia had no choice but to let the child have its way and grimly wed its father.

The couple moved to London, and to a mossy flat on the second floor of a Victorian block in Paddington. Christopher worked in an office in Shepherd's Bush, Lavinia declared her life ruined and began a doctoral thesis, though she was unable to walk far out of the house before collapsing into disabling floods. To the irritation of her husband, she peppered her melancholy conversation with French turns of phrase ['il faut le faire', 'quel dommage', 'tu es vraiment un con', 'bon sens'], citing a need to keep up the tongue she had spent so long improving during her university years.

All of which coloured the world into whose arms baby Isabel would fall. Having historically been judged an insignificant period, contemporary thought has highlighted the importance of a child's early experience. According to Mr Rogers, his daughter's start had been cheerful, his wife judged it to have involved nightmarish adaptation to unimaginable misery. Isabel wasn't sure.

She had been joined two and a half years later by a little sister, then a little brother. Her room was painted sky blue and she had a furry tortoise called Mully and a much chewed woollen rug called Goobie. She was driven around Hyde Park in a nylon pushchair, and her mother gave her husks of bread to tear up for the pigeons. Some weekends, she would be taken to her grandparents' house in the country, sleep in a yellow room and swivel on a leather chair until it squealed. She had a pile of books, including one about a princess who lived on the moon and was lonely until she made friends with a star called Neptune. She had toys too: cubes you had to find spaces for in a wooden block, plastic circles you stacked up on a pole and a liquid-filled ball which changed colour as you shook it. There were friends around. Luke, the toddler from downstairs with blue eyes and a skill at acrobatics on the carpet, and later came Poppy, brought around by her schoolteacher mother, always dressed in purple with an orange cap.

There was no work to be done, days could be spent exploring the living-room, learning how to tear the lining out of the sofa cushions, what would happen if you threw the bulbous glass ashtray on the floor or what the telephone cord was like to chew. In the kitchen, there were biscuits you could lick, drop on the ground and drive around the black and white tiles until they had collected dust, before deciding they might be tasty after all and watching Mummy's face as it changed from white to red when she bent down to sweep you off your feet, prised your fingers loose, threw the fibry cookie in the bin and pretended to be cross – though you knew you only had to give a smile and everything would be forgiven. Daddy disappeared at dawn and returned in the night, and always smelt the same, though it was rougher against his cheeks at dinner time. He'd put you on his shoulders and you laughed because everything seemed small from above and you could touch the light bulb and watch it dance. Later on there was school with the corridors that smelt sharp like lemons, and learning to do numbers, and how did the teacher know when you cheated and did an 8 with two oos stuck together instead of in that proper, difficult way?

There were lots of questions. What did the people who lived inside the TV do when the set was turned off? How did they have enough room and change so fast? Why did Mummy smack her when she'd thought of giving them some milk – she was always saying how healthy it was – and drained a pint into the vent at the side? There were other things: if the earth was like a tennis ball which floated in space, then what did space float in? Was there a bigger room in which space floated? Maybe there was someone looking at the earth like she looked at the ants in the crack on the garden wall? And where had Mrs Brithton, the caretaker, gone? She used to play with her in the morning, then went to sleep. Only she went to sleep for much longer than Isabel was allowed. She slept for weeks, and when Isabel asked Mummy where she'd gone, she fumed and said poor Mrs Brithton should be left to lie in peace. What did that mean, and what did it mean when, later, Daddy explained she had gone to heaven which was a special place, a little like the funfair they'd visited at Christmas, with the toys you had to throw loops around and you could keep them, but they hadn't been able to throw very far and ended up with a plastic frog, oh, it was an oily green thing which looked at her in the night, but it couldn't see her if she put her head under the sheets? Mrs Brithton had gone to heaven, and that's what happened if you slept too much, now Isabel would get up early. Sometimes she saw the moon floating in the corner of the window, why didn't it bump into aeroplanes and why wasn't it there during the day, or only sometimes? Maybe it was shy, she would make friends with the moon.

Then Mummy got fat and suddenly there was a yellow

cot and smells. She and Daddy only paid attention to the
screaming thing. When they tried to play, they were like
Granny when you knew she really wanted to be somewhere else, the garden and roses which bit when you
touched them. At first, she didn't like the thing, but gradually it started smiling and following her around the house.
It was called Lucy. Lucy did anything you told her, so she
was named slave and Isabel was queen. Isabel told the
slave she had a host of secret powers: she could talk to
the black and white cat downstairs, who wouldn't talk
to Lucy because it didn't like her. She could talk to birds
as well, and it made Lucy cry because there were so many
birds, and not one ever squeaked to her.

The queen and her slave had a favourite game where
they sat in two laundry baskets in the kitchen which were
Viking ships like in the book Grandpa had given them.
They had to conquer a foreign land which was the table,
and seize the enemy's treasure which sat in the larder.
They made up a Viking language which annoyed the non-
Vikings in the flat because they wanted a straight answer
to how many potatoes the queen and her slave wanted for
dinner.

Food was interesting. Isabel had 15p a week to spend
on sweets; there were two shops near by, one run by Mrs
Hudson, another by Mr Singh. She alternated between
them, because she didn't want either to go out of business.
She knew what she could buy with her money; a packet
of crisps, five cola sweets, one stick of liquorice and two
flying saucers filled with sherbet. Or she could have a
packet of mints, two liquorice sticks and four flying saucers. Then again, she could spend everything on a sherbet
dip with a red lolly. At school, Julian told her that if she

let a Mars go stale and posted it to the company, they'd send a letter back with two new ones. She did it three times, then they told her not to be greedy, so she started with the people who made sherbet dips. It was five packets before they realized.

'So that's my strange childhood, I was nasty, shy and something of a menace all at once,' said Isabel at twenty-five, suddenly withdrawing from her memories with the embarrassment of someone shocked at how her enthusiasm might have overridden conversational propriety.

'Sorry I went on. People's childhoods are a little like their dreams, interesting for two minutes or ten, and then simply obscure. I suppose they're always far more interesting to the teller than the listener. They come out so jumbled, some bits seem clear, like they happened yesterday, then there are long stretches when you don't remember a thing. I never know whether something happened at the age of two, five or eight, I don't know whether it's a photo of something I'm remembering or a story someone told me or whether it's actually a memory. Anyway. My God, is that the time? I've been blabbering for ages, and you've been doing a great job at not looking bored.'

'I'm fascinated.'

'You mean you're well brought up.'

'I've rarely been accused of that.'

I looked down at the table and our empty glasses. 'Shall we have something else to drink?'

'What are you having?'

'A beer. What can I get you?'

'Oh, a glass of milk.'

'Of milk?'

'What's so funny?'

'At seven-thirty in the evening?'

'It's no crime.'

But in the course of negotiating my way towards the counter of a bar in Clapham [none of whose customers looked like they had emptied a glass of milk in two decades], I was assailed by doubts, doubts which indirectly culminated in the temporary interruption of Isabel's life-story in the name of a few questions and a couple of drinks.

'Could I have a Heineken and a glass of milk, please?' I asked the barman, who looked as if he might have found a more lucrative career as a heavy-weight boxer.

'A what?' he bellowed, indicating a conceptual rather than auditory problem.

'It's not for me,' I answered defensively, 'it's someone who's, she's, well, she's driving home.'

'Watch you don't go with her, my friend,' advised the barman with an insolent wink.

I had been certain that a linear narration of childhood was the way to begin. Every biography opened with the early years garnished with anecdotes extracted from the subject's later poems or prose, episodes transcribed from the reminiscences of loving aunts, ambivalent siblings or obscure school friends making capital of their incidental connection to the great sailor or statesman who happened to have had the adjacent desk in extra maths and made the peashooter to fire pellets at the biology teacher.

Why then, so early on in this biographical venture, before we had even covered the chink in the latency period playing stethoscope with the neighbour, did I feel that to begin this way would mean leaving something out? If it had been good enough for Perugino and Picasso, why was the standard method suddenly unsuitable for Isabel?

I wished my biography to be exhaustive and yet it struck me that this would require not just the past, but the particular way in which the past coexisted with and emerged from the present. The linear method of arranging biographies, beginning with the earliest incident and ending with the last, was certainly faithful to the demands of objective history. Kindergarten did come before the tetanus jab on the calendar, so there seemed a strong argument for placing its bead in the correct part of the chronological necklace. But if events happened in an order which could be plotted on a historical axis, they were rarely remembered in such a clean way by their subject or indeed revealed thus to outsiders in Clapham bars.

It was hard to remember whether the holiday in Wales had taken place before or after Grandma's operation, learning to make biscuits certainly happened much before changing schools, so why did the former seem as clear as if it had occurred yesterday and the latter gave off the dim light of the sun on a December day?

Though a life might in some analogies be compared to an alphabet starting at A and ending at Z, it could never be experienced in such a grammatical strait-jacket. It resembled the efforts of a muddled child unsure of his letters. One would enter someone's life at Q, and then be shuttled back to D, concern would shift forward to S, hover in the advancing present of R before briefly dipping back to G to pick up something which happened at fifteen, an association triggered by a song on a jukebox or a photo fallen out of a forgotten book on the migration patterns of the Balinese gull.

There was an argument for stabilizing the mess and arranging things as best one could. Yet there was also an argument for letting a little of this complexity into the picture. Isabel and I had been sitting in a Clapham bar for two hours, I had known her for a few weeks, but a worthy chapter on the early years could only be founded on a dozen conversations extending over many months, then carefully retrospectively assembled, a period during which the present would have itself advanced and thrown up an ever-changing perspective on the past. Our initial conversations did not even dwell primarily, like good biographers', on our initial, childhood moments. The discovery that Isabel's father had worked for a food conglomerate came only two months after I had met her, the anecdote about the slave and her queen had to wait until the conciliatory second stroke of an argument half a year later over who had forgotten to give back a rented video to a shop in Queensway.

'Thanks,' said Isabel, as I returned with the milk and a glass of beer.

'Aren't you worried about cholesterol?' I asked.

'I've got the opposite problem actually. My doctor told me I should have dairy products as often as possible. It's funny, because that's what I like to do anyway. What do you usually drink?'

'It depends, but I have far too many cups of coffee.'

'You'll develop hairy hands in later life if you continue to do that,' she warned.

'Where did you hear that rubbish?'

'There was a piece in *Marie-Claire*.'

I was now troubled by another and associated assumption behind biographies; that when they were serious, they had no author. They simply had a subject whose life was ghost-written, approached from a perspectiveless standpoint by a writer who was never more than a name, and whose motives in picking up a pen were draped in mystery [requiring me to exit the show at the earliest opportunity – or as soon as the drinks were paid for]. A biographer would efface himself or herself like a shy host, marshalling guests to speak at correct moments, but rarely intruding to lend judgement, or if judgement there was, then it would be measured, mature, rarely a biased or passionate outcry.

Signs of the independent life of biographers are disappointingly scarce. At the end of the acknowledgements, a coy hint occasionally protrudes. One may be fortunate enough to find the place or date of a book's completion. In his work on Proust, George Painter subtly let drop London, May, 1959, and Richard Ellmann introduced his life of Joyce with Evanston, Illinois, March 15th [my birthday] of the same year.

Though generous, one might be excused for longing to know more. Where in London? What was the weather like in May 1959? Did the editor invite Painter out for lunch to celebrate publication day? Italian or French? And where on earth is Evanston, Illinois? Can one find drinkable coffee there?

In the preface to a later edition [this time he was in Hove, and it was 1988], George Painter wrote that his book was, 'again dedicated as before to my wife Joan Painter, now forty-seven years after our marriage'.

Scholarly spouses are a tempting secret. Who was Joan

Painter, how did she feel about her husband devoting gallons of emotional energy to this nervous, turn of the century French genius? Did she like Proust or might she have preferred Tolstoy or even Arnold Bennett? Did they have a secret nickname for him, jokes about George spending the holidays with Marcel again? Could it be valid to spare curiosity not simply for Proust's life, but also for how Painter discovered the life, the bits which bored him, the times he had to go to Paris for research, what hotels he stayed at and if he ever spent the afternoon in a café opposite the Bibliothèque Nationale dreaming of giving it all up for a teaching post in the Dordogne?

These are heretical thoughts, though biographers, with their insatiable curiosity, should forgive readers for turning a little of the substance back onto them. Is there not something unbalanced in the way one is required to be fascinated by the subject of biography while rigidly uninterested in the author, as uninterested as in the voice which answers directory enquiries, a voice subservient to its message? [To consider the voice as a person might dangerously threaten one's priorities. The superiority of the train station phone number could recede at the idea that the operator was a human being, had a house and possibly children but definitely a toothbrush, realizations which might lead to questions like what colour was it, had this person been rejected in love, did they swim breaststroke and how long did their lamb need in the oven?]

But the absence of biographers from their text should not be explained simply through modesty. Richard Ellmann would, if asked, no doubt have genially explained where the best diner in Evanston, Illinois, was, or what his wife ['. . . Mary Ellmann, who has improved it everywhere, both in conception and expression . . .'] thought of the book, or what led him to find an affinity with Joyce or how his children reacted to their father vanishing to the library for days on end. Holding himself back from such digressions was not just good manners, it is part of the philosophical premiss underlying biographical writing: namely, that one never simply aims to write a *view* of a life [the view from Evanston with a wife and kids of an Irishman living years before in a land far away], but rather, one tries to write that life *itself*, as free as possible from the distorting perspectives of prejudice and sloppy scholarship. In this light, a bad biography is precisely one where the author intrudes too much on his or her subject, where one finds out more about the author's complexes than those of the grander figure one has paid to learn about.

'I don't mind orange juice,' I explained to Isabel in further reaction to her enquiry. 'It's just I'd far rather drink water than the artificial stuff which most of the time passes for juice but isn't.'

'Really,' she replied, 'water's crap. It's so boring. It's so, you know, *watery*,' she elucidated with a raise of the shoulders.

'How do you feel about the fizzy variety?'

'I guess that's a bit better.'

'Actually, I prefer drinking grapefruit to orange juice,' I reflected, 'because somehow, it's easier to make it fake and yet taste OK.'

'You're right.'

If people had simply one life, then it would be vital for biographers to remain out of the picture, so it could be carefully and unbiasedly reconstructed away from the meddling interference of competing egos and taste buds. However, we have as many lives as we have people to converse with. In the company of one's mother, certain things are spoken of and others not, policemen make us feel one way, members of extreme religious groups another. The relativity evokes Heisenberg's Uncertainty principle, called in to explain any situation where the observer both watches and simultaneously affects the thing being watched. If you spend time staring down the microscope at some atoms, Heisenberg is said to have said, you'll make them so self-conscious, they'll start doing things they hadn't in private, the equivalent of suggesting that spying through a telescope at your neighbours is likely to cut short their plans for cuddles on the living-room floor.

When I had been standing at the bar, I had cast an eye back at the table, and seen Isabel rapidly brush a hair away from her cheek. It had been a tiny gesture, one of the many she had displayed without raising my attention as we talked. But because she had not now known she was being watched by curious eyes, it hinted at the way she might appear to a commuter on a train or to a tourist on the escalator of a department store. The gesture spoke of who Isabel was in a world which did not know her, of the way she was when she believed herself alone. This realization had none of the lurid shades carried by the word voyeurism, Isabel was not in the process of rolling down her stockings, simply brushing back a hair. What was important was not *what* she was doing, but the barely perceptible change brought on by the belief that she was doing something unnoticed. Had I told her the truth, it might have produced a moment of embarrassment akin to being recognized by a friend in a street down which one was walking un-selfconsciously, doing something as benign as whistling or planning the evening meal – but nevertheless doing so with a presumption of anonymity.

Biographies seem largely oblivious to the implications of Heisenberg's theory. They aim to present the 'definitive' life, the authentic version which Bloggs, responsible for the last stab, failed to grasp because he hadn't talked to the head waiter at the Hôtel du Cap and overlooked the memoirs of the subject's chiropodist. The prejudice is similar to the one encountered in the field of psycho-analysis, where therapists struggle to be invisible, where one cannot ask if they liked a recent film, where they prefer to take their holidays, or more pressingly, what they think of the dazzlingly personal material one is spilling out. The aggression voiced towards them may be nothing other than discomfort at the power-imbalance one registers whenever there is only one person answering questions, revealing things about themselves while the other listens, inciting a monologue to which they have no intention of replying.

Ghost-written biographies appear as the heirs of a sad nineteenth-century industrial movement, manufacturing what Virginia Woolf described as 'an amorphous mass, a life of Tennyson, or of Gladstone, in which we go seeking disconsolately for a voice or laughter, for curse or anger, for any trace that this fossil was once a living man'.

Yet they should not obscure an alternative tradition embodied in what must be the supreme Heisenberg biography, Boswell's portrait of Johnson, which presumed that an honest account of a life could only arise from a relation-ship between author and subject – a work which was hence as full of the idiosyncrasy of the biographer as that of the doctor.

'I'm starving,' said Isabel, standing up abruptly and taking her bag off the window-sill. 'Do you want to come home for supper? I could rustle up some fish fingers or something.'

'Oh, very *cordon bleu*. Sounds great.'

'Spare the sarcasm. You should consider yourself lucky to be invited.'

'Nobody can write the life of a man, but those who have eaten and drunk and lived in social intercourse with him,' Johnson had warned Boswell – and the scribe had taken him at his word. 'I generally have a meat pye on Sunday,' he had reported, then went on to justify a description of a meal at his house: 'As dinner here was considered a singular phenomenon, and as I was frequently interrogated on the subject, my readers may perhaps be desirous to know our bill of fare. We had a very good soup, a boiled leg of lamb and spinach, a veal pye, and a rice pudding.'

'What are we going to have with the fingers, then?' I asked.

'I don't know, maybe new potatoes or some rice, or perhaps just a salad. I've got a few tomatoes left. I could cut them up and mix them with some cucumber for a Greek salad.'

Why not then begin the process quite differently? Instead of disappearing behind an impersonal chronology of Isabel's life, was it not more honest to begin with a brief account of how I had come to know her, what my impressions had been and how they had evolved, what I had grasped and misunderstood, where my prejudices had interfered and how my insights had been formed? In response to Heisenberg's Uncertainty principle, I would need, for a time at least, to privilege the early dates over the early years.

II

THE EARLY DATES

A party, half-past eleven, Saturday night, London. Voices, music, dancing. A young man and woman are talking.

SHE: You're so right.

HE [*Long hair, leather jacket*]: I'm glad you agree. Some of those Hendrix moments have been like God to me, do you know what I mean? The sky, it opened, like, it opened. Do you know what I mean?

SHE [*nodding*]: Sure.

HE: I always say a prayer to Hendrix before I go on stage. It sounds silly, right? You think I'm silly.

SHE: I don't, I'd do that for Hendrix. So where do you do gigs?

HE: I was in LA last year.

SHE: Really.

HE: I've been to Tokyo a couple of times as well.

SHE: That's great.

HE: Man, it's heaven.

I had been at the party for an hour or so when I first laid eyes on her. She was standing in an alcove of the living-room of a house in Belsize Park, whose walls were decorated with a set of Indian prints displaying an athletic couple in successive erotic states. The guitarist pointed to these intermittently and each time elicited a muffled giggle from his companion. I stirred the ice in my second, and if the evening were to continue in such a manner certainly not my last, vodka tonic, and settled back into a maroon sofa.

I knew her type exactly; the sort of woman who reserves an exaggerated respect for louche males involved in the seedier side of the arts business. Though herself conventional, she would attach herself to such a figure in an attempt to escape the sterility of her existence. She would mistake his stubble for social commentary, accompany him on the road for a few years, perhaps acquire an addiction and a child, and end up being rescued by her family from a caravan site a decade later. Her opinions would be the predictable brand of post-adolescent middle-class nonsense. She would mix a certain unreflective left-wingism with a materialist attachment to household appliances, she would a few years back have flirted with vegetarianism but settled for mild sentimentality, reflected in her membership of groups devoted to rescuing panda bears and endangered Australian anteaters.

Content with the psychological portrait, I planned not to give her another thought, and wandered into the kitchen in the hope of meeting someone more congenial. Sadly it was deserted, but a copy of the previous day's paper lay open on the table at an article forecasting a collision between the earth and a meteor the size of a railway terminus.

'Oh my God, save me,' said the afore-labelled woman, hurrying into the kitchen an instant later.

'I'm sorry?' I replied.

'I'm being pursued,' she announced, shutting the door behind her.

'By who?'

'Why do I always get into these situations? He's the brother of a friend, and he's supposed to be giving me a lift home – and of course, he's got the wrong idea. I think he's dangerous too, not in a serious way, just mildly psychotic.'

'Only mildly?'

'If he comes in, can we pretend we're deep in some conversation?'

'Should we just hum Christmas carols otherwise?'

'I'm sorry. I must be being very rude.'

'Do you want some wine?'

'No, but I'd love one of those carrots. I've never mastered the knack of being hungry at the right time.'

'Why?'

'Well, it's always now I get peckish, then of course I'm not that hungry for breakfast, but get starving around midday. I'd die for a biscuit as well.'

We located one in a tin by the stove. A brief introduction followed.

'So who do you know here?' I asked.

'I'm a friend of Nick. Do you know Nick?'

'No, who's Nick?'

'He's a friend of Julie. Do you know Julie?'

'No. Do you know Chris?'

'No.'

'So why did you have to get a lift with old Hendrix?'

'Oh, he lives near me in Hammersmith. I don't know what it is about me. I'm always friendly to people when I shouldn't be. I haven't really mastered the art of how to freeze someone out. Maybe I'm afraid of offending them, that's why I have to be friendly.'

'You want everyone to love you?'

'Don't you?'

'Naturally.'

'But thinking about this Hendrix guy, if there's one thing I hate, it's people who try to be fashionable. I don't mind people who are fashionable, but it's the effort that's pathetic. It's like people who try to impress you by how clever they are. If someone's read the unabridged works of Aristotle, they should have more tact than to ram that information down your throat.'

'Have you got someone in mind?'

'Yeah, well. Sort of. Anyway, don't pry, we've only just met.'

'So?'

'I bet you've already forgotten my name.'

'How could I forget a name like Harriet?'

'Quite easily. The more pressing question is why you can't remember a name like Isabel?'

'How did you know I'd forgotten?'

'Because I was the same for a long time. Then I read an article on the name problem in the paper. Apparently, it happens to people who are worried about the appearance they're making, so they can't concentrate on the other person.'

'I'm glad to know that's what it is.'

'I'm sorry. Was that rude? I'm a rude thing, it's something you should know.'

She smiled briefly, then looked thoughtfully away. She had medium-length dark brown and lightly curled hair. Her skin was pale under the bright fluorescent kitchen light, there was an incongruous mole on the left side of her chin and her eyes [at that moment focused on the refrigerator door] were an unremarkable hazel-brown.

31

'What do you do for a living?' I asked to cover the dripping tap.

'I hate that kind of question.'

'Why?'

'Because people assume you're just your job.'

'I won't.'

'Look at those magnets stuck to the fridge. They're all famous people. There's Carter, Gorbachev, Sadat, and that looks like Shakespeare. Isn't he sweet?' she said, unsticking the magnetic figurine and stroking its bald plastic head.

'I work for this stationery company called Paperweight,' she continued. 'They do exercise books, pads and diaries, and now they're expanding into rubbers, pencils and folders. I've got the title of production assistant. I haven't always wanted to do that, and I may do something else later, but it came up, there were bills to pay, you know, the usual story.'

There was a pause while two guests walked in, picked up a bottle of wine, then walked out again. My impression of Isabel had by this stage undergone some alteration since the initial judgement so conclusively reached only minutes before. No longer was she a pop-star groupie or patron of Australian anteaters, and though I didn't quite know what she could be instead, the shifting impressions were reminders of the degree to which prejudice [both favourable and unfavourable] were affecting my reading. They evoked the egocentric way in which our view of others remains dependent on their attitude towards us, the frightening ease with which we may decide that Stalin was not so bad when he spared us the gulag, or the guest at the party was quite interesting once it was our postcode she requested.

'Do you brush your gums regularly?' asked Isabel.

'I don't know.'

'I didn't know either,' she said, 'but I went to the dentist today and found out I wasn't. Apparently it's a huge problem. Almost forty per cent of people have bad gums, and it leads to terrible complications when you're older. The real mistake people make is to think that just because they're brushing vigorously, they're doing some good. In fact, the best thing is simply to apply the brush and sort of rotate it like this very gently . . .'

Loopy girl, I thought, nice smile. Coy. I wonder if she likes gardening? though when it came to dialogue, I asked, 'Have you ever used an electric brush?' and Isabel answered yes, but not often, it belonged to her mother and it hadn't worked for a year.

Without knowing others properly, we shamelessly generate thoughts of who they are: one might declare it impossible to meet someone and suspend judgement as our ignorance would require. A certain habit of speech, readership of a newspaper, the shape of a mouth or a skull, these breed whole beings, we can predict how someone will vote or want to be kissed after only the briefest discussion concerning dentistry or the location of the bus stop.

This foolhardy process of acquaintance is akin to cracking open a novel and at once forming an idea of the characters. To qualify as a good reader, one would of course wait until the author had had a chance to set things out rather than rush into naïve identifications and caricatures. Then again, I had a problem with such patience, for I rarely finished novels. I would pick them up, read a few pages, then find something more appropriate on television. The curse had dogged my relationship with Jane Austen's *Emma*. The book had travelled with me across the Atlantic, to Glasgow and Spain, but still it had not been perused past the early twenties.

As a bad reader, I could nevertheless claim a certain confidence regarding Emma's character, future and my ability to recognize her at a party. In fact, from the very first sentence of the book, I had come to clear prejudices:

> *Emma Woodhouse, handsome, clever, and rich, with a comfortable home and happy disposition, seemed to unite some of the best blessings of existence; and had lived nearly twenty-one years in the world with very little to distress or vex her.*

Imagine I had been interrupted by a news bulletin and would never have learnt more. It would have been no reason to refrain from a portrait. I would have ascribed Emma the face of one of her namesakes I had known and tried to seduce at university. She had shoulder-length brown hair, a haughty demeanour and a ruddy complexion which might have been termed English. She was always cheerful and moved in a pack of girlfriends who, as one passed them in corridors, would often be laughing at a joke someone had just made. The first syllable of her surname evoked rural life, forests and the green with which I would colour her eyes, the second was a reminder of a red-brick country house which was on the front cover of a history book I owned and would now become her home. 'Handsome, clever, and rich' would bring to mind someone confident, quick-witted and sharp, perhaps psychologically like my cousin Hannah. Emma also seemed a touch spoilt and ridiculous; to talk of comfortable homes and happy dispositions was mockery because every home is dysfunctional and people with happy dispositions are comic in literature, which is predominantly written and read by melancholics. The idea of the girl living to be twenty-one with little to distress or vex her would, in the vengeful spirit of those whose adolescence had left scars, lead one to hope she wouldn't reach twenty-two without something redemptively catastrophic occurring.

Such a prejudiced reading of Emma was not in the end so far from my cursory reading of Isabel, though I would have been happier to drive home the latter than the former.

'That's so kind of you,' said Isabel, 'you know, if it's a problem, I can take a taxi, or go with Hendrix.'

'It's no hassle, it's in my direction,' I lied, for something had made me reluctant to part without exchanging phone numbers.

By the time I left Isabel in Hammersmith and arranged to go swimming with her the following weekend, I thought I knew who she was once more. After all, it is not ignorance which damages the clarity of our portraits, but the accumulation of knowledge. It is the length of time we spend with others which muddies our schemas, forcing us to acknowledge that we cannot cohere the man or woman we have known for twenty-five years into a tidy whole, a tacit recognition of the fact that others are in fact as complex and unknowable as we – something we rarely find the patience [or to be kinder] the energy to contemplate after brief acquaintance.

Spared the paradox of knowing too much and hence understanding nothing once more, I moved within the confines of my psychological tool-kit, which provided a set of general answers founded on specific experience to such questions as 'Are blondes kind?' 'Is it wise to trust smokers?' or 'Should one believe people who say they don't get angry?' I slotted my unknown character into the group of known characters who most immediately came to mind, reserving the right to alter the picture should new and incompatible information arrive.

My friend Natalie was the starting point of my understanding. Isabel might have been unique, but the imagination did not read her as such, preferring to collapse different people into one. Dreams reveal how people share identities in the unconscious, hence the confusing dreamer's report that he or she has spent the night with Caesar, though this was not quite the Caesar of history books but 'really' or 'at the same time' the local baker or their cousin Angus. The mind is a master at recognizing congruencies, when it is awake, largely at the physical level, and when uninhibited in bed, at a psychological one, leading us to witness uncomfortable unconscious twinnings; that our girlfriend shares the symbolic category of our great-aunt, that our golfing partner plays an unconscious Orson Welles in *Apocalypse Now* – congruencies we find hard to forget the next time we kiss or propose nine holes.

So Isabel was Natalie, and because Natalie had once told me she had been shy as a child and yet was now confident, I imagined a similar process had been at play. She must have taken a decision to wear her self-consciousness on her sleeve and refused to be embarrassed at things which had historically been a source of shame. This was perhaps what gave her an aggressive edge, notable when she had suddenly asked if I remembered her name. There was a disregard for the minor social conventions in the way she had spoken of her dentist and her eating habits. From this, I imagined it would be hard to shock her, and that she would think the very idea pretentious. The social indicators were vague. She lived in Hammersmith, an area housing all classes, and worked in a business which was distantly artistic enough to count as more than an administrative job. Her earrings hinted at foreign travel, perhaps the Far East or Africa.

In forming ideas before it was time, I risked being as foolish as tourists who arrive in a new land, and attach overwhelming importance to the externals of their trip, whether there are trolleys at the airport, if the taxi driver uses deodorant, how long the queue is at the museum gates – and use these details to come to such nonsensical conclusions as, 'Spain is so aggressive', 'Indians are polite' or 'she's delightful'.

The following weekend Isabel and I met to go swimming, and I learnt a few more things. She lived in a flat on the top floor of an Edwardian block in a street off Hammersmith Grove.

'Be careful not to park under the trees in front, every bird in London seems to treat the place like a bathroom,' she warned when I called to confirm.

I rang the bell and through the intercom she said, 'I'll be ready in a minute. I'd invite you up, but the place is a pigsty,' and was down before I could protest.

'I've just had my mother on the phone,' she apologized, shutting the car door and reaching to find the seat-belt.

'The woman is undoubtedly mad, it's a miracle she hasn't been locked up.'

'What's so demented about her?'

'She's spent half an hour telling me I don't eat enough, and says it's no wonder I never have any nice men to go out with. She's become obsessed with what I eat, it's some psychological control thing, every time she calls, she asks for an inventory of my fridge. Can you imagine, a mother doing that to her grown-up daughter? Oh, turn left here.'

I swung into the main road.

'Damn,' she said.

'What?'

'I meant right. I never know the difference.'

Once in the pool, Isabel explained how she couldn't dive because she hadn't mastered the way to stop water going up her nose. She still had to pinch it shut, but laughed and said she wasn't prepared to demonstrate this ungainly act in a crowded municipal bath. We did some laps alongside floating granny-whales, and she told me she had only recently started doing exercise again, having not done any since she was a teenager. She always got bored during sport, she didn't really see the point. She wanted a goal when she did things, that's why she wasn't a great one for long hikes through the countryside, she preferred the city. What was the thrill of tennis, for instance? You just shot the ball backwards and forwards. Or skiing? She'd been two years ago, ten of them in a chalet in France, and though it had been fun at night, the days bored her. She'd experienced what sounded like an existential crisis in a cable car.

'I was looking up at the mountain, and I thought, "Oh my God, I'm going to have to go up and then down, and then up and then down." It seemed like what that Greek bloke...'

'Tantalus?'

'No.'

'The other one.'

'Sisyphus.'

'Like what he had to do.'

We reached one end of the pool, and turned to back-stroke for the return journey. A group of children had arrived and competed to cause the bigger splash at one end of this un-Hockneyish Hammersmith pool.

'Do you know something odd?' she asked. 'Both Camus and Beckett really loved sport. Camus was a goalkeeper for the Algerian football team and Beckett was in *Wisden* for having done something great in cricket.'

'So?'

'Well, it's funny how they always went on that everything was meaningless, but then they took sport very seriously, which I think is pretty meaningless. Maybe you need to find life meaningless before you can find sport meaningful.'

The digression over, I learnt that Isabel had gone to school in Kingston where her family still lived, a local school with poor teaching but where she had insisted on going rather than face the private boarding school her mother had wished for her. She hadn't performed as well as she might, she'd been smaller than the other girls, but it had made her street-wise. She'd gone on to Queen Mary College, part of London University, studied a salad of European literature and been somewhat 'boy-crazy'. She had been working for four years, and enjoyed it intermittently, though sometimes dreamt of giving it up to become a gardener. She had a younger sister called Lucy, with whom she had a love-hate relationship, and a brother who was still at school, sulked and wore 'galumphing' boots. She rarely went home, her mother was too wearing for that. She worked in the education department of the local council, and having once espoused feminist ideals, now warned Isabel that if she didn't marry soon she would be left a spinster, that men didn't like the clothes she wore [why didn't she choose more feminine things?] and that she should accept more dinner invitations. There was no time for much on the father, simply that he was kind but a little ineffectual, frustratingly incompetent.

We got out of the pool and separated to change according to our genders. Once outside, I proposed lunch in a sandwich place a few yards down the road. It was crowded at this hour on a Saturday, but we waited and were eventually given a table in a corner by the door.

'What do you think I should have?' she asked looking at the menu.

'I don't know.'

'I think I'll go for avocado and bacon, with maybe some turkey as well.'

I chose a cheese and tomato number, and we began chatting aimlessly while our stomachs rumbled in post-nautical hunger. The bustling atmosphere led me to ask Isabel if she liked living in London.

'Oh, I don't know. A lot of friends I knew from university have left London. They've gone to provincial cities, or else to Europe or America. I've got a good friend who moved to New York. I don't particularly like London, but at the same time, I think it's granting too much importance to the place you live if you actually move to another one. In the end, all cities are the same, so you might as well stay where you are, where you know how the phone and transport system work, and get on with what matters.'

To be including such details in a biographical effort was to run a danger of exaggeration. Was there really room for sandwich descriptions and light banter between two people over a snack?

Boswell seemed to have felt implicated of a similar charge as he trailed behind Dr Johnson, but he was ready with a defence: 'I am fully aware of the objections which may be made to the minuteness on some occasions of my detail of Johnson's conversation, and how happily it is adapted for the petty exercise of ridicule, by men of super-ficial understanding and ludicrous fancy; but I remain firm and confident in my opinion, that minute particulars are frequently characteristic, and always amusing, when they relate to a distinguished man.'

After all, it was precisely this attention to the minute particulars which had saved for posterity Johnson's answer to the question of whether London was a good place to live, which was not a million miles away from the spirit, if not the splendour of what Isabel had just said.

The real difference with Boswell's defence of Johnson was that it would have been impossible to call Isabel a man and presumptuous to call her distinguished. I might have been accused of an absence of empathy by an ex-girlfriend and thereby grown unexpectedly interested in the possibilities of biography, but why was this interest focusing on someone I had barely swum twenty laps with?

'The most tiring thing about swimming,' said Isabel running her hand through her hair to check if it was dry, 'isn't really the swimming itself, it's getting changed and going there and having a shower and so on. I must say, if I was very rich, the first thing I'd do would be to buy a private swimming pool. Can you imagine? Every morning before work, you could just go swimming for twenty minutes, then feel ready to face the day.'

'But maybe you'd just get bored and not use it.'

'Perhaps. Or else get depressed about being so rich you had a pool in your house. I guess the great thing about not having money is you can imagine how everything would be well if you did have some. But if you're rich, you've only got yourself to blame.'

'Or your parents.'

'Well, we're all allowed to do a bit of that,' she said, and smiled teasingly – just in time for the plate of sand-wiches which landed between us.

Though normally phlegmatic in my concern for others, I realized that our conversation had, despite its outward banality, grown filled with a power to fascinate and enchant.

'Oh shit, it's collapsing everywhere,' said Isabel of her sandwich, which was something of an exaggeration, because the three-layered beast was limiting its collapse to the lap of her skirt.

'I can't believe it, I've got tomato all over this, and it's only just come back from the cleaners. I'm sorry, can I borrow your napkin?'

While Isabel scrubbed, I noticed how she hadn't put her beige pullover on properly after swimming, and a washing label had been left sticking its tongue out of the collar. The contrast between our conversation, her scrubbing and this label hinted in a very obvious way at a more private Isabel – and I suddenly felt the unique and no doubt pathological sense that there was no reason why my interest in her should not stretch as far as her approach to the weekly wash.

To answer those holding that the nobility of biography and the baser realm of human attachment should never be mixed, one may suggest a connection between attachment and the biographical impulse, that is, *an impulse to know another fully.* Every attachment involves a more or less conscious process of biography [as one works out dates, characteristics, favoured wash cycles and snacks . . .], much as a true biography demands a more or less conscious emotional relationship between author and subject. What else could account for the gargantuan energy required to finish such a book?

Richard Holmes, the biographer of Shelley and Coleridge, once movingly compared the biographer's task to following a subject's footsteps through time. He also added a crucial requirement for such an undertaking: 'If you are not in love with them, you will not follow them – not very far, anyway.'

Boswell had felt much the same, writing that he was 'conscious of a generous attachment to Johnson, as my preceptor and friend . . . I thought I could defend him at the point of my sword.'

And even Freud, no fan of the art of fencing, was in agreement: 'Biographers are fixated on their heroes in a quite special way. In many cases they have chosen their hero as the subject of their studies because – for reasons of their personal emotional life – they have felt a special affection for him from the first.' [The rest of the passage grows a little more caustic, though not to quote it would be disingenuous: 'They then devote their energies to a task of idealization, they obliterate the individual features of their subject's physiognomy; they smooth over the traces of his life's struggles with his internal and external resistances, and they tolerate in him no vestige of human weakness or imperfection.']

I began seeing Isabel more regularly. As we were walking along Shaftesbury Avenue one evening and had stopped to look at the window of a newsagent, I was overwhelmed by an urge to kiss her.

'What are you doing?' she asked, withdrawing from my muddled pastiche of an embrace.

['I came to suspect that there is something frequently comic about the trailing figure of the biographer: a sort of tramp permanently knocking at the kitchen window and secretly hoping he might be invited in for supper.' Richard Holmes, *Footsteps*.]

'What am I doing?'

I no longer knew, and instead collided with a green litter bin which noisily spilt three crushed cans onto the pavement – but she had ideas of her own, and a protest I could not ignore.

'I don't want to be difficult, but we don't know one another well enough for me to feel this is right. We sort of know one another, and I know that's enough for most people, but I don't want to rush into anything. It's not that I'm against this, it's just that, well, and this might sound weird, but I want us to learn more about one another first.'

'How do you mean?' I asked, bending down to gather the debris of my collision.

'I don't know: other relationships, friends, work, hang-ups, everything. People never seem to do that till it's too late. Does this seem crazy? Do you mind?'

Did I mind?

There was no time to mind: there was too much to learn.

III

FAMILY TREES

Biographies rarely pass their first page without inaugurating research into the family from whose bosom a noble subject has had the fortune to drop. Though Isabel had spoken of a continuing struggle to cut through her umbilical cord 'with a saw', it was natural to express an interest in her family tree.

There was something enticingly logical about these plants, the way they enabled one to follow a series of alliances and births which had led to a chosen creature. Some branches were vital, and fed into successive twigs, others abutted abruptly with maiden aunts active in village fêtes or confirmed bachelors who took snuff and were caustic in the company of women. There was a feudal side to trees, the way they displayed the matches which separated a lineage from the rabble, the pure blood which ran in the veins and irrigated sets of receding chins.

I had recently come across a tree of the Grosvenor family at the back of a biography of Lady Lettice, found

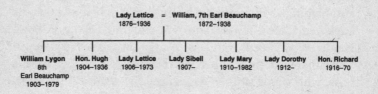

in a rack in a second-hand bookshop on the Charing Cross Road, and had been inspired to imitate the spirit of its elegant symmetry.

'You know, it's funny, I don't know exactly how old my father is. He's a bit older than him,' replied Isabel as we waited at the traffic lights at Hyde Park Corner on our way to the theatre and she pointed to a man talking on a carphone in a chauffeur-driven Jaguar beside us.

'Except he's lot poorer, and probably has less hair. He never had much hair, even when he was young. I know there was some talk about him having a sixtieth birthday party some time ago, but he said that wasn't anything to celebrate, so the idea was dropped – finally, it's green – and I can't remember when that was. He's always seemed a certain age, sort of a cardigan-wearing age. Come on, Gran, move it,' said Isabel by way of encouragement to a car which looked as though it wished to remain at the lights until they changed back to red.

'What about the rest of your family?'

'What about them? I sometimes think I was dropped here by a passing stork, family is an odd concept. I have no idea how my cousins, second cousins and all that works. Because of the way my parents got married, sort of in a hurry by mistake, some sides of the family stopped talking to us altogether. My posh grandparents, my mother's parents, were the problem. They thought my father's family weren't grand enough. They were also anti-Semitic. My father's grandfather, God, that takes us back years, was Jewish and had emigrated from Poland. He lived in Leeds, and was apprenticed to a lawyer. Then there's a story where he married the servant of his boss, who was a simple Yorkshire lass, a good Protestant, who ended up being called Reitzman, because that was my great-grandfather's name. What lane should I take?'

'This one.'

'Thanks. So then they had my father's father, who changed his name to Rogers and who I remember vaguely from when I was young. He and my granny lived in Finchley, and their house smelt like a hospital because my grandfather had a skin complaint and had to rub cream all over himself. Both of them died within about six months of one another when I was seven or eight. On my mother's side were the rich grandparents. My grandfather had served in the army, had been a general in India, so there was lots of India memorabilia, and a sad atmosphere that nothing was going to be as good as it had been on the shaded veranda out in the Punjab. Then there's my aunt, my mother's sister, who went out to America, probably to escape her family, and now lives in Tucson with her husband Jesse who is a biologist. She's become completely American and her children – I don't know much about them or like them much either – play baseball and do cheer–leading and that kind of thing. The man she married was related to the guy who invented the stapler.'

'Eh?'

'Well, someone had to. Anyway, that's one branch of the cousins, then on my father's side, there's a brother and sister. Or rather, brother Tony's only half there, because he flipped out in the sixties and now lives in a caravan in Wales. He writes Beat poetry and used to be a friend of Ginsberg, at least that's what Dad told me, but when I read a book on the Beats, there was no sign of him, so maybe it was just Dad's way of trying to make his brother more respectable. Then there's my aunt Janice. She's pathologically conventional and xenophobic. She's never left England even for a holiday, cleans her house ten times a day and is obsessed with finding hairs in her food. She nearly had to be taken to hospital when she found one in a risotto Mum made.

'So that's a guide to my family, who I hope you'll never have the ill fortune to meet, but at least they've saved you from my collection of car music. They've even made the trip to the Barbican fly past. And there's a parking space, so we're really in luck,' exclaimed Isabel, reversing her car between a concrete mixer and a van.

Whatever the claims to completeness, Isabel's family tree could not at this stage have been considered anything but an unfinished plant given the stretches she had ignored or claimed never to have known. No wonder biographers could build up their genealogies only after consultation with a succession of family members, corroborating their stories with public records and birth certificates. The complexity of family structures was a sobering reminder of the challenge of biographies, and the respect owed to the energy required for their research. They offered a vision of a logical, intact world, every last stepchild and letter would be traced and a victory scored in the eternal war waged against forgetting.

It could explain our admiration for the thorough way a biographer like Richard Ellmann had approached Joyce's family history. There is something extraordinary about a man who would unearth the precise chronology of Joyce's father's school career, who discovered that the boy entered St Colman's College on March 17th, 1859, and, not liking it much, left on February 19th, 1860, not forgetting to tell us that seven pounds of tuition remained unpaid.*

But biographers, in their archival zeal, are prone to overlooking a small but significant feature of the way we experience our family trees; despite our efforts to recall the year Dad was born and the name of our second cousin from Nova Scotia who married the girl from Perth [was it Bronwyn or Bethany?], we often cannot recall half our story. Our genealogy is sunk in shameful darkness, dates and names are as shaky as those of the kings and queens learnt by rote at school, we are as unsure of where we have come from as where we are heading.

Amidst our admiration for Professor Ellmann's precision, a nagging doubt therefore risks creeping in. Did James Joyce, the subject justifying the titanic research, actually have an idea of these facts about his father? He may have had a general picture of him not much liking St Colman's College and coming from a family with money problems, but did he really know his departure date had been February 19th and not the 18th or indeed the 20th? Did he know it had been seven pounds of tuition and not six?

One suspects not, which is where sceptics may let out a polite cough. Before opening the archives, a distinction may need to be made between two sorts of biographical information: on the one hand, facts which a person can remember about his or her family, and on the other, facts which belong to this family but remain unknown to the subject.

The distinction seemed to leave room for a new form

* Richard Ellmann, *James Joyce*, Oxford University Press, 1982.

of biography, far less accurate than that of the old, but concurrently far more authentic. This genre would leave out of the story of a person's life everything which they did not themselves remember of it, it would reflect how *they* understood their family tree rather than the totality of dates and facts which might objectively have been attached to it.

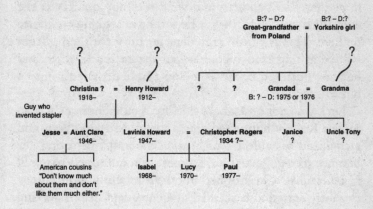

Isabel and I had been driving to the Barbican Theatre to see a production of Lorca's *House of Bernarda Alba*. Given the conversation, what happened once we had taken our seats was a noteworthy [or for Isabel, simply horrific] coincidence.

'Oh my God, I think that's my mum over there,' she gasped.

'Where?'

'By the pillar. Careful, don't look. What is she *doing* here? And what's that dress? It looks like a willow tree. Where's Dad? I hope she didn't come with one of her gentlemen friends. She's really too old for that.'

'Did you tell her you were going?'

'No, I mean, I said I wanted to see the play, but I didn't let on I had tickets for tonight.'

'She's talking to someone. Can you see?'

'Phew, that's my dad. He must have gone off to buy programmes. And he's about to sneeze. Look, there we go, aaahhtchooo. Out comes his red handkerchief. I just hope they don't spot us and we can escape quickly at the end. With any luck, they'll be too busy arguing to glance up here. This is prime argument territory for them, Mum will be asking Dad where he put the car park ticket and he'll get flustered because he'll just have dropped it into a bin by mistake.'

Luck was not on Isabel's side, for a moment later, Christopher Rogers happened to glance up to the gallery and recognized his eldest daughter, in the midst of trying her best not to recognize him. So that she might cease to dwell in ignorance, Christopher stood up in the middle of the elegantly suited and scented audience, and began making the vigorous hand gestures of a man waving off a departing cruise ship. In case Isabel had not spotted this maniac, her mother was in turn informed of her eldest daughter's location, and decided that the presence of four hundred people in the auditorium should be no impediment to her desire to shout 'Isabel' at top pitch and with all the excitement of a woman recognizing a long-lost friend on the deck of an in-coming cruise ship.

Isabel smiled feebly, turned a beetroot shade and repeated in panicked diction, 'I can't believe this, please let them shut up.'

Not a second too soon, Lorca came to the rescue, the lights faded, and Mr and Mrs Rogers reluctantly took their seats, pointing ominously to an exit sign by way of interval rendezvous.

An hour and a quarter of Spanish domestic drama later, we found ourselves at the bar.

'What are you doing here, Mum?' asked Isabel.

'Why shouldn't I be here? You're not the only one who does fancy things with your evenings. Your father and I have a right to go out once in a while.'

'I'm sure, I didn't mean it like that, it's just I'm surprised at the coincidence.'

'Where did you buy this dress? Is that the one I paid for at Christmas?'

'No, Mum, I got it myself last week.'

'Oh, well, it's very nice, pity you don't have more of a cleavage for it, but that's your father's fault. You know what all the women in his family are like.'

'How are you, Dad?' Isabel turned to ask her father, who was looking up at the ceiling with an intent expression.

'Dad?' repeated Isabel.

'Yes, darling, how are you, my bean? Enjoying the show?'

'Yup, and you? What are you staring at up there?'

'I'm looking at the light fixtures they have. They're new tungsten bulbs, Japanese things, quite wonderful, they use only a small amount of electricity but give off a very nice light.'

'Oh, great, Dad. And, ehm, there's someone I'd like you both to meet.'

'Delighted,' said Mrs Rogers, confiding in me almost at once: 'She's a lovely girl really,' in case my theatre companion had inspired doubts to the contrary.

'Thanks, Mum,' said Isabel wearily, as though the statement were no one-off.

'Don't mind her, bean, she's had a hard day,' explained Dad, now looking more horizontally at the world.

'My day would be fine if I wasn't lumbered with someone who kept losing tickets to the car park,' snapped Mrs Rogers.

'Dad! You haven't?'

'Yes, I'm afraid I have. They're so fiddly these days, they fall right out of one's hands.'

A bell sounded and a canned voice informed us in dulcet tones that the performance would soon be resuming.

'I'm sorry about that,' said Isabel when we were back in our seats. 'I'm sure Mum only came because I told her about this play, and she always wants to imitate what I do. Sometimes I wish my family was a bit more normal.'

'They seem fine.'

'I don't know, they're so odd. They were the sort of parents who always stood out at school meetings, my mother resembled someone about to suggest cocktails on the veranda in a Noël Coward play, my father had the manic glare of an Einstein *manqué*. They're misplaced in the modern world. Dad can't operate any modern technology, however interested he is in light bulbs. He shouts down the phone as though it were wind operated. He loves to cook, he makes jam, and my mother sings in a choir. When I was a child, we could never travel without drawing attention to ourselves. If we went out to a restaurant, someone would order a bizarre dish, my sister was a great one for that, a few years ago, she was saying she couldn't have anything with nitrates in. And my father used to ask waiters in crummy establishments who the prints on the wall were by. As though a pizzeria could have a Rembrandt or Titian above the salad bar. I suppose my father's sweet in that respect, he's always engaging people in conversation in the unlikeliest places. At petrol stations, you can leave him alone for a minute, and he'll have made friends with someone, and be in the middle of a discussion on oil filters, the government road-building programme or the best way to roast a chicken. That drives my mother insane, she thinks he's doing it to annoy her, but in fact, he's just un-self-conscious, a big child, really.'

At the end of the play, so as to avoid the congestion in the car park, Isabel and I slipped out before the final curtain call.

'I hate the actors looking so pleased with themselves when they bow,' she whispered. 'It destroys all the illusions they'd built up during the play. You realize they're just late twentieth-century Brits, not broody Spaniards with marriage problems.'

We had also intended to avoid Isabel's parents in the foyer, but the plan went awry when we crossed them in the lift down to the car park.

'Now I know the last thing on your mind would be to go off and have dinner with two frightfully boring people like us, so I won't even ask,' began Isabel's mother, thereby both asking and generating guilt were the implied offer to be refused.

'Stop doing that,' replied Isabel.

'Doing what?'

'The martyr thing again.'

'I beg your pardon? I'm simply giving you the option to eat with us. We made a booking at a lovely restaurant just near here, and we'd be delighted if you and your friend could join us. Christopher, will you please tell your daughter to stop looking at me like that?'

'Bean, don't listen to a word your mother says. Go and have dinner as you planned, and we'll see you in a couple of weeks for Lucy's birthday.'

'Thanks, Dad, bye, Mum,' said Isabel as the lift doors opened at the requisite level.

'Isn't Dad a sweetie?' she asked when we reached the car, her face radiant at the suggestion.

We drove across the city, and ended up in a wall-carpeted Indian restaurant near Isabel's house, where the conversation returned to parental matters and further elucidated the particular nuance which the Rogers had succeeded in giving Tolstoy's dictum about unhappy families.

Isabel's mother had historically considered her three children a nuisance, until they reached maturity and awoke her to a sense of desertion and the end of her home-making vocation. The paradox for the deserters was that the wished-for audience they occasionally granted their mother did not go beyond reverting her to an earlier mode of emotional absenteeism. The only way for Isabel to feel wanted was to pretend she permanently had better things to do.

'She's going to be furious I didn't want to have dinner with her tonight, but she's also going to admire me for it,' said Isabel, glancing down the menu and alighting on a tandoori.

It was no coincidence, for though Mrs Rogers valued

emotional warmth, in her particular mental constellation, her ability to display it was subservient to an imperative to freeze in contact with the emotional sensitivities of others. She had a satanic ability to sort true vulnerabilities from false ones, could tell when Isabel's moan at the behaviour of a friend was simply that or genuine pain at the oddity of others, and lost no time in flailing the wound were it to be the latter.

The maternal grandparents were from wealthy landed stock, people who wept for weeks at the roadside death of their golden retriever but did not blink at consigning a child to boarding school before it had been potty-trained. Mrs Rogers's father enjoyed his whisky, or was an alcoholic, depending on one's position vis-à-vis the drinks cabinet. He combined a conservative belief in the role of Church and state with a feudal sense of his rights. He liked to fire rifles over the heads of picnickers who unpacked their hampers on his field, had ridden a bull through a nearby village shouting Latin obscenities and had been involved in an affair with the wife and daughters of a local solicitor. His wife had endured her husband with dignity and the development of facial tics and intestinal disorders.

The daughter had not emerged unscathed. Her emotional balance relied on an ability to complain about everything, and would have suffered had anyone been foolish enough to alleviate her of her lot. Mrs Rogers needed obstacles and found them in her parents, the husband she had unwillingly married, her children, the government, the press and in her bleaker moments, humanity.

She had a veneration for strong men [one side rather

fancied someone who would ride through a village on a bull], but had married one of the mildest brands available [it was hard to imagine Christopher riding a pony at a funfair]. Unwilling to blame herself for the discrepancy, she daily chastized her husband for not being someone else – usually, though not exclusively, the artist Jacques who she had encountered in her university years.

A small house in Kingston meant living in a style far from that to which she had been accustomed, so Mrs Rogers developed a taste for sardonic remarks as to the wealth of others, which might in some circles have been taken for socialist leanings and in others for jealousy. She projected her discomforts onto the world stage, those around her were quickly made aware that they were living in a decade which heralded a return to the Dark Ages. When asked for evidence for this shift in the global economy, enquirers would be regaled with tales of the garishness of the new Kingston shopping centre, the demise of the local arts cinema and an increase in dog fouling on the common.

In her spare time, she collected teapots in the shape of animals; there was a line in cats, dogs, rabbits, giraffes and hedgehogs. She also owned a set of lamps in the shape of flowers. A large tulip illuminated the living-room, while in the hall a rose shone a pink half-light onto disrobing visitors. Another interest centred on embroidered screens designed to cover inert fireplaces: she had over twenty, though her house lacked any fireplaces, let alone an inert one.

'It's a way of taking out her sex drive,' explained Isabel, uncharitably I thought, for she knew how to do this directly when she wished.

She had had affairs in the course of her marriage, kept in view of Isabel, who had frequently been asked to participate in sessions of reconciliation between her mother and father [it had fostered the impression that she was the only adult in the family, not an amusing realization when she longed to make her own mistakes]. The most developed liaison had been with the father of a girl at Isabel's school, a car dealer who had sold the family a discounted estate model, but whose dominant purpose was to strike life into Mr Rogers. Sadly, when his wife anonymously sent the family some photos showing her husband and Mrs Rogers in a state of undress on a beach in Patmos [Lavinia had claimed a trip to Jersey with her reading club], Christopher lacked the decency to grow jealous, preferring to digress instead on the island's relation to sections of *The Iliad*.

'Do you think this dress really makes me look flat chested?' interrupted Isabel, her mother's comment having been of apparent subterranean concern all the while.

'Oh, I hadn't . . . I mean . . .'

'I don't think it does particularly, not more than usual. I may not have impressive . . . you know, but that's nothing new. I'm sorry, is this embarrassing?' enquired Isabel, noticing a light blush across her companion's cheek.

'Not at all. This madras, God, they've gone overboard with the spices in the kitchen,' I answered, pointing to a pair of swing doors at the back of the restaurant.

'Mum always passes judgement on my clothes. She finds elaborate, quite poetic metaphors for them. She tells me things like, "That makes you look like an intergalactic space stewardess," or, "It's a dress that wouldn't have been out of place on one of the daughters of the posh family in *The Little House on the Prairie*." '

Behind such criticism, Mrs Rogers waged an exhausting wardrobe competition with her eldest daughter. Unable to accept the verdict of her age, Lavinia could not spend more than a few minutes with a stranger before informing them that she and Isabel had once been mistaken for sisters.

The pretensions of her appearance were matched only by those of her conversation. One could not mention a book which Lavinia had not read or more often reread. Isabel had a few years back challenged her to relate the plot of a panoramic Russian novel whose virtues she had been extolling during dinner. 'Don't be so stupid,' Lavinia had snapped, but by her irritation and discomfort admitted fraudulence. She rarely had the grace to do so directly. Her belief in knowing it all meant she could only be challenged by a bet, the last recourse when dealing with someone who could not be convinced.

'So what about your father?'

'Oh, he's lovely by comparison,' said Isabel, the radiant smile reappearing, 'just rather eccentric.'

Mr Rogers had escaped his wife's complexity with interest in the peripherals of existence. He could entertain a conversation of many hours' duration on the second downward clue of *The Times* crossword, the migration of African birds, the effect of carbon dioxide on the synapses of the brain, not to mention the pros and cons of buying a water purifier or the gradual supersession of the sewn bookbinding by its glued counterpart – but remained at a loss to understand the role allotted to him in the family drama.

Everything one said threw him into deep thought, whereby he would roll back his eyes, lift up his head and enter into a phase of saying 'Yes' in rapid succession, though the comment which had elicited this might have been no greater than, 'It's getting harder to find red apples these days.' He believed people were good if only they cared to realize it, and though this lack of scepticism had led him to be passed over for promotion by younger and more hardened colleagues, he seemed not to mind as long as he could keep a roof over his family and continue reading the diaries of his beloved Pepys. His other-worldliness was found charming by many, particularly women, so that without trying he found himself bewitching dinner guests with his wonder that Pepys should have been born a hundred metres from Gough Square where Samuel Johnson was to take rooms in the next century.

Listening to Isabel, I thought of the many different times her past must have been related over meals both spicy and less so, and how each telling would subtly have differed, both out of Isabel's semiconscious impression of what was valid to her companions and the active channelling of their questions. It was like showing a guest around one's house, only to be interrupted by a curious, 'What's in here?', a diversion from the predicted tour for the sake of a particular cupboard or attic room – a diversion akin to my having asked Isabel exactly what sort of affairs her mother had had, my curiosity born [as it too often is, or perhaps only can be] out of a search for parallels with my own life, out of a quest for an identity which would be thrown into sharper relief by the experiences of others. How much of our interest in dinner companions and in biographies is not at base a desire to find out, 'How do *I* differ from this friend, Napoleon, Verdi, or W. H. Auden?' and hence indirectly, 'Who am I to be?'?

Though what Isabel was relating had happened long before, the story was not fixed. There were pauses which had nothing to do with mouthfuls when Isabel seemed to reach sensitive material which had not been ironed by frequent tellings, moments when she became dreamy and fell into the conceptually paradoxical process of asking herself what this self in fact felt, rather than reporting to an ignorant outsider things she knew full well already.

'I suppose I'm Dad's favourite in the family,' said Isabel after such a pause, 'I've got more sympathy for him than the others. He had a rather stern father and difficult mother, whom he loved but who he always had to take care of, to calm down when she was in a stew. By marrying my mother, who's always climbing onto her high horse, it was as if he was recreating the situation he'd known as a child. It's only recently I've begun to de-idealize him a little, but I still want to know what he thinks of things I'm doing, or people I'm going out with. I look for his approval and opinions about silly details, like what sort of loudspeakers to buy or books to read. My sister thinks I'm a noodle, but probably only because she's jealous. By the way, this is a fantastic curry. Is yours really too spicy?'

Much of the distinctiveness of Isabel's story was captured in the rhythms and expressions of her language. I was beginning to recognize her linguistic idiosyncrasies, the areas in which her English differed from that spoken on the radio, the uses she made of words and phrases out of psychological rather than grammatical choice. In Isabel-English, people who were evil or cruel were simply 'noodles' or more often, 'monkeys', which suggested a benevolent approach to malfeasance, a misdeed performed by a naughty child and not an intentional immorality. When she behaved unreasonably, she would label herself a 'nong' [or even 'Mrs Nong'], which did not appear in the dictionary, but suggested someone childishly clumsy and inept. There was a cockney lilt in certain of her words, her property was missing its *e*, her tea cups lacked their *p*s and little was *liole* – these items socially contradicted by her World Service pronunciation of 'perpendicular' and use of 'disenfranchizement'.

A chance to meet Isabel's younger sister came the weekend following our Indian meal, when Lucy dropped off some clothes she had borrowed.

'Come up, munchkin,' said Isabel through the intercom and pressed a button to release the door.

A moment later, a tall young woman entered the living-room, hugged her sister and displayed a smile sufficient to remove any physical prejudices which her nickname might have evoked.

'Hi,' she said extending a hand, 'I'm so pleased to meet you.'

'Don't exaggerate,' said Isabel, 'you haven't spoken to him yet.'

'But I can tell,' she said, fixing her grey-green eyes on mine.

'Do you want a drink?' asked Isabel.

'Thanks. A gin and tonic would be great.'

'Be serious, it's three in the afternoon and you're in Hammersmith, not Hollywood,' she said, a cockney lilt covering the second clause.

'Oh, a Perrier then.'

'I only do *eau du robinet*.'

'Don't worry then. So tell me exactly what you do with your life?' Lucy turned and asked me, with a touch on my knee to lend emphasis to her enquiry, thus revealing what Isabel later explained her sister spent much of her time doing whenever there were males in Isabel's vicinity.

'What do I do?' repeated Lucy, to whom I had returned the question. 'Ha,' she laughed, 'I don't know, I guess I'm a student.'

'Why do you guess, Lucy? You are a student,' interjected Isabel.

'Well, it's only fashion,' she said biting her nail, 'not like what you did or Dad or Mum.'

'Doesn't matter,' answered Isabel, 'it's a great thing to do.'

'I suppose so,' replied Lucy, as though she had never thought about it in those terms before.

Lucy suffered from what Isabel called 'the typical sandwich problem', being stuck between an older sister and a younger brother. It was a way of explaining an unusual number of neurotic traits compared to her siblings, problems which Isabel had a tendency to feel guilty about, as she had been the top half of a sandwich of which Lucy was the more neglected filling.

Lucy lacked confidence in her intellectual capacities. Afraid a conversation might grow beyond her comprehension, she had a habit of deflating matters to levels obviously below her. To discuss the politics of the Prime Minister would lead her to wonder how he combed his hair, consideration of a recent novel would elicit remarks on how the jacket cover matched the author's eyes.

Her behaviour towards Isabel veered between admiration and jealousy. Though it was hard to imagine, she had been a scrawny and unattractive child, in the shadow of her more popular older sibling. She had imitated her in everything, and this had continued into adult life and the realm of men. Unfortunately for Isabel, Lucy didn't just want a boyfriend like hers, she frequently wanted exactly hers – and had gone out with two men indecently soon after their relationships with her.

When the criteria of interest was not her sister's link with them, Lucy searched for characters who would treat her badly. Her masochism went beyond the emotional tease frequently captured by the word, it included cigarette burns, beatings and an inability to tolerate the kindness owed to a farm animal. Mrs Rogers was sure who was to blame.

'Watching the way you treated her as a child, it's no wonder she turned out like that,' she accused Isabel.

Wherever the true responsibility lay, there was a note of paranoia in Lucy's behaviour which Isabel could do nothing to alleviate.

'You think I never work hard enough,' she snapped at Isabel, in reply to a remark that it was hard to concentrate on studies when the weather was so warm.

'I didn't say that,' replied her sister, 'I know how hard you work.'

'I gather that's not what you told Dad. I spoke to him yesterday.'

'How do you mean?'

'He said you told him I was worried about my exams.'

'You were.'

'But you don't have to report that to him.'

'I'm not reporting anything, he just asked me how you were.'

'Yeah, well, I don't want him to think I do no work.'

'He doesn't, he knows you work a lot – and certainly more than Paul.'

Paul was their younger brother, the apple of his mother's eye, who had received the double attention owed to a boy who was at the same time the youngest child – but who failed to excite much sympathy in either Lucy, Isabel or Mr Rogers.

The sisters had spent their childhood orchestrating a Spanish Inquisition against him, once convincing him that if he ate a small frog people at school would stop their bullying and become his friends. Desperation made him swallow the wriggling creature Isabel had found in a pet shop, but he soon realized the deception, and from then on, ceased to care if he had friends or not. He had grown to love vigorous sports and had a pugnacious character, considering a Saturday evening well spent if it had included five pints of beer and a fist-fight ignited by the gladiatorial [if not philosophical] question, 'Do you have a problem, mate?'

'So I guess it's the average dysfunctional set-up, the usual rather fucked-up family,' sighed Isabel once her sister had left the apartment, an unresolved argument hovering between them concerning who had said what to Mr Rogers. 'Now I'm no longer living at home, I try not to think about it too much, but I suppose you can't really forget where you've come from. You carry it with you all the time: a problem your parents had is going to be your problem at some level. Mum was screwed up by her mum and so screwed me up, you know, the Larkin stuff. Still, there's no point frittering the afternoon away with moans. I'm sorry, I'm being a very bad host, do you want some biscuits?'

The traditional family tree, emerging as it did from the feudal age, was primarily devoted to stressing lineage and dates of birth and death. But in a more psychological age, was the primary responsibility still to record such factual details? Listening to Isabel's description of her family, I wondered if one might not inaugurate a different structure, one which traced not what lands, titles and estates moved down the generations, but rather the passage of emotional dispositions, in short, a [Larkinesque] tree of family fucked-upness?

Isabel's inheritance from the merry hoard was constituted in part by an ambivalence as to whether she should

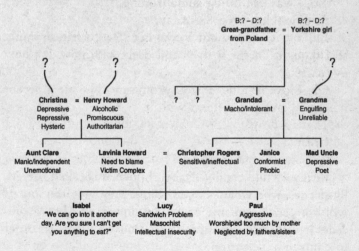

take any of it seriously. Reading of the deprivation of the unemployed, the decline of living standards and the suffering of cancer patients, she doubted the legitimacy of the expression of these suburban complaints and tended to offer biscuits [chocolate or oatmeal] instead.

A brief outline of the tree of fucked-upness was therefore concluded with a digression on how ridiculous it was to harbour resentments at events in childhood.

'After all, my parents did the best for their children, and the same for my grandparents. So it's really a pity to spend your life worrying about what happened to you at the age of two.'

However, when Isabel went to celebrate her sister's birthday at her parents' house a few weeks later, the story grew more complicated.

'I'm not bothering you, am I?' she asked, giving me a ring early the following morning.

'No, I was just doing some ironing.'

'At nine thirty on a Saturday?'

'I know, it's crazy, but I couldn't sleep. I hate ironing, so I thought I'd get it over and done with now. It's only five shirts.'

'Oh, I love ironing. If you promise to buy me a decent lunch, I'll give you a hand with it.'

'That's a deal.'

'Great.'

'So how was the birthday?'

'Really awful,' replied Isabel, but then checked herself, like a guest who worries that the joke they have announced will not prove amusing to fellow diners, and hence precedes it with 'You know, it's really not so funny' in order to dampen expectation.

'It's just I got annoyed with my mother in a childish way,' she continued.

At the end of the meal, Mrs Rogers had mockingly alluded to how upset Isabel had been when, many years before, she had thrown away 'a stinky old blanket' Isabel had used as a bed for her teddy bear.

'What's so wrong with having been upset about that?' Isabel had asked.

'Oh, well, it was ridiculous, you made a drama that lasted for weeks. I wonder whether you've even forgiven me now,' replied the mother.

Relating the incident, Isabel remarked with a wry laugh, 'And in fact, it's funny, but I realized that at one level I *hadn't* forgiven the old witch, there was still a "me" at the age of six somewhere in "me" at the age of twenty-five and this little person was indignant with my mother for doing what she did.'

In the scale of abuses which adults regularly inflict on one another, what Isabel had suffered in childhood deserved more ridicule than pity. And yet judged on the childhood scale, these were dramatic events, which could excite and sadden way past the age when to do so was deemed respectable in mature company. The loss of a blanket at the age of six could not be considered with the same robustness as the loss might elicit at sixty.

Isabel went on to recall how she had once drawn a house in kindergarten and proudly shown it to her mother, who had made her cry by replying in a teasing voice, 'That's not going to be much good, you've forgotten to put in a door. How do you expect people to get out?'

Why would anyone bawl at such minor criticism? Yet if viewed from where Isabel had stood, it might have been a symbol for an attitude of permanent derision of things in which she had invested her energies.

One could imagine the defensive layers which had coated Isabel's sensitivities since then, for she could now endure the most scathing conversations with her mother, or for that matter, fall into a vehement row with a taxi driver in a London street, be called a harlot, insult the man back with equal force – and all the while not show offence. Yet beneath this adult invulnerability, there lay a network of ancient hurts which were as laughably small when seen from afar as they were deadly serious from close-up; they were the hurts of a thin-skinned child rather than an elephant-skinned adult.

So whatever gratitude Isabel felt towards her parents, whatever her inclinations not to exaggerate her history, enough had happened to fill a list on that notoriously hubris-prone subject:

What I would never do to my own children

1) 'I'd never force them to eat overcooked broccoli,' explained Isabel later that morning, stretching the sleeve of an ageing white shirt before applying the iron.

'How do you mean?'

'My mother spent my childhood on a crusade to make me eat every noxious vegetable around. What's more, she'd terrify me with stories of starving Chinese children who'd be far nicer to have at the dinner table than me. She once said she'd found a pretty Chinese girl, Xanshi, who ate whatever was in front of her, and she'd be swapping us as soon as the adoption papers were ready. I started crying my eyes out, I think because I always had this fear Mum wasn't happy with me. She'd make comments to Lucy and me about how she could have finished her Ph.D. and would probably be presenting an arts programme on the radio by now, if only it hadn't been for us. I'd never want to see my child turn round at the age of fifteen and sneer, "I never asked to be born." '

'You didn't?'

'I know it's a cliché, but it seemed dramatic at the time.'

'What did your mother do?'

'She was quite frank; she said she hadn't asked to be born either, but the same misfortune had happened to her, so we might as well both get on with it.'

2) Spraying the collar of a better preserved blue shirt, Isabel went on to blame her father for not giving her enough of a sense of the world's economic realities. Because of an old-fashioned, potentially chivalrous but practically damaging belief that women were not to be plagued by material concerns, he had been absent [or staring at the ceiling] at the crucial career decisions, and had never pushed Isabel as hard as he had pushed Paul.

She had been unable to do wrong at school, which was pleasant had it not implied an insulting lack of discrimination between the effort of an A grade and a Z – both of which were great achievements when she was their author. Isabel had hence worked with the energy of someone fighting to get approval – because universal admiration had seemed simply another, if milder, form of neglect.

3) 'Nor would I be so liberal about sex. My parents tried hard to be modern, but ended up unnaturally open. I remember being sixteen and telling them oral sex was great. My mother just said, "Yes, you'll find it is, but it's hard to do well."

And she put me on the pill. No thrill in shuffling off to the doctor, she just came into my room and said that as I'd been seeing a boy, I'd better get some "protection".'

4) 'Then I suppose I'd try not to get favourites in the family. I know my father preferred me to my sister, which might be lovely, but was in fact very complicated. Because I loved Lucy, I felt bad knowing Dad was being more affectionate with me. If I didn't get on well with her at times, it was mostly out of a sense of guilt, it was too much to always look after her and play big sister. And I think that in turn impacted on Paul, who had to bear the brunt of Lucy's insecurities. She's always teased him and tried to cause fights between my mother and him, because he's her favourite, which rightly bugs her too.'

5) 'Nor would I use guilt as a weapon to get things out of my children. My mother frequently asks me to do things she knows I have no time for or inclination to do, and then she'll reply, "Oh, well, I knew it. I know how you feel about me. I must seem like such a silly old woman now you're grown up and taking care of yourself." One of her closest friends died of leukaemia recently, and when she rang to tell me, I was on the other line, so of course I said I'd finish with the call and talk to her, but she said, "No, no, don't do that, darling. I just wanted to let you know, but I realize how busy you are, so I don't want to

keep you." As though I was going to be too busy to talk to her when her best friend just died!

I can't stand martyrdom as a way of influencing people. If you want something, you have to say it directly, not try and force it out of the other person by making a long face. I hate the way my mother hides behind her own self-criticism. She'll say, "I'm so boring for you," just so as to prevent herself being disappointed. She caricatures herself, and rather revels in it. She's like one of those fat people who prefers to buy a T-shirt saying "Danger, Fat Person" rather than go on a diet.'

6) 'I'd also try to respect the boundaries between myself and my kids more. My mother sees my love life as a natural part of her business. Once I was going out with a boy she really liked, and I later learnt she stayed in touch with him even after I'd ended the relationship. From when I was young, she'd confide in me about things I didn't want on my plate. When I was eleven, she told me she thought my father had been having an affair, which was a projection if ever I saw one, and that she found her marriage very difficult, which isn't something you say to a child unless there's a real reason to do so. Only the other day, she phoned me up at around ten thirty in the evening, and started telling me how bored she was with my father, and how it must be nice for me to have "choices". Then, just to prove her point, she said, "Listen to how your father snores, it's been more than a quarter of a century that I've had to put up with this noise," and she placed the receiver over his nose so I could hear.'

'Hear what?' I pruriently asked.

'You know, those snoring noises, chhhhhummmm,

chhhhhhummmm, chhhhummm. I mean, poor man. What business is it of mine? She brings me into the marriage bed. I think there are laws against that.

'OK, that's five shirts done. Do you remember the number of the Ritz by heart?'

However long the list and whatever her efforts, Isabel nevertheless displayed an ironic assurance that she would in due course stumble upon new and more inventive ways of creating resentments in her own children – and therefore that child-raising could only be approached with a desire not so much to succeed as to limit the severity of inevitable failure.

IV

KITCHEN BIOGRAPHY

Isabel had a box of chocolates in her fridge, a birthday present from her American aunt. It had been christened Continental Selection and came in a brown carton with a pink bow, the individual pieces berthed on two layers of corrugated-plastic cots.

When Isabel went away for a week on business, because I lived relatively close by she asked if I might drop into her flat to water a plant she owned, a green creature whose biological name I never learnt, but whom she called Gripper, an allusion to its clinging, sharp-pointed leaves.

'Have anything you like from the fridge. It's all yours,' she added, and when I arrived to fulfil the watering task, I believed her.

There was not much inside its bowels. A jar of olives, Spanish, but apparently *à la Grecque*, a bottle of ketchup, a tub of margarine, two apples, a carrot, some medicine labelled BY PRESCRIPTION ONLY, a jar of pesto, some black cherry jam, a tin of tuna and sitting coyly on the third scaffold, a little to the left of the milk, Continental Selection.

Outside the fridge, history was being made on the football pitch, so before watering Gripper, I took the box from its chilly tomb and went to sit in front of the television. I hadn't thought greed would undo so many. One or two might have been enough, if the game hadn't taken a turn for the worst, if I hadn't been such a fool. By the time I turned off the set [the chosen team shamefully defeated], twelve had been devoured. I hastily compressed the foil wrappings into pellets, and buried the evidence at the bottom of the bin, rearranging the survivors so as to diminish the scale of the massacre. The thought of Gripper crying out for a glass of water in the corner of the room did not, members of the jury, cross my mind for a moment and I left the flat absorbed in the failure of the English goalkeeper to defend the nation's honour.

'He's dead,' exclaimed Isabel on her return, grief tangible down the telephone line.

'Who?' I asked, trying to remember her family members most likely to suffer cardiac arrest.

'Gripper, he died of thirst.'

'I'm sorry to hear that,' I replied, at that moment realizing the enormity of my crime.

'You didn't water him, did you?'

'Yes,' answered the murderer with the automatic deceit sparked by situations of extreme guilt, 'yes, I did. It was just very hot, it's been so hot here. God, it's been hot, unbelievable really. I've been sleeping with the windows open . . .'

'You're lying. You didn't water him, the earth was completely dry. I wish you could be honest, I don't mind, it's lying I hate. What's more, you left the light on and ate all my chocolates.'

'I didn't.'

'You did.'

'I only ate a few.'

'You hoovered up everything worth eating. Who do you think I am? Someone who's going to get fat on a bloody lemon parfait?'

It was time for reparation, so after work I stopped off at a department store, which carried a range of ruinously priced chocolates from two of the more morose countries on the European mainland. Yet faced with Belgian and Swiss confectionery, I realized my inability to answer any of the questions Isabel had so forcefully put to me.

Why *was* it inconceivable that she should eat a 'bloody lemon parfait'? What was a lemon parfait? What constituted a more desirable chocolate? A truffle, white or brown, filled with liqueur or caramel? And therefore, who *did* I think she was?

These were grand questions to confront in a department store. I noticed a headscarfed woman growing impatient with my nail-biting hesitation between boxes, but they surely merited the dilemma at hand. Since disenchantment with linear biographies had set in, I had been searching for suitable themes through which to observe Isabel's life. I had not imagined being distracted by something as humble as her appetite at this precocious stage, but her question had sharply highlighted my ignorance of the issue.

Based solely on a consideration of the time taken up with ingesting it, food is to be counted as a significant part of any life. Isabel spent ten minutes eating breakfast, twenty snacking through lunch, and forty-five munching dinner. A quarter of an hour a day was taken up with apples, nuts, crisps and chocolate biscuits. She had therefore spent some 13,685 hours of her life in the process of eating – not to mention the time spent anticipating or regretting binges, something which probably brought the figure closer to 15,000 hours.

But food rarely rears its head in works of biography. While studies of his life make us feel we know him better than he knew himself, Coleridge's taste in spring vegetables remains an edifying mystery. Despite the ample information on their careers, we would be unable to say whether Abraham Lincoln preferred eggs poached or fried and whether Baron Hausmann liked his lamb medium or rare.

E. M. Forster once moaned appetitively of a similar lack of culinary enthusiasm in fiction [whose historical connections with biography are marked]: 'Food draws characters together, but they seldom require it physiologically, seldom enjoy it, and never digest it unless specifically asked to do so. They hunger for each other, as we do in life, but our equally constant longing for breakfast and lunch does not get reflected.'

If it fails to be, it is perhaps out of a prejudice that there are certain activities which reflect our individuality better than others. Forster's biographers overlook his favourite foods [aubergines, spotted dick] because they choose to locate the essence of his identity in who he slept with or voted for [young men, the Liberals].

Yet it seemed a person might be present in their minuter actions and inclinations, in areas one had previously thought non-symbolic and hence forgettable, ways of drinking from a can or manoeuvring chocolate raisins from their packet. Anyone who hears a lover account for the demise of their passion will recognize that we are prone to locating the essence of a person in what we publicly dismiss as trivial, yet privately hold as vital. The lover may cite the rejected one's taste in religion, profession or literature, but this lacks the explicative power of the crumbs which follow, namely that the ex happened also to gulp loudly between mouthfuls, did not replace their knife and fork symmetrically and mopped up gravy with a piece of bread, details which one intuitively knows to be far closer to the grounds of the relationship's demise than anything yet outlined.

Haughtily dismissed as irrelevant to the revelation of character, appetite may deserve to be recognized as the gateway to its secrets. Had Dr Johnson not wisely explained to Boswell after that famous meat pye, 'Nobody can write the life of a man, but those who have eaten and drunk with him' [and shared a few chocolates, he might have added, had Continental Selection been available in Oxford Street in 1776]?

For Ximenes Doudan, on earth in 1843, sniffing out the tastes of the stomach was a symbol of duty for the true biographer: 'I cannot cure myself of my biographical passion. If I knew where one could read how many grains of salt Caesar put on his eggs, I'd leave this minute to go and hunt out this precious document. I'm suspicious of great minds who don't like little details – they're pedants.'

It is no surprise if the culinary information we do have on biographical figures has a power to fascinate: is there not something captivating in the idea that the Marquis de Sade had a soft spot for meringues, that Rousseau sang the praise of pears, that Sartre had a horror of shellfish, that Proust ordered roast chicken from the Ritz and that Nietzsche delighted in steaks served with omelettes in apple marmalade?

Because the headscarfed woman had by now twice dug her trolley into my ribs, I cut short my hesitation and gambled on a box incongruously labelled Zurich Delights.

'Thanks so much,' said Isabel when I presented it to her. 'Look, it's got a picture of the lake, and portraits of famous Swiss people. You really shouldn't have bought this. I just lost my temper for a moment, as Gripper lay dying and everything, but the chocolates don't matter at all. Why don't you help me with them? I'm too fat anyway.'

I was not going to risk a second error, so though the box lay open before us while Isabel and I played a game of chess, I forbade my hand from reaching for one.

'Go on,' repeated Isabel, noticing this abstinence, 'they'll just go stale otherwise, or make me obese.'

One side of me was salivating to respond to the offer, but another needed more information, needed to know precisely which chocolates Isabel favoured, and hence indirectly [with particular reference to the lemon parfait], who Isabel was.

A small map came with the box, indicating the qualities and fillings of each specimen, so I interrupted our game for an investigation.

'Zurich Delight' Range	Isabel's Evaluation out of 10
Hazelnut Slice: Finely chopped, roasted hazelnuts blended with extra-smooth praline, covered in smooth milk chocolate and sliced into individual pieces.	7
Walnut Truffle: Caramel truffle with fresh cream, sprinkled with finely chopped walnut pieces and covered in a double layer of rich milk chocolate.	11

Limmat Truffle: A delicious truffle flavoured with oil of oranges, mixed with flakes of wafer and covered in smooth milk chocolate.	5

'Oh, enough, you monkey,' interrupted Isabel, 'can we get back to the game? Just because your knight's in trouble, doesn't mean you should change the subject.'

'Still, what do you make of the Zwingli twirl? It has a praline base, with a lightly whipped, brandy flavoured—'

'Shush, I hate brandy, I can't stand whipping and I want to finish the game before *Gardeners Today* comes on.'

Reluctantly, I returned to the task of rescuing my knight, though his valiance and black armour were incapable of averting death at the hands of a pawn some ten minutes before the start of the aforementioned programme.

But what did all this mean – the chocolates, that is? I had been as biographically passionate as Ximenes Doudan with his wish to unearth the amount of salt Caesar had put on his eggs, but what could the chocolate verdict tell me of who Isabel was? What would Doudan have learnt had it been twelve grains Caesar had sprinkled rather than eleven or perhaps even ten?

When food is considered in a psychological light, numberless theories may follow as to its meaning. Edible products cease to inhabit the domain of common sense; a fondness for radishes is no longer just a fondness for the root of a conciferous plant, it accedes to the symbolic level where, depending on one's analytical inclinations, it may become a sign of cold-bloodedness, paranoia or liberality.

Isabel had never systematized her theories between food and personality, but certainly assumed they were worth having. One of her occasional supermarket occupations was to pass a 'trolley test' on people, whereby she would deduce, on the basis of items in a shopping bag, something about the owner's life.

'Look at that weirdo,' she whispered to me a few days after our chocolate reconciliation, while we waited in a supermarket queue behind a tall moustachioed gentleman paying for a tube of anchovy paste and a bottle of walnut oil.

'Definitely a child pornography type, you know, deflowered-virgin fantasies – but ultra-right-wing at the same time, probably in favour of capital punishment for stealing car radios.'

'Shhh, not so loud.'

'Don't be ridiculous, he won't hear. And look behind us, there's a really defensive one.'

The shopper in question had rushed to set the plastic barrier marked NEXT CUSTOMER to defend her two tinned tomatoes, six onions, three tins of tuna and one jar of HP sauce. Every time the rubber carpet inched towards the laser scanner, the woman would readjust one of her items, and checked carefully that none of Isabel's food was straying across the boundary.

'But you can't make snap judgements on people like that,' I protested.

'Why not?'

'Because they might not be true.'

'So?'

'Well, how would you like it if someone judged you on what you ate?'

'I'd think it was fine, it's probably a good way of getting to know someone.'

Isabel hated to divide her attention between eating and an activity other than talking. Heights of depravity were reached by people who watched television while they ate; indeed her anxiety about a sterile marriage was symbolized by the fear that 'Hubby and I would end up in our semi-detached bungalow watching the news with a TV dinner on our knees'. I had heard her condemn a friend of her parents as 'someone who reads magazines at dinner', and she had mentioned in a tone of disgust a boyfriend who had glanced through the sports pages while he ate. Even when she was alone, despite the minimal evening meal she might prepare, she still refused to countenance dividing her attention between a piece of toast and the next day's weather forecast. She had a trace of an aesthetic approach to eating which placed the functional, nutritive dimension far below the sensual one. It led to condemnations of fast-food restaurants not on the basis of the food they served [some of which she liked, particularly the french fries doused in ketchup], but rather the way people ate there coarsely and anonymously.

But even within the appetitive realm, meaningful ways of eating would have to be separated from purely contingent ones. Our impressions of people are rarely based soundly on example. We may feel someone to be socially nervous, but be at a loss to say exactly why, until a more skilled observer reminds us of an occasion when they greeted us by offering both their cheek and their hand, awkwardly withdrawing each at the inappropriate moment.

I knew Isabel was impatient, she was someone who

swallowed rather than chewed Vitamin C, but the representative example of the trait had to wait until an evening spent in a pizzeria. It emerged that whereas I adopted a systematic approach according to which pizzas were divided into slices, she chose a meandering route which stopped at all the most tempting moments first, eventually leaving her with the inferior crust which she had generously offered to me with the prediction, 'I'd burst if I ate another mouthful.'

Nothing in Isabel's shopping basket spoke of complicated or lengthy cooking rituals, there were no vanilla essences, cake mixtures or joints of beef. The impatient cook lacks faith in time as a benevolent force, the delay succeeds only in increasing risk and exposure. It might have explained Isabel's fondness for pasta, embodied in three packets of linguine on the rubber carpet. She faulted most pasta for not tasting enough of tomatoes, and had therefore taken many tins of concentrate, so the ratio of concentrate to chopped tomato would be approximately 3:1. Aware this was not the norm, she retained greater insecurities concerning the results of this dish than others [given her level of kitchen confidence, Isabel always sought to reduce expectations in the hope of gaining credit if the food was edible].

When Isabel was not eating pasta, she was frequently in the habit of eating parts of herself.

'What are you doing?' I asked when I noticed her putting most of her hand down her mouth before our departure for the High Street.

'Oh, nothing,' she replied, and rapidly hid her hand under a cushion.

I left the room for a moment, only to return to see her

doing much the same thing, though on closer inspection, she seemed to be gnawing at a specific spot between two fingers on her left hand.

'Have you got a blister or something?' I asked.

'It's just a piece of hard skin,' Isabel answered, reddening slightly.

In two spots on each hand, at the base of the index finger, she had areas of dead skin, which she would pick at during uncomfortable thoughts [quite what these might be was another question. It seemed Isabel's anxieties focused around a range of issues.

1. Whether she was ugly, and if so, to what degree. There were periodic crises as to her weight, particularly after she had not been swimming in a while. I was surprised to learn that the thought of being too fat could cast a shadow over an entire day.

2. Whether she was in the right job.

3. Whether she had any real friends – this concern could have been dietetically linked to her reluctance to eat alone in restaurants, which required the belief, in the face of others' doubts, that one potentially had other people with whom to sit.

4. Whether she was wasting her life, should read more or focus her activities].

'What do they taste like?' I asked of these dead skins.

'Oh, a bit like chicken,' she answered, 'just less tender.'

Isabel enjoyed a good relationship with chicken. It was the thing she most often cooked for dinner. She liked to chop a breast, fry it, then make a light cream sauce with mushrooms and a trace of paprika.

It was significant that the piece Isabel was buying from the supermarket had had both the skin and bone removed.

She tended to be wary of foods which showed too much of their natural origin. In lettuces, she would pay a little more for prewashed and selected leaves and avoid having to tear them off a threateningly earthy head.

This wariness might have explained the absence of fruit from the basket. She had once found a worm in a peach, and had never consumed another. She avoided grapes with seeds in, and didn't like berries because they harboured small insects. Psychologists might have connected this with her attitudes to travel, for she had never been the back-packing sort, tending to stay at home or go away only if a modicum of comfort was within reach.

'Cash or cheque?' enquired the cashier.

'Oh, cash,' replied Isabel, startled from a melancholic daydream.

'Eighteen thirty-three, love. And there's a carrier if you need it.'

'It's not getting any cheaper,' murmured Isabel.

On reaching the car a few moments later, I attempted to lighten the mood with a hypothetical scenario.

'What do you think you'd eat if you were designing an ideal last meal on earth, you know, whatever the cost, if you were given completely free rein to choose; Beluga caviare, a side of Kenyan antelope, quails' eggs, pastries from Paris . . .?'

'Don't, I feel like retching at the thought. Anyway, how do you mean my last meal?'

'Well, you know . . .'

'No, how would it be the last? Would I have reached a very old age, or would I be facing execution? Would I be committing suicide? Would I believe in God?'

'What would that matter?'

'Someone who believes in God from a Christian perspective could happily order a ten-course meal, unsickened by the idea that it would really be the last. They'd think they'd survive in a bodiless form, which would be ideal for anyone into chocolate cake but with a cellulite problem.'

'Do you believe in God?'

'That's a big question for an underground car park. Not the sort of God who lets you eat. If I really had to prepare a last meal, I think I'd be so anxious, I'd eat both my hands, not just those dry bits I showed you.'

Isabel's reluctance to engage her imaginative capacities in planning a last supper turned out to have been linked in part to the onset of a mild stomach flu, which sent her to bed and a bowl of clear soup shortly after her return home.

In reducing Isabel to a mute and pained shell quite at odds with her normal temper, the overnight illness was a small reminder of how the stability of another's personality was largely an illusion founded on an unstable balance of physical particles, and how the healthy self we optimistically refer to as 'ourselves' was but one possible character among a range of monsters lying at the whim of our organs.

Illness may cruelly transform us into incapable representatives of the chosen self, the arm we ask to move remains arrogantly limp, our gentleness gives way to an appalling shrillness, the sharpness of our mind to intolerable lethargy. More than the physical pain it inflicts, illness, like blinding love, has the capacity to unnerve us with the thought, 'Will I ever be myself again?' It scrambles our habitual mental functioning, opinions which had seemed reliably our own appear as foreign as the course of a dream in which we leave domestic comforts for a perilous life in a savannah.

A biographical reluctance to remember the stomach might in this light stem from a more forgivable reluctance to acknowledge the times when this organ, and the body in which it is housed, force us to languish in those twilight states where we are severed from what we precariously call our selves.

V

MEMORY

Prompting someone to remember their past is akin to forcing them to sneeze at gun-point. The results are fated to disappoint, for true remembering, like sneezing, is not something one can do at will. Of course there is something that ordinarily passes for remembering, the mechanical reflex when you ask me what marks I finished secondary school with and I reach into the filing cabinet to tell you, but this is a paltry cousin of the phenomenon in question. A genuine collision with a fragment of our past should strike us with an immediacy which defies temporal distance; it should not seem a memory at all, but something occurring in a pocket outside time. The true memory dissolves everything which happened between itself and the present. At thirty, we are suddenly back in the forest and twelve years old on a camping trip eating sandwiches filled with pink fleshy ham, a memory not forced on us by another's intrusive question but suggested by an incidental encounter with the smell of a similarly constructed sandwich three decades later in a train station café.

'Yes, it's the, whatever it's called, that Proustian moment thing,' spotted Isabel's friend Chris, with whom I had been sharing the thought [second-hand and as yet unlabelled], while the three of us sat in a pub and Isabel silently picked wax tears off a candlestick, divided them into pieces and re-fed them into the flame.

'Have you read Proust?' Isabel looked up and asked Chris sceptically.

'Me?'

'Yes, you.'

'Sort of, well, no,' said Chris uncomfortably, 'I mean I have it, and I've read some commentaries on it, but it's really a question of finding a holiday long enough to . . .'

A way of judging a writer's stature might be the extent to which their ideas have been assimilated by those whose holidays never stretch far enough to allow for a reading of the original. Unfortunately I too had not read more than twenty pages of the work and, judging by the look which Isabel had given Chris, it seemed best to pursue another topic or propose a lift home.

But the matter appeared relevant once again a few weeks later, when Isabel and I were sitting on the garish sofa of a friend of mine, an orange structure covered with an assortment of coloured cushions. One of these was made out of blue fluffy felt, which I noticed Isabel taking up, stroking once or twice, then briefly bending down to smell.

'What are you doing?' I whispered, while our host had gone to prepare drinks in the kitchen.

'It's funny, but this cushion is made out of exactly the same material as my pyjamas when I was a child. Do you know the ones I mean? They were a one-piece jump-suit type, this kind of deep blue as well, with a large zip at the front, then feet made out of soft plastic and sewn directly into the material. The best times of my childhood were in them, you felt so protected and at the same time so free. I remember having a bath, being put into one and wandering around the house in my little shell. For some reason,

I remember it being sunny, and the house filled with the orange light of the sun at dusk. It was the time when my mother would be getting my sister and me ready for bed, and my father would be coming home from the office. Mum tended to be far more relaxed with the babs in the evening, she'd have a glass of wine and a cigarette and even become quite gentle. Do you think I could ask your friend where he got them from?'

I might only have dipped a toe in Proust, but I had read enough of an insightful book on him by Samuel Beckett to know that what Isabel had unexpectedly recalled of her childhood on the sofa might without too much presumption have been identified as a Proustian moment. Proust's thoughts on memory had introduced a rich but biographically complex method of evaluating the resurrection of the past. The most common but unsatisfactory way was through voluntary memory, witnessed during a conversation before the lights went down at the cinema, when I had asked Isabel where she had spent her childhood summers. 'Oh, Lausanne, a house by the lake owned by friends of my parents. Do you fancy more popcorn?' The memory had not stepped onto the stage unprompted; it was therefore going to be surly and a prelude to a change of subject, it was the reheated dish rather than the ingredients spitting petulantly in the frying-pan.

In involuntary memory on the other hand, without a question being asked, one would be hurled by a random piece of the present, by the famous madeleine or the less celebrated felt cushion, into the arms of the past, a past which would be as real as the present, existing through every sense. One could never predict when these illuminations would occur, one would simply stumble on something which had been a part of and hence resurrected a lost world.

The next time Isabel and I went swimming, the chlorinated smell of the pool chose to evoke what she had done with her childhood summers far more skilfully than my cinema enquiry had been able. On our third lap, Isabel was splashed by a paddling infant, who made her wipe water away from her eyes and remark, 'God, that takes me back.' I turned around as though the infant was an acquaintance or the offspring of one, but Isabel swam on and began to speak of another chlorinated pool she had known in her childhood. From its side one had been able to see across Lac Léman to the French Alps, some still snow-capped in summer. She had learnt to swim there, staying in so long that the tips of her fingers grew wrinkled, 'like a fisherman's hands', her mother had said. There were large yellow towels in a store-room with cobwebs and wasps. Isabel had built a towel tent holding two corners with her toes, and placing the other end above her head. The sun shining through the material gave a golden luminous interior in which she felt snug. Outside, stranger things went on. Her mother laughed exaggeratedly and the grown-ups spoke French. She didn't like them, or the way the older man called her 'my little princess' and kept patting her on the head when handing out an extra serving of spaghetti. Every summer for five years the family returned to the house and its pool, and though Isabel had forgotten the room she slept in and the faces of their hosts, the smell of municipal chlorine carried her back to the atmosphere of those days more effectively than had my cumbersome question of the week before.

I began to wonder if one might arrange the past not according to the familiar chronology, but by pioneering the use of the Proustian moment, following the triggers of smell, touch, sound and sight around which the scenes of a life had crystallized.

But the method had its complications when compared to a more traditional chronology. Here was Nietzsche's life as one had come to relate it:

1844 – Born in Saxony
1865 – Taken to and flees from a brothel. His friend, the famous Indologist Deussen, remarks: '*Mulierem nunquam attigit.*' ['He never touched a woman.']
     – Discovers Schopenhauer
1867 – Begins military service
1869 – Appointed professor at Basle University
1872 – Publishes *The Birth of Tragedy*
1876 – Meets Wagner at Sorrento
1879 – Gives up teaching
1881 – Stays in Sils Maria, Engadine, Switzerland
1882 – Conceives the idea of Eternal Recurrence
     – Falls in love with Lou Andreas Salome
1883 – Death of Wagner
     – Publishes *Thus Spake Zarathustra*
1889 – Sees horse being beaten by coachman in Turin. Embraces horse screaming, 'I understand you.' Becomes insane
1900 – Dies

Such an ordering of events was at some level premised on the idea of a linear relation to time, of certain memories lying further back in time than others. But the Proustian moment revealed that, subjectively, the distance separating us from an event did not indicate its distance. When he had fallen in love unrequitedly with Lou Andreas Salome in 1882, Nietzsche might have remembered 1865, the date when he had rushed out of a brothel, more powerfully than he had in 1872, in which he had merely published *The Birth of Tragedy*. When memory was as powerful as actuality, a life was lived in tandem rather than sequentially, we could experience two sections of time at once. Nietzsche might in 1889, on embracing the horse, which precipitated his madness, have felt the same outrage at the cruelty towards animals as he had experienced during military service in 1867.

This further complicated the definition of a chronologically significant event. Biographies rely on butch criteria, a life is plotted according to the markers of death, marriage, professional appointment, murder and military campaign – whereas when we remember our past, far less tangible images haunt us. We may not even remember anything as robust as an event, we simply recall a mood, an atmosphere devoid of story. It was therefore unsurprising how often one might be lost in the past yet claim one was in the process of thinking nothing.

Isabel and I were in a coffee shop off the Farringdon Road on a Thursday evening after work when she suggested just such a thing. We were both in a silent mood liable to follow days of chat in the office, but I felt that the length of her silence could have signalled a problem, so I enquired what was on her mind.

'Oh, nothing,' she replied, brightening with a smile.

'Nothing?'

'Well, you know, this and that. Nothing really.'
'Great, I was just wondering. Do you want some cake?'
'I'm fine.'

Much of our time is spent thinking nothing much really. Next to sleeping, it may be our most popular pastime. Even great men and women, subjects of the densest chronologies [Tolstoy, Florence Nightingale, Henry IV] must have spent sections of their lives thinking nothing much really, sitting on trains and horses, in conference rooms and in soapy baths, letting things float through consciousness without being able to sum up the situation with the sort of clarity that would allow them to blow a trumpet and announce, 'Ich bin ein Berliner' or 'Paris is perhaps worth a mass after all'.

When we speak, we make efforts to make sense to others, to present them with a point or two, and hence do not let them share the more confused process unfolding in consciousness. Even characters in fiction largely lack the requisite complexity of thought, their ideas are extracted from the mental goo and slapped on the page with a tidy, 'he thought', 'she thought'.

When Anita Brookner wished to tell us what was going on inside Edith's head in *Hotel du Lac*, she set up a sedate scene of cogitation:

'The company of their own sex, Edith reflected, was what drove many women into marriage.'

Contrast this with Joyce's efforts when he wanted to tell us what was going on in Molly's mind in *Ulysses* [in a monologue which Jung told Joyce had taught him more about female psychology than anything he had ever read, and Nabokov judged to be *'entre nous soit dit*, the weakest chapter in the book']:

It makes your lips pale anyhow its done now once and for all with all the talk of the world about it people make its only the first time after that its just the ordinary do it and think no more about it why cant you kiss a man without going and marrying him first you sometimes love to wildly when you feel that way so nice all over you you cant help yourself I wish some man or other would take me sometime when hes there and kiss me in his arms theres nothing like a kiss long and hot down to your soul almost paralyses you then I hate that confession . . .

If one assumes Brookner is realistic and Joyce eccentric, it is because when we talk to each other in coffee shops, we communicate in Brooknerish sentences and not Joycean ones. If I tapped her gently on the shoulder and asked Edith what she was thinking in her armchair, she would have answered, 'Oh, I was just reflecting how the company of their own sex drove many women into marriage.'

But Edith wouldn't actually have been thinking things so cleanly to herself, she would have behaved in a rapid, digressive, associative, babbling Molly Bloomish way. Then again, the clean up is what society forces on us, we cannot spew the syntax-less goo in our consciousness. We have no choice but to package matters in sausages we learn to construct when we learn to speak, made up of a verb, nouns, a sprinkling of adjectives, neatly wrapped in full stops. When we communicate, we struggle to make sense to others, and we know what we mean long before anyone could understand what we have in mind.

'So I dida literature paper too, you know,' replied Isabel, then decided she might want a little cake after all.

'But whatever I was thinking,' she continued more charitably on her return from the counter with an almond and chocolate roll, 'I was just a bit lost in my tea.

'You see, camomile is always a reminder of being ill as a child,' she explained, stirring a now half empty cup decorated with a logo of the 1984 Olympics. 'My mother had this idea that camomile could cure anything, so whenever one of us had something wrong, I can hear her saying, "I'm going to brew you a good camomile and you'll be better in a tick." I don't know if she had any medical evidence for this, but her enthusiasm was enough. Brewing a cup confirmed your departure from the land of the healthy. So I wasn't really thinking much, I was just lost in some clouds.'

Clouds of time were sealed in other senses and beverages. From inside freshly milled coffee arose, genielike, the figure of her father on childhood Saturday mornings, the time when he would treat himself to a steaming espresso and declare [away from the ears of his wife] that a man could not wish for more than this. He would sit down with the paper in the kitchen, and something about his good mood made Isabel, Paul and Lucy stay at table chattering even after they had finished their own breakfast. Occasionally he would turn and give one of them a wink, and they would laugh and ask him to wink again. Sometimes he would sing them songs and take one of them on his knee. He did a good 'Waltzing Matilda' and an appalling 'John Brown's Body', so bad they would scream at him to be quiet, laugh and put their fingers in their ears.

She remembered thinking that her father had been alive for ever, he was so tall and old and seemed to know everything. One school term, they had been studying the Industrial Revolution and Isabel returned home and asked him if he remembered the time before there were trains.

Thoughts of her father drifted back in a coffee shop in Covent Garden. Though he himself never smelt of coffee grains, in Isabel's imagination, coffee and father always came under one heading.

'Further evidence of my Oedipal fixation?' she asked as we left the shop, a packet of Colombian beans wrapped up for his birthday.

Continuing this Proustian investigation, Isabel told me that inside ginger biscuits were trapped the morning breaks of her primary school. A bell would ring at eleven, and the children would run out of the classrooms and form a long, noisy queue in the dining hall. There were only a few ginger biscuits in the tins laid out along the metal counters, and the other choices were horrible: there were strange custard creams, sickening digestives and boring shortbreads. Isabel had perfected a way of choosing the desk nearest the door and running very fast down the left side of the courtyard. She ran so fast, one time she slammed into the deputy headmistress carrying a small plant to the biology room, and scattered it in the ensuing collision. Terrified at what she had done, she froze dumbfounded.

'Well, aren't you going to say sorry?' asked the earth-splattered teacher.

And all Isabel had been able to answer was 'Ginger biscuits' – and burst into tears.

Yet more Proustian associations lay in bubble baths, vehicles that carried Isabel back to a trip she had made to New York at the age of eleven. Her father's firm had sent him to close a deal, and the family had been treated to a week at a business hotel in midtown Manhattan. Isabel had been thrilled at the luxury of the place, at the television with thirty channels, at the lobby with the large swing doors and a room perched on the thirty-ninth floor of a sixty-storey building. She had made friends with the elevator-man, and he had taken her to the top floor. It looked just the same as the others, though he told her that in high winds you could feel the building moving. That night, there was a storm and she was glad they were only on the thirty-ninth floor. It was then she had had her first bubble bath and marvelled at the green liquid expanding into jagged chunks of soft light white honeycomb. She had looked at it like a Saharan child touching snow, and spent an hour moulding it into shapes. She had built igloos, then mountains with ski slopes, then the bubbles began to die, and the game turned to icebergs floating in a green sea, then all she was left with was a sweet oily smell that remained until the next time she bathed.

However many memories were to be found in sights, tastes and smells, Isabel judged music to be her most evocative Proustian medium.

'Could you turn it up a liole [sic]?' she asked, when Joan Armatrading's 'Love and Affection' came on the car radio during a night-time drive.

'Do you know I first heard this song at Sarah's fourteenth birthday party? I spent most of the evening hiding in the bathroom, or in the kitchen helping with the washing-up. The place was packed, and people were eating sausages with a pungent relish – which is probably why I remember someone wanting to kiss me. And I spilt something on my dress, apple juice, I think.'

When Isabel listened to music, she often added a Proustian track containing a particular time and atmosphere, so that when she returned to the piece, it would secrete from among its vocals and instrumentation the circumstances of the original recording.

The way the Proustian track was laid down did not follow logical patterns; she might have owned pieces for several years without imprinting time, others carried memories which were not connected to the music's original performance, but had later become glued by association. She had never heard the REM song 'Rockville' on a drive back from a wedding in Fort William to Glasgow, and yet it now reminded her of the journey she had made with a fellow wedding guest. It was a September day, and storms had blown in from the sea, covering the hills with several inches of snow. The windscreen wipers had rubbed furiously, and the car heater blasted warm air, lending a comforting contrast to the fury of the elements outside. The song evoked the flavour of the journey rather than particular events, these were poetic, sensuous memories rather than narrative ones; the smell of hot car seats, the feel of steamed glass, the patterns of the snowdrifts on the roadside, the dramatic break in the clouds as they reached Glasgow.

Isabel had begun buying her own music and imprinting memories on it in early adolescence, and from then on, her collection provided both a map of her evolving musical taste and a reference to the settings in which she had formed it.

Her first tape had come from HMV in Oxford Street, she was thirteen, had kissed a boy in her class and sworn never to do so again, and it was entitled:

Abba: The Hits

On the cover stood the members of the group in flared satin trousers and silk purple shirts, bathed in a hazy orange light. The record included 'Dancing Queen', 'Take a Chance on Me', 'The Winner Takes it All', 'Chiquitita', and 'One of Us'. She had spent the summer of its purchase in shopping centres with a small band of girls, Sarah, Tammy, Janet and Laura. She recalled her wish to be someone else, specifically Grace Marsden in the class two years above, who had ample breasts, long hair and clear skin. Isabel had been unable to look at herself in the mirror, a pus-filled growth had sat at the base of her nose for a week and she had considered hanging herself – which was perhaps not compatible with the tunes of Abba, but they had been responsible for the few moments of happiness. There was the energy and speed of 'Dancing Queen', which she and Laura had played at volume, jumping on the bed until Laura's father, a solicitor who had left his wife for his legal assistant, shouted at them to be more mature.

But several layers of memory might sit side by side in a single record, reflecting the different times it had been heard, like cutting a cross-section through the earth on the site of a long inhabited city which showed up layer upon layer of successive settlement.

Beneath Abba's primary Proustian layer sat a holiday in the Algarve, where Isabel had gone with Chris, his girlfriend and her sister. They had rented a flat and car for a week, and had played the tape driving down the winding roads to the beach and night-club. Isabel had been in search of frivolity, which had come in an affair with a

German from Lübeck, a submarine engineer who at the end of the holiday revealed himself to be married with a young son – which had not prevented Wolfgang from colonizing 'Our Last Summer', and turning it into a reminder of the time he and Isabel had spent the night in his jeep and watched the dawn break over the sea.

The final Proustian track had been laid down at the most recent office Christmas party, where 'Take a Chance on Me' had captured the pink decor of a restaurant and bar in Piccadilly, the tears of Sally Welch, the receptionist whose boyfriend had left her that night, and the mixture of alcohol, flirtation and loneliness which had accompanied the occasion.

Then came:

The Best of Blondie

This time, Isabel was fourteen and spending her afternoons trying on make-up and her friends' clothes to the sounds of 'The Tide is High', 'Hanging on the Telephone' and 'Heart of Glass'. Her skirts were growing shorter ['Looks more like a belt than a skirt,' her mother had said sarcastically at the sight of one], the first mini had made an appearance along with black tights and high heels. When her parents spent the Easter break with her grandparents, Isabel took Laura to a night-club in Notting Hill, they wore eyeliner and mauve lipstick and gained entry as two youthful sixteen-year-olds. They were bought drinks by Italian language students, one of whom, Guido or was it Giovanni or even Giacomo, Isabel had kissed while under the effects of two strawberry daiquiris, which she later vomited in a drain off Ladbroke Grove.

The record had made its second appearance when Isabel

moved into her flat in Hammersmith at the age of twenty-two, where it became her cleaning tape, the music she would put on while she vacuumed the bedroom and tiny living-room, dusted the bookshelves, attacked piles of washing up and did her best with the bathroom. Her hatred of the routine was such that she needed music with energy enough to prevent her collapsing on the sofa as soon as she had begun.

Leonard Cohen: Greatest Hits

This opus carried Isabel back to listless afternoons spent in her bedroom in her mid-teens. The dominant colours of the memory were purple, which had been the shade of her duvet, and creamy yellow, which had been the colour of the album jacket. Her mother was giving her condemning stares, accusing her of looking like a street urchin, making no effort to talk to the family and doing nothing at school – none of which Isabel contested, she simply asked in a low monotone if she could be left alone. It was not a wish likely to be granted by a mother who saw it as an insult when someone refused to fight back. Her rage had been such she had once slapped Isabel hard on the cheek after she had refused to deny trying drugs. Isabel had sat immobile at the kitchen table and not blinked in case the tears she felt welling up had cascaded out. It was then she had uttered the notorious line suggesting she had never asked to be born.

By the time she reached:

Bob Dylan: Infidels

things were looking up. For a start, the record had been a present from Stuart Wilson, Isabel's first boyfriend, who revealed that one could sometimes talk to boys as easily as if they were girls. Stuart was seventeen, had left school the year before and now worked in a youth travel agency near Victoria Station. The relationship lasted a year, during which the couple spent hours in street markets looking for clothes, hunting in record stores and fumbling on Stuart's bed at his parents' house in Enfield.

Stuart had had the uncanny ability to make Isabel feel understood while rarely speaking. Dylan had been central to the feat, though one could have chosen worse vehicles for it than 'Sweetheart Like You', 'Tangled Up in Blue' and 'All I Really Want to Do'. He had initiated a phase covering the middle stretch of adolescence during which Isabel's tastes in music and boyfriends had gone hand in hand. Enquiries concerning another's life had ended shortly after one had discovered their three favourite bands.

But by the last year of school, greater maturity had entered both relationships and musical collections, and Isabel acquired a version of:

Mozart: Violin Concertos Nos. 3 and 5

It contained a school trip to Paris with ten girls and the art history teacher. They had stayed in a threadbare hotel in Montmartre, where she had shared a room with the deputy head girl who had a place at Oxford and was going to die of cancer a week before her twenty-fifth birthday. They had toured the museums, written postcards to friends from a café on the rue de Rivoli and spoken appalling French to young men willing to forgive the detail if they smiled. Listening to the concertos specifically evoked the train journey back to Calais. Isabel remembered the green plastic seats, and the view out of the window on to the bleak Artois countryside. She was nostalgic at leaving the city to return home and the constraints of her family, yet it was only a few months later that she finished school and, with a place assured at London University, began a year of work and travel abroad. She went first to Berlin, where she worked for a translator and fell in with a group of Americans, one of whom left her with a copy of:

Highlights: Don Giovanni, Die Zauberflöte, Le Nozze di Figaro, Così Fan Tutte

It was to capture a confusion of memories of her year abroad. Inside 'Se vuol ballare' was a small café she had frequented at the corner of Meineckestrasse in Berlin, 'E Susanna non vien!' held the approach to the Opera House, in 'Come scoglio immoto resta' lay a view of Deauville where she had spent the summer season working at the reception of a hotel, while her sleeper pulling out of Milan station found itself ominously packed into 'Don Ottavio, son morta!'

VI

THE PRIVATE

We read biographies under the common, though perhaps contestable, impression that some parts of a life are more significant than others. In whatever way the work has made us curious, it remains a flirtation, that is, it will not disclose what it latently suggests, unless it favours, like an unfair parent, one part over another. For a time, we are amused to learn how Einstein blew soap bubbles as a child, Churchill's way of sharing his cigars with Stalin at Yalta and Bertrand Russell's feelings towards the Stilton at Trinity, and yet, if fed no more than this, we may close a biography with the frustration of a diner hungering for a plate of profiteroles who is told that the kitchen has just sold its last.

It is the private life we seek, suspicious of what is left of a life when it contains only what others are supposed to know. 'No one likes to be pitied for his faults,' wrote the French aphorist Vauvenargues in 1746. Quite true, but more or less irrelevant for the aphorist's biographer, whose curiosity would be limited to the painful private moment which had sparked the polished maxim. Whereas Vauvenargues had toiled to make out of his personal experience something applicable to the whole race, something to outlast the age of wigs and carriages in which he had lived, something which might be understood in Taipei and Caracas in centuries he could not imagine, the biographer would see it as his task silently to undo the careful knitting, to destroy the seamless prose, to detect beneath it exactly who had pitied the aphorist and for what and for how long, and had it ended in a duel or a broken heart? The maxim would be dishonest until it had been returned to the personal roots from which it had tried so cunningly to escape.

What could account for this desire to collapse a public life into its private dimension? Perhaps a resentment at the public side's uniqueness, the temptation to reveal that the great man or woman had not escaped the ordinary follies. In his aphorisms, Vauvenargues may have been a genius, in the life which inspired them, he was incontestably human – with all the weaknesses we ascribe to our species. Moreover, to think only of what had led him to his thoughts would be a comforting antidote to the power of the thoughts themselves. Curiosity about others is a favoured choice when skirting introspection – one may substitute the inner struggle by battling with the estate for quotes and permission for the letters.

The modern biography can nevertheless be accused of a curtailment of imaginative possibilities in limiting its quest for the private self to the perimeters of the bedroom. Take the opening of Philip Larkin's 'Talking in Bed':

> Talking in bed ought to be easiest,
> Lying together there goes back so far,
> An emblem of two people being honest.
>
> Yet more and more time passes silently.
> Outside, the wind's incomplete unrest
> Builds and disperses clouds about the sky . . .

It may seem an evocative poem to those familiar with the tongue-tied discomfort that accompanies the end of unfulfilling sexual encounters, but to someone of a biographical mindset the issue has little to do with rhythm, metre and the influence of Thomas Hardy, and much to do with who the poet was lying in bed with in awkward silence, what had happened in childhood to make it hard for him to find his tongue and if he had embraced a woman when a chap would have been preferable.

Separating the biography from the polite memoir or academic monograph is the idea that the biographer should metaphorically sleep with his or her subject – the corollary of a non-literary idea that the crowning act of two people's acquaintance unfolds after the enquiry of whether the light should be left on or off.

'I mean, it's counter-productive, she's always going to bed with people before they even know her name,' explained Isabel of her Brazilian office colleague Graziella, presenting an implicit challenge to the notion while opening a tub of cottage cheese for her lunch. 'And then she's surprised when it turns out they're not really suited, or they never call her back.'

'But perhaps Gabriella is only doing it out of lust,' I suggested.

'Graziella, not Gabriella.'

'Tricky, you must admit. I haven't slept with her and the name's already slipped my mind.'

'That's not the problem. It's just she wants someone to snuggle with on Sunday evenings, but doesn't know how to get intimate properly. The bed seems a handy way out of the dilemma.'

Isabel may have sympathized with Graziella's desire to

Right
Isabel's mother sitting
on her mother's lap,
her aunt Claire on the
stone steps of the garden
of their house in Essex.

Below
Maternal grandparents,
left, paternal grandparents,
right.

Mr Rogers, *above left*,
his wife, *above right*.

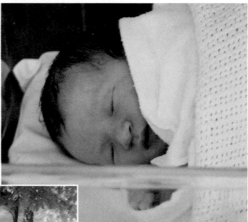

Above
Isabel after two days on earth.

Left
Isabel on a pony in the Jardin
du Luxembourg, Paris.

Above
Coming second in a school race.

Below
Isabel with spaghetti.

Above
Isabel holding her brother Paul.

Left
Isabel's sister, Lucy, and Paul.

Above and right
Two of Isabel's best childhood friends
and neighbours, Luke and Poppy.

Above
'Tracy's at the far end, I'm next to her, then that's Susan [twice divorced already], I forget who she's sitting next to, but nearest to us is Nicki Dawnay. She got thrown out for cheating, now she's with the police in Hull.'

Above
The two Rogers pets: Cassandra
the cat and Churchill the dog.

Left
The front of Isabel's secondary
school.

Below
Mr Frank Whitford gave Isabel
extra English tuition.

Teenage friendships. *Top* Laura Greenman (left) and Lisabel McDermot. *Left* Isabel's sister at eighteen. *Above* Best friend Sarah at sixteen.

French crush, Bertrand Denis, *right*, first love, Stuart Wilson, *below*.

Boyfriends. *Clockwise from top left* Andrew O'Sullivan, Guy Stricks, Michael Catten, Wolfgang from the Algarve, Isaac Davidson. *Below* Breakfast 'post-coital somewhere'.

Above
Colleagues from work at the local restaurant, the Devil's Dinner. (From left to right) Roxanna, Louise, Tim and Sue.

Right
Isabel's house off Hammersmith Grove, with her car, Bug, parked in front. Her flat was on the top floor.

disclose her private self, but she rejected the chosen means. Though sex was a symbol of intimacy, it did not in itself assure that two people could become intimate. The symbol might even impede the realization of the condition it symbolized – sleeping with someone as a way of avoiding a more arduous process of acquaintance, like buying a book to save one from reading it.

'So what should Graziella be doing to be happy?' I asked with a godparent's concern.

'I'm no expert,' said Isabel, replacing her cottage cheese in the fridge, 'I simply think it isn't always a good idea to go to bed with someone unless you've gone through some intimate stuff with them before.'

'Like what?'

'You know, getting jealous, swearing, showing your devious sides, throwing up, picking your nose, cutting your toenails.'

'Why?' I asked obtusely. 'Is there something about your toe . . .?'

'No, they're fine.'

'So?'

'Well, it's the idea of cutting them that's sort of private. If a nail is on a foot, then it's OK, but once it's off, it's waste. It's the difference between seeing hair on a person and finding old hairs in the bath.'

'But why is cutting your nails more intimate than having sex?'

'It's only that the person you have sex with should also be someone you wouldn't be embarrassed to cut your toenails in front of.'

Subtly but importantly, Isabel was redrawing the definition of the elements required in order to understand the private self, her list standing in contrast to the naked criteria of modern biography. But given the discrepancy, on what basis was a life to be cordoned off as private? Perhaps according to how vulnerable it revealed us to be. Toenail cutting was private because its unaesthetic quality required generosity from an observer, like the trust required to emerge for breakfast without grooming or make-up. The private life contained whatever needed to be viewed with kindness or compassion, it was the record of our exposed moments.

The process of intimacy therefore involved the opposite of seduction, for it meant revealing what risked rendering one most open to unfavourable judgement, or least worthy of love. Whereas seduction was founded on the display of one's finest qualities and dinner jackets, intimacy entailed a complex offer of both vulnerability and toenails.

According to her criteria, Isabel's private self was more in evidence than I had assumed. She had grown comfortable enough to display her vocabulary of swear words, she had shown certain of her more devious sides, she even admitted to lying about the extent of her reading of Susan Sontag.

'How do you mean?' I queried.

'Well, you know the time we were talking about photography, and I started going on about the old witch? I'd never read a word she'd written.'

'Not one?'

'No – I think I was trying to make you feel small at the time, so . . .'

To admit to such tactics might have exposed Isabel to the same vulnerability as the bedroom, whereby one would finish and wonder, 'Do you think much less of me now?'

The private parts of a life were those which threatened to take up more than their share of influence in understanding a person. Isabel's reluctance to reveal her Sontag subterfuge was based on the fear that it might alter my view not just of her reading matter but of her entire intellectual and even moral capacities. There are things we learn about others which unreasonably impede our ability to consider them in a rounded way again, single details, for instance the revelation of a certain physical deformity or unsavoury habit, an extra nipple or taste for auto-erotic asphyxia, which will dominate our thoughts whenever their name is mentioned.

It could have explained the tact required before withdrawing an object from one's nose in company.

'I'm sorry, it's not very hygienic, I know,' apologized Isabel, who had been unexpectedly witnessed in the act while reading a newspaper on her sofa.

'That's fine,' I replied, unable to judge this on the level of the three papillae. 'What are you going to do with it?'

'Oh, I normally just roll it into a ball.'

'And?'

'You know, if there's a bin near by, I'm not going to avoid it, but otherwise I'll just shred it around the carpet. The best snot is dry and stays in one piece, the worst is when you have a cold, and everything breaks up. You know the halfway stage between the need to pick and blow when neither quite does the trick? Maybe you'll take out a bit, then it breaks off midway and you've got to do your best to hide the remains.'

Isabel explained how changeable were the colours of her mucus. It had to do with the quality of the air, so in the city it would emerge sooty and black, and in the country yellow like beeswax. She was awed by the size of certain pieces, their uneven texture reminiscent of the walls of prehistoric caves.

'Do you often stick them to . . . ?'

'I've stopped now, but at school and at home, I used to glue them to the side of a desk or the back side of a cupboard where we kept the silver. Or if I was the only one reading it, maybe the paper.'

'And eat them . . . ?'

'I tried, but mine are too salty.'

A few weeks later, a little after eleven on an unusually warm summer's night, the phone rang in my flat. I was in bed watching the news, following the story of identical twins separated at birth who had both married left-handed flautists. I chose to ignore the phone and let the answering machine respond.

'Oh, damn, I guess you're not in. Isabel here. I'm sorry to call this late, but I did the most stupid thing today. I lent my keys to my boss, which now means I can't get into my . . .'

I realized the problem and therefore at once offered Isabel a bed in my apartment, though she found the suggestion hard to accept.

'That's kind, but I'll just sleep on the floor.'

'What a good idea. Or, no, even that's too comfortable, why don't we put you at the very top of a cupboard or on the balcony?'

'Don't tease. I'm sorry, I'm just so embarrassed.'

She eventually camped down on the sofa which stood outside the bedroom. The flat's open plan meant privacy was limited, and Isabel cried, 'Don't look' as she dashed from the bathroom to the sofa in a T-shirt I had lent her.

Perhaps because of the uncustomary nature of our situation, we expressed prompt tiredness, and turned out the lamps amidst an exchange of goodnights.

I tried to sleep, but the heat and the presence of another body in the adjoining room did not afford the requisite peace. I opened my eyes to sketch thoughts on the ceiling, readjusted the pillows, worried about the crack on the wall opposite and wondered whether Isabel had yet slipped into dreams, trying to interpret the occasional creak and shuffle from next door. We were in the delicate period after two people have wished one another good night, and remain aware that they may both still be awake, but feign unconsciousness so as not to deny the other their rest. As time goes by, it becomes ever less possible to interrupt the companion, and one is left with the mild panic of the insomniac at the prospect of a long night alone, listening to what may now be signs of sleep, a light snoring or limbs stretching under the covers.

'Are you asleep?' asked a little voice from next door.

'Completely, and you?'

'Me too.'

'Good.'

'It's so hot tonight.'

'I know.'

'Can I open the window in the living-room?'

'Sure.'

I watched Isabel climb off the sofa and walk to the window, her figure silhouetted by the orange street light.

'That's better,' she remarked. 'I'm a really bad sleeper,

sometimes I just read all night, then arrive shattered at the office. I think it's a habit from when I was young. My sister and I used to share a room, and we'd never get any rest because we'd chat for hours.'

'About what?'

'Oh, anything and everything. Mostly very smutty, silly stuff.'

'I can't imagine you doing that.'

'Why not?'

'I don't know.'

'Shall I tell you a secret?' proposed Isabel.

'Yeah.'

'Promise you won't tell anyone?'

'Of course not.'

'OK, well it's to do with my sister and me.'

'And?'

'No, I can't. It's too much of a secret.'

'Go on, you can't start and then stop,' I protested, the word secret having whetted the imagination.

'Oh, all right then. As long as you promise not to repeat this to a soul. It's just that, well, the first kiss I ever had was with Lucy.'

'You combined both lesbianism and incest in your first kiss?'

'We were fascinated by why people snogged in films all the time, so one day, I suggested that we have a go ourselves. We went into the store cupboard – I suppose because we instinctively knew it was a bit weird – and opened our mouths in imitation of what we'd seen. It got slobbery and we started giggling but couldn't stop for ages, because it was quite pleasurable in a way. It was probably my first sexual experience. After that, every time

114

we were watching a film where people kissed, we would look at one another and the giggling would start up again. Even now, when I'm in a cinema with Lucy and there's a kiss, I'll wonder if she's thinking the same, but we've grown too embarrassed to talk about it. So that's the secret. You promise to keep it to yourself, won't you?'

If secrets have such power to ignite our interest and yet are frequently so unsensational when told, it is perhaps because we unconsciously imagine our own when the word is used rather than the less spectacular items others label as such. We call a secret those aspects of our personality which we suspect do not fully belong to the race. A secret is the dismal and embarrassing side of our uniqueness, a moment when we leave the expectations of society not for the sake of genius or heroism but for values we fear the social world condemns or at best sneeringly tolerates; the secret that I am incontinent, in love with my sibling or attracted to the same sex. No wonder children have the most secrets, for their lack of experience means they are most sensitive to the strangeness, the privacy of things they have done or felt. At the end of a long life, one imagines the stock of secrets diminishing, for what had previously seemed an aberrant and shameful deed appears to fit more harmoniously into an understanding of what it means to be human. In this sense, the tendency of others to spill secrets may stem less from cruelty than from an ability, as an outsider, to recognize that what is deemed private in fact belongs to the province – far wider than the narrow strip the secret-holder imagines – of the normal.

Something about our situation meant that there was not long to wait before Isabel spilt another secret. The

Rogers family had been using the same dentist in Baker Street since Lavinia and Christopher had moved to London a quarter of a century before. Dr Ross was a garrulous Australian with a love of horse-racing, his office was covered in equestrian trophies and pictures of an equine-looking wife. He had imposed braces on Lucy at twelve, and pulled out Isabel's four wisdom teeth at eighteen. He had done root canal work on Mr Rogers and filled a number of cavities in Mrs Rogers' molars. But the rest of the family had been spared a detail of his activities.

'It sounds bizarre, but he was one of those men who could get me to do more or less anything,' revealed Isabel, now sitting up on her sofa bed.

'At twelve, it was always boys who were looking for me to be decisive, and of course I wasn't. I thought it was weird that he should have been interested in me, I mean I was just a child, and he was so old, but then, I did have something of a father complex. I had been to see him alone once, Mum had dropped me off in late afternoon. I can't remember what he had to do with my teeth, but one minute he was brushing around in the back, and it was just the usual dentist intimacy that means nothing, full of neutral comments like, "Your upper teeth are lovely, you know," and then, without changing his voice or putting on a different tape – it was Verdi as ever – he suddenly said, "The receptionist is leaving, and after that we'll be alone. No one needs to know, and if you don't wish to do anything, I will stop at once." I didn't understand what he was talking about, but he started kissing me in a very gentle, almost professional way. It lasted a few minutes, then he stopped and said, "Now you know how it's done," as though this was a continuation of the treatment. I couldn't believe it, but I was also pleased, because I had a bit of a crush on him, to be honest.'

'Then what happened?'

'Well, I didn't have many appointments, only maybe twice a year, and when I did go next, it was all back to normal. He wasn't ashamed, he felt he'd been doing me a favour. We never referred to it again, and we even started talking about other crushes I had.'

It seemed an intelligent choice, so Isabel and I abandoned hope of immediate rest by falling into the mutual interrogation commonly reserved for the truth games of prurient adolescents.

'I can't go through with this,' she protested when it was her turn.

'But you promised.'

'I'm too embarrassed.'

'You made me tell you everything.'

'I'm sorry.'

'Why can't you say?'

'Because,' she said and stopped as though it were explanation enough, coyly pulling back the covers to her chin.

'It's not very many you know,' she resumed after a moment spent lightly chewing the end of the sheet.

'I don't mind.'

'I'm quite square.'

'So what?'

'Or maybe I'm not. Maybe it's too many, perhaps I'm a real slut. Oh, all right. I'll tell you.'

Isabel shut her eyes, frowned with concentration and began mumbling numbers. A moment later, like the solemn official of an election result, she announced, 'Oh, I've probably snogged about seventeen people. As for going the whole hog, that would be much less, around nine or ten.'

Name	Snogged	Whole Hogged	Age
Lucy Rogers	X		9
Dr Ross	X		12
Charlie Brint	X		13
Giacomo ?	X		14
Bertrand Denis	X	Sort of	15
Stuart Wilson	X	X	16–17
Frank Whitford	X		17
Roger Boyd	X		18
Patrick Armstrong	X		18
Tom Greig	X	X	18
Andrew O'Sullivan	X	X	18–19
Guy Stricks	X	X	19–20
Wolfgang ?	X		20
John Water	X		20
Alfred Buren	X	X	21
Jeremy Bagley		X*	20
Isaac Davidson	X	X	22
Michael Catten	X	X	23–25

* Someone Isabel had spent a night with during a skiing holiday, who had declined to kiss while making love.

'I wondered how Isabel had "sort of" lost her virginity at fifteen but definitely lost it at sixteen.

'Because I was an idiot,' she explained. 'It was on my French exchange. I was sent away to a family in the Dordogne. Actually, it was with the daughter of this man my mother had had a thing for at university.'

'The artist.'

'That's right, Jacques. He was no longer an artist though, he went on to work for the oil company Elf and became a big-wig there. He bought himself a flat in Paris and converted a barn in the Dordogne. He married the daughter of an art dealer, a very rich woman with one eye that doesn't open. They had two kids, Bertrand and Marie-Laure . . .'

'How do you mean, one eye that doesn't open?'

'I don't know why it doesn't, she's got a lazy eyelid muscle or something. Anyway, the girl is my age and Bertrand is a year older, and I was doing an exchange with her to try and get my French better for O-level. Marie-Laure had spent the summer with Mum, Dad and me the year before in Cornwall. She had been a pain, always telling us that Cheddar wasn't as good as some fancy Camembert "Maman" bought for her. I was dreading another summer with her, but then I met her brother and, well, everything changed.'

'What was he like?'

'Sixteen, drove a moped, smoked – enough to spark a crush. I was in the midst of my blushing phase then. Anything remotely sexual would start it off, even if we were talking about the mating rituals of farm animals. One evening in the Dordogne, something had set me blushing at dinner, and afterwards I went out onto the stone steps outside the kitchen and listened to the crickets. Bertrand joined me, I tried to talk to him, but he never liked to talk much. So we just sat there, and suddenly he said, "You're very attractive when you go red. It brings out your cheekbones." No one had ever used the word attractive to describe me, nor had been brutal enough to refer to my blushing, which meant I turned even redder than usual. I was so confused and embarrassed and in love yet knowing I was making a fool of myself, I started crying.'

'What did he do?'

'Nothing for a moment. As I remember, he tried to light another cigarette, but because of the wind, the matches kept blowing out. So he gave up, and started kissing me.'

I swallowed.

'Are you falling asleep? You must be so bored,' asked my narrator.

'God, no, it's the opposite.'

'Don't lie.'

'I'm not.'

'It's such an average story.'

She was right, there was nothing extraordinary here, and yet the tale was gripping, narratives of physical desire having a power to hold the attention whatever the outward drama. Once a story is set in motion, we may revert to the condition of generic cave people, crunching woolly mammoth ribs by the camp fire, longing to find out an answer to the question considered so vulgar by the educated literary critic, namely, 'What happened next?' The essence of suspense may lie in nothing more than a lowly concern with the circumstances in which Troilus and Cressida get it together and why. Though only five stories exist in the world, we can happily hear them repeated, relishing local particularities, the fact that in this retelling, Cinderella met her suitor on a train and not at a ball, or that in another, the prince metamorphosed into an earplug, not a toad.

'If you really want to know, Bertrand's parents showed up or we were interrupted in some way, and I went off to my room, but in the middle of the night, he came and climbed into bed with me. It was the first time I'd been in a bed with anyone but a teddy bear so I froze rigid, even though one side of me was thinking, "God, wait till you tell Sarah about this." '

'Then?'

'Well, we sort of fooled around, and it was one of those typical adolescent things where no one quite knows what's going on; someone who blushed at the mention of farm animals certainly wasn't going to take charge.'

'So you . . .?'

'Kind of, I mean, it sort of happened for a minute, then he started muttering something in French and it was over. I immediately thought I'd be pregnant, but it turned out the sheet had had the honour.'

'With whom did you eventually properly . . .?' I euphemized.

'Oh, with Stuart I was telling you about the other day. We even had a manual. I still have it at home somewhere, full of diagrams, bearded blokes, a lot of lace, and rather seventies pictures. We went out for a year. It was great, very easy – but that probably says more about how uncomplicated I was in those days. It was puppy love. The real love stories happened later, and they were more of a mess. God, listen to me. *The love stories*. It sounds like I'm ninety, I've only had one or two.'

There was a pause, Isabel changed position to lean on her other hand.

'You know, it's really getting late,' she said, 'and I can't imagine you'd want to hear them.'

But I did, and as we ran into the early hours of the morning, the question was why.

What does one hope to learn of someone by hearing who they have loved? Why does this issue seem so central to understanding the mysterious segment of a life we deem private? And therefore what is it we reveal of ourselves with our choice of lover?

In so far as we desire what we do not ourselves possess, our loves trace the evolution of our needs, from a comforting kiss with the dentist to the qualities of the character Isabel might next uncover if we did not fall asleep. But lovers are not chosen according to a perfect match between emotional void and amorous candidate – and in this sense are a complicated guide to inner needs. Many had been picked not because Isabel judged them suitable, but because it seemed suitable for her to have a hand to hold. We may be forced to identify our lovers from a cripplingly small pool of choices. In trying to explain the more inexplicable love stories, one may have to answer the question, 'Why them?' with the gloomy thought, 'Did you see the others?'

Besides such administrative problems, there was also a medley of psychological injunctions which might prevent one from reciprocating the love of an apparently ideal soul in favour of an unsatisfactory but puzzlingly more seductive one. In the eccentricity of our choices, we reveal the nuance we impose on the supposedly straightforward but practically knotted process of giving and receiving affection. Unable to fall in love coincidentally, we remain hemmed in by criteria. The criteria may be benign, a preference for cheerful eyes, mathematicians with broad foreheads or débutantes with narrow ankles, or they may comprise less pleasant callings, a compulsion to wed aristocracy, alcoholics, hysterics or those who have been abandoned by their mother. To speak only of the assets we choose in others neglects how much time we spend appeasing our historically determined, often unconscious psychological needs, compatible poles on the sado-masochistic dial, common neuroses rather than shared tastes in opera or winter sports.

Isabel summed up the points on her compass as such: 'Bastards who I love, nice guys who love me and who I end up despising. And more recently, OK guys who I make an effort to stay with to try to be an adult.'

She had met Andrew O'Sullivan, a Glaswegian Ph.D. student, in her first term at London University, and appointed him representative of the second of these tendencies. The relationship had been founded on what Isabel called her Saul Bellow fantasy.

'You see, normally, I like to be in control of things, and take responsibility, but another side of me wants to throw myself at the feet of stable, solid men, like women in Saul Bellow novels. I want someone to look after me so I can be pampered and spoilt. I know it's not respectable, but at one level I need someone who will take care of money, food and where to live.'

To anyone suffering from a fantasy of passivity, Andrew O'Sullivan could not have been more apt; he was an ideal companion for a shipwreck or plane crash, he would have known how to light a fire with two sticks, build a tent from a rug and bamboo canes and attract the attention of rescue services with a pocket lighter. In non-disastrous life, these capacities manifested themselves in a dexterity with insurance claim forms, household wiring and the two fiddly screws which came with Isabel's wall-mounted phone.

A feature of what makes a man useful in a shipwreck is his ability to block a part of his imagination, the one skilled at envisaging a band of pirates slaughtering the passengers or a typhoon turning a difficult situation into a funeral. While this block is welcome in emergencies, it may present problems on quiet spring days when there is a need for an imaginative understanding of another's muted dramas. Isabel recalled an occasion when she had told Andrew about her mother's affair with a car dealer. He had waited until the end of the story with wide-eyed patience, then reflected, 'It's so weird,' the last word stressed as though he had learnt the initiation rights of a lost tribe.

With the capricious movement of disenchantment, Isabel noticed her growing irritation with a watch Andrew owned. It was made for divers, with a thick metallic strap, a broad screen with dials measuring air pressure, the time in five different countries and a chronometer. Andrew had a habit of turning to it during lulls in the conversation and asking, 'Well, did you know it was four thirty in the morning in Tokyo?'

Eight months into the relationship, the watch ceased to be merely an instrument of time-keeping and acceded to the fatal rank of a symbol for Andrew's more rigid qualities. Isabel did not notice anything new, she had always known the watch and Andrew's corresponding aspects, but she might read the same element in two different ways depending on which side of the love line she was standing.

We never misunderstand people as extravagantly as in our emotional life, for never are we more committed to a person's aptness than when we have fallen in love with them, never do we seek to forget with such vehemence their more inconvenient evils. The state of love is the masterful symbol of what it means to get people wrong, to write bad biographies.

It is neediness which might fairly be held responsible for this shambolic psychological effort, for it is when we need to have children or would go out of our minds at spending another Sunday alone, that we cease to consider others with requisite impartiality. We are fooled into an acknowledgement of only some of our wishes, the wish for a face to kiss predominant among these, and meanwhile forget our enthusiasm for open air sports or Early Modern history. These also comprise what we wish to share with another, but they can be sacrificed in the name of a cuddle, like the ballet schools or amusement arcades a government shuts down for the sake of a war effort.

Had Isabel been asked for her opinions on Andrew when she had been in love with [and blind to the faults of] a second man, she would no doubt have lucidly explained his shortcomings, but in the confusion of her early university months, Andrew fulfilled a primitive need which rendered his more pedantic characteristics invisible.

But Andrew had lit a fuse which could only hasten his own destruction. Isabel's need had blinded her to certain of his faults, but his skill in satisfying the core of the need meant he had gradually allowed her the comfort to notice a host of things wrong with him – like a starving motorist in a roadside restaurant who registers only once his hunger is a little satiated that the vegetables left on his plate are criminally overcooked, the meat too salty and the decor of the dining-room execrable. Ironically, we gain the security to discover faults in others as a consequence of the very strength these faulty characters have been generous enough to grant us.

Isabel grew more difficult in the hope of provoking an ill-tempered, though live, reaction. Unfortunately, the tactic had the opposite effect, whereby her moodiness turned Andrew into the very nursing, stable figure who had elicited the difficulty in the first place. He asked her to explain her discomforts and tried to make sense of the elaborate excuses.

'So if I'm understanding you correctly, what you're saying is you want us to be closer without actually being closer?' Andrew would repeat like a student enunciating characters of the Chinese alphabet.

'Oh, I don't know what I want. I just need to be alone,' Isabel would answer, as confused as he about a situation in which much had been invested, but which had grown mysteriously maddening.

She began to let the relationship run down. Arguments which at the beginning would have been properly repaired were now patched up with a shrug or a tumble into bed.

' "Maybe you're just afraid of your emotions," Andrew once said to me,' remembered Isabel. 'I should have replied, "I'm not afraid of my emotions per se, I just don't want to have any with you." '

That Isabel did not was partly the result of her changing circumstance and character. University had made her more confident, she had forged friendships with people whose lives made Andrew look frustratingly staid. Whereas she now wished to go out at night, he saw no reason to stop staying in as they had done comfortably until then, suggesting that she play him more of the music she pretended to frequent clubs for.

Had Isabel not met these new friends, the problems might never have arisen, and Andrew continued to please, like an idyllic romance thrown into disarray only by departure from the quiet holiday resort where it had been forged. A compatibility which we prefer to explain by psychology might in the end be better understood with reference to the environment. The apparent stability of certain locales means that only a few sides of a person are revealed, so few that the other partner may end up under a false impression that there are no others. It is as if two people who were the best of friends in a city where they met for dinner twice a week had gone on a camping holiday and there identified a host of unpleasant traits they had never witnessed before, but which made further dinners impossible. What had seemed inherent compatibility was restricted to a particular environment. It was the confusion of a person whose wealth has accustomed him to smiling faces, and who has ended up forgetting the connection between the smiles and the money, believing it is his very being that others smile at, only to realize, when bankruptcy strikes, how he had mistaken a relative response for a natural one.

Isabel's inability to be frank with Andrew sprang from a shameful fear of being alone, a fear which meant she tried hard to cling on to those aspects she had loved in him. Realizing Andrew might be someone other than she had supposed had none of the coolness of finishing a biography with the thought, 'Well, Mountbatten wasn't quite the hero I imagined.' Isabel could only give up on her Mountbatten with an assurance that there would be someone there to replace him – but until she had met Guy, the necessary courage was lacking.

Guy was a music journalist who had invited her to a party after a press conference and on the way home kissed her in the doorway of a boarded shop in Soho. He had then reneged on his promise to call and seemed always out of his office when she tried. She had given up on resuming contact, when he showed up at the door of her college room clutching roses and an excuse that he had been held up on an assignment in Manchester. Attraction vanquishing suspicion, they made love three times in her room.

'And after that, well, how can I put it,' smiled Isabel, 'I knew it had to end with Andrew.'

But there were problems in being honest, so Isabel cited a need to devote more time to her studies, presuming Andrew would feel better at being dismissed for the sake of a textbook than a journalist. That he did not drove him to an agonizing search for why he had failed to satisfy her.

'He even asked me if I thought he was bad in bed.'

'What did you say?'

'I told him not to be silly, that he was fine.'

'And?'

'Oh, he got all sarcastic about my use of the word fine. I think he wanted something a bit stronger.'

Isabel's guilt manifested itself in a desire to remain good friends with Andrew. It meant she could escape the brutal shock of ending a relationship by continuing to enjoy its best parts, namely, Andrew's conversation, rather than his presence in her bed and his diver's watch on her night-table – though even if she had found him dull, Isabel would have continued to see him, for she had a resistance to letting people drift out of her life. She recalled her last day at school, when she took the phone number of Yvonne Dowler, a girl she had always done her best to avoid, not because she wanted to see her again, but because the end of any possibility of doing so had seemed morbidly final. Isabel and Andrew therefore went on trips to Kew Gardens and walks around Bloomsbury. It might have been pleasant for Isabel, but there was no way Andrew could see these encounters as anything other than confused attempts to patch things up. Only after his attempt at a kiss on the platform of Leicester Square Station did Isabel learn the impossibility of the friendship.

While Isabel finished her story, another part of me sum-moned the thought of how differently events might have sounded had I heard them recounted by Andrew O'Sulli-van on a train trip to Scotland. From the other side of the dividing line separating victim from executioner, the tale might well have been unrecognizable. Instead of a buffoon with a diver's watch and irritating gentleness, one might have found a woman who had not known what she wanted, who had played games and been unfaithful, who might have had her equivalent of a diver's watch – details which, because she was the narrator, remained censored by our natural blindness to what others find to condemn in us once our back is turned.

129

Then again, the different ways in which a person can leave another means we cannot necessarily take the person who has been thrown out of an apartment as the rejected one. We may sometimes want to pack our bags but unconsciously ask others to pack them for us.

Isabel had been embarrassed at the way Andrew had annoyed her, embarrassed because she felt this annoyance to reflect a private dissatisfaction, like the diabetic guest who must decline a soup with a trace of sugar in it knowing he or she is alone with the complaint. But this might have overlooked the extent to which Andrew himself was an agent of the story. The reason why he had become annoying to Isabel might have stemmed from a frustration with her of which he was not fully aware, and hence could not but hide. He might have tried to understand Isabel's objections to him, but his real struggle [of which this outward struggle was but a pale model] could have been his need to understand what *he* objected to in her. There may have been a complex contract between them to negotiate the separation, a contract as a collusion between two people to hold to a version of a story which both of them would deep down know to be untrue, but formulate to satisfy other demands. Andrew to Isabel: 'Let me leave you in such a way that I will be the victim.' Isabel to Andrew: 'If you must leave, allow me to believe that I am the executioner.'

If Andrew had been one answer to Isabel's fantasy of passivity, then Guy was an answer to a different emotional puzzle.

On one of their first evenings together he had smiled knowingly and remarked, as though pointing out the colour of her dress or a painting on the wall above, 'You're a very selfish person, aren't you?' It might not have been an ordinary fixture of a romantic dinner to find one partner calling another selfish, but in order for Isabel to feel understood, it was no use suggesting her eyes were a beautiful brown or her desires selfless. Though flattery might have been pleasant, criticism seemed truer.

A rocky fourteen months ensued. There was enough goodness in Guy to lead Isabel to fall in love, but never quite enough for her to be less than miserable once she had done so.

'Things were very much up and down, sometimes so lovely that we'd think of marriage and kids, then completely awful,' remembered Isabel. 'It might have carried on like that for ever, but without having planned it, I found myself ending it all of a sudden one evening. The break came after a magazine Guy had been doing a story for had cancelled a contract. He came to my room and started pacing and calling them bastards. I tried to calm him down by saying it wasn't so bad, and that made it worse. He told me how spoilt I was, how I'd always been given everything on a plate. He'd said it before, but this time I got angry, because he'd promised not to keep coming back to it. I told him to stop pitying himself, and it must have struck a chord, because the next minute, he was coming towards me, enraged, his fist in the air. I don't think he meant to hit me, but the angle was wrong and my eye got in the way. It was a big mess. I started crying, he panicked when he saw what he'd done and started getting towels and stuff. There was a fundamentalist Christian girl who lived opposite, she heard the noise and came in. She was a tiny thing, and Guy was huge, but she shouted at him to get out, and Guy picked up his jacket and did as he was told. She was so sweet, I'd never spoken to her during the two terms I'd lived on her corridor at college, but she took me to hospital and while we were waiting, suddenly it seemed insane that I'd been in this kind of situation, because if there's one thing I can't stand, it's physical violence. I put up with a lot from Guy, and I might have put up with a lot more, but blood and stitches were the limit. It was like coming out of a tunnel, and I told him that very night I never wanted to see him again.'

It seemed strange to imagine what might have happened if Guy had not had his story cancelled by a magazine, if he had not miscalculated the angle of Isabel's eye, if there had therefore been no blood and no hospital. Guy would certainly have been the same person, but his ability to hit a girlfriend would have stayed safely hidden in the realm of possibility.

When people criticize biographers and novelists for paying so much attention to extraordinary stories, while our lives largely go by without punch-ups and dramatic events, one might answer that stories are not unreal or irrelevant, but simply the outward manifestation of contradictions which are not usually granted the opportunity of expression [or rather only in slow or indistinct ways]. How does one know if a boyfriend is ill tempered or violent when his professional life is placid and easy? How do we know if we are courageous until a lion roars at us in a jungle clearing? If Oedipus had chanced on someone else, if Anna Karenina had not bumped into Vronsky, if Emma Bovary's husband had won the lottery, their lives would certainly have been quieter, but their characters would not have uncoiled themselves before us.

In accounting for our love of story-filled lives, escapism seems too brutal a word, suggesting that these stories have nothing to do with us, rather than that they reflect dormant fragments of ourselves. The drama that Oedipus lived is not any less our own because we married well and live in a leafy suburb. The extremes of biographical lives are fuller articulations of ourselves which the environment has curtailed. The life of Nelson may be fascinating to someone who would not dare to row across the Serpentine because, containing in a fully developed form so many of our half-formulated fantasies, it constitutes an exercise in self-knowledge.

Isabel couldn't understand quite why she had gone out with Guy. Was it out of a masochistic desire to prove herself good in the eyes of a disapproving father? So what was the relation between this symbolic father and her more than approving real one? But wasn't he more like her mother than her father? Had she chosen him because he had been very good looking? Or was it out of social conscience and middle-class guilt? Had she loved him because he would not love her back? Could she therefore have ended it precisely when he might [despite the punch] have begun to do so?

But one couldn't suppose that Isabel was always the best person to locate answers to these questions. Had she minded that Guy had not wished to stay friends with her after apologizing for the violence?

'No, actually, not. Not once I was over the separation. Perhaps I would have liked to remain friends with Guy, he was always fascinating, and very good company, but no, actually, I don't mind at all. I mean, if someone doesn't want to see me, then I really don't want to see them. I liked

Guy, but I'm not going to humiliate myself by pursuing a friendship with someone who's not interested. And anyway, is Guy in fact that interesting? Perhaps he isn't, and even if he was, what stops him being interesting is his apathy in returning calls from people who want to see him. I'm not saying I mind, because one thing is certain, I really don't, but it's just that . . .'

'Isn't the lady protesting a jot too much?'

'Why? What are you saying?' replied Isabel, a sudden indignancy in her voice more apt for someone unfairly slandered. 'What do you mean?' she repeated.

'Oh, I don't know, you were just going on a lot.'

'So?'

It was one of those moments when one thinks [and how arrogant, or simply useless the thought always is] that one has an insight into someone's character which they are hiding from themselves, and that one may hence make the fatal claim, 'Over your feelings towards X, I think I may know you better than you know yourself . . .'

'I'm sorry, I was wrong,' I replied instead, eager as a caveman not to jeopardize hearing what happened next.

'Do you want another one of these?' I added, offering Isabel the packet of chocolate raisins which we had opened as the alarm clock reached two thirty.

'Thanks,' she said, and came over to the bed to take one, then sat cross-legged on a chair in one corner of the room.

'I'll never know for sure what went on with Guy,' she resumed, 'which was the problem with my other big boy-friend, Michael.'

I had encountered this problem a long time before I learnt its name. Isabel and I had been aboard a crowded bus on Shaftesbury Avenue when I noticed her turning around to address a suited figure who had tapped her on the shoulder. He had been too short to reach the handrail, sweated profusely, and sported thick spectacles of the type which get broken by bigger boys on the school playground. They had exchanged a few words before we stepped off at Cambridge Circus, where I asked who it had been.

'Just a friend I haven't seen in a while,' replied Isabel and changed the subject to rain clouds.

It was a while before I matched this apparition to a certain Michael Catten, who Isabel was now describing as 'the most sensual man I ever went out with'.

I blinked, and once more recognized the devious ways in which the imagination could stumble in its interpretation of another's words. In my understanding of Michael, I was at the mercy of Isabel's descriptions, and now suffered the correction which can be awaited whenever someone who has merely been explained collides with their dimensional representation. No wonder the photographs included in biographies could bewilder, like seeing in the flesh someone one had previously only imagined from the timbre of their telephone voice. After a hundred pages in which Lady Loughborough had assumed the shape of a tall, severe schoolmistress with her hair in a bun [as much due to the author's disabilities as to the distraction of the audience], the reader would turn to a shot of Clarissa Loughborough at the beach in Cannes two years before the Great War and be surprised by the unconventional way she held her parasol, her lively eyes and affectionate glance towards her children playing beside her in the sand.

It made the task of understanding Isabel's passion more challenging, especially after she remarked, 'I'm a little cold, you don't mind if I just tuck myself in here?'

She rose off the chair and landed on the far corner of the bed, from where she continued her story without interruption. Unfortunately, the sight of her toes rising in a small tent formation beneath the duvet only inches from mine meant that most of the tale was lost in the maelstrom engendered by such proximity – so much so that I took in no word of what she said until I awoke from my reverie to find her asking, 'Have you ever had such a devastating break-up?'

I nodded vaguely but sympathetically.

'Do you want to lean against the headrest?' I asked. 'You look awfully uncomfortable there on the edge,' I added altruistically.

'Oh, all right,' she replied with mild surprise, and rearranged herself beside me.

Something about the situation acted as a reminder that the customary bedroom biography comprises only a fragment of the people who have wished or who one would have wished to enter it. Though consummated affairs are granted the prestige and exposure of everything which falls into our naïve category of an event, we may have far more to learn in rescuing from the realm of contingency the stories which fail to happen; those who have been desired or who have desired in vain. The kisses we do not have may be more interesting than the ones we do.

The first choice who would not let themselves be chosen lived at home.

'It happened when I was around ten, and we were all sitting at table celebrating Dad's birthday,' remembered

Isabel, one hand playing with the area of dead skin on the other.

'Not your . . .'

'Wait. Anyway, my mother had made an enormous dinner, lots of members of the family had come over, and we'd cut out paper decorations and bought presents. After the food, Dad stood up and called for a bit of quiet to make a toast. "Now I'd like to thank a very, very special lady in my life . . ." he began, and I remember at once assuming he was going to talk about me. I looked down at my plate imagining the eyes around the table would be turning in my direction, but then Dad came to the end and said, "And this special woman is of course my wife Lavinia, who has cooked us such a lovely dinner, and . . ." I suddenly felt incredibly confused, partly angry at him, partly at myself for being such a noodle. It was worryingly late for such a fixation. I was ten, and should have repressed things a little more by then.'

This doomed scenario of love was by no means the only one Isabel had had to endure.

Name	Desired her Unrequitedly	Desired him Unrequitedly	Age
Dad		X	10
Heathcliff		X	12
Tim Jencks	X		13
Charlie Brint		X	13
Mr Heskett		X	15
Ophelia Kempton	X		18
Vaclav Havel		X	23

There was Heathcliff, who twelve-year-old Isabel had dreamt might answer her confused emotions amidst the bracken on the Yorkshire moors. His heart was in demand, for eight other girls at Kingston Secondary had fallen for the hero of that year's set text, but Isabel felt superior to the competition, particularly the arrogant Valerie Shifton who got As but understood nothing of love and anyway had a fat behind. Isabel had imposed a Yorkshire holiday on her family that summer so they could visit the Haworth parsonage where Emily Brontë had grown up. The rain did not let up, Lavinia sprained her ankle and Isabel recognized early on that she had been driven not by an interest in the Brontës' kitchen but by an irrational wish to spend a night with a fictional character – and once the truth dawned, she grew sullen at having missed out on a canal holiday with Sarah and her fifteen-year-old cousin who was said to open beer bottles with his teeth.

But Heathcliff had proved as deaf to Isabel's advances as Isabel to those of her classmate Tim Jencks. They had both acted in the Christmas pantomime, he as the rear section of a cow, she as a princess captured in a raid by vengeful pirates. During rehearsals and subsequent performances, Isabel had swooned over a captor wearing a pair of felt trousers, a ripped linen shirt and a sailor's hat, who in class answered to the name Charlie Brint but was now known as Captain Hook. After the first scene, the princess and the cow were off stage until the curtain call, so Tim did his best to charm Isabel, suggesting he was not simply the tail-end of a ridiculed animal, and later gathering the courage to invite her to the cinema. Sadly, ten minutes before the appointment, Charlie casually asked

Isabel whether she wished to join him for a hamburger and, ready to walk to Islamabad if Charlie was involved, Tim saw *Raiders of the Lost Ark* alone. Isabel returned home with a gherkin and mustard scented kiss, and later learnt from a long letter delivered by hand that she had broken someone's heart, much as the pirate had by then broken hers.

Such tragi-comic misalliance evoked the cruel uncertainty of our effect upon others, evident in the way one may hastily deliver a piece of banal advice to a friend in trouble, which they surprise us by cherishing for the rest of their days. 'I'll never forget the way you told me, "Always take your time when you do things," ' they inform us of a statement one had made with no investment twenty years before, a truism to release us from a tiresome phone call. And if this were not unfortunate enough, the one meaningful speech we did make to this friend, the one time we spoke with sincerity and conviction, this part of ourselves has left no trace in their mind, for they now shrug their shoulders and accuse us of confusing them with another.

Tim Jencks's feelings for Isabel had been as irrelevant to her as she had been to Charlie Brint. When, three years later, Brint invited Isabel out for dinner and she refused, it showed how the reception of our selves and ideas has less to do with their qualities than the states of mind they encounter. 'Take your time when you do things' can be as significant when one needs to hear it as bewitching smiles are insignificant when one is happily engaged.

It could have explained the behaviour of Mr Heskett, Isabel's politics teacher, a one time Maoist with a seductively crisp voice and a fiery contempt for the social system. Unfortunately for his student, this had not translated into a fiery contempt for his wife, though Isabel had done her best to wear short skirts during hockey games and sprayed a light film of her mother's perfume over an essay entitled 'The Labour victory of 1945'. Her love had led to an encyclopaedic knowledge of Heskett's wardrobe, the rotation of his shirts, the cut of his salt-and-pepper jacket and his habit of blinking before sneezing. Isabel judged her most erotic early experience to have been a school performance of *The Killing Fields*, where she had taken a seat beside Mr Heskett and sat with her elbow against his, feeling his warmth and movement in ambiguous delight while political massacres unfolded on screen.

The most recent unrequited love was for the Czech president and playwright Vaclav Havel. Isabel had read his plays, the letters to his wife from prison, his essays and judged him to be the solution to her adult years. When pressed on the question of Mr Havel's physical appearance, she conceded that this might leave features to be desired, as would the language barrier between them.

A new formulation of her adult and as yet elusive ideal man was hence arrived at: *a cross between Vaclav Havel and Heathcliff with a voice like Mr Heskett.*

More than aware that there were some discrepancies between myself and this trinity, I nevertheless decided it would be foolish to suppose them insurmountable.

'Can I see your foot?' I therefore asked.

'Why?'

'Just let me see.'

Isabel slid her leg out from beneath the duvet, and I leant down to examine it.

'You know, I think you really need to cut that nail on the second toe. Doesn't it hurt?'

'Ehm, yeah, a little,' replied Isabel, baffled.

'So what do you think about my being eligible to attend the operation . . .?'

'Oh,' she smiled, 'I guess we know one another well enough for that by now.'

'Only for that?'

'Are you trying to add yourself to a little list I've been boring you with, by any chance?'

'I always liked the number eighteen.'

VII

THE WORLD THROUGH
ANOTHER'S EYES

The epitome of empathy is said to be the capacity to look at the world through another's eyes. Though our glance on the planet is largely distorted by our crooked perspectives, we may nevertheless, with luck or agility, accede to a privileged glimpse of the view from another's shoes – and in the process claim to have been able, for a moment at least, to surmount our relativity.

Such a possibility might have seemed abstract or plain eerie until, a week after our embrace had heralded a more classic form of intimacy, Isabel and I started a discussion on a trip she was due to make to Athens. Her company was shipping its first products to Greece, and she, her boss and the director of marketing were travelling to discuss arrangements with a local manager. The trip initiated the recognizable pattern of Isabel's departure phobia. She wondered what to take with her, the dilemma hung on two skirts or one, and whether something more informal was needed for the weekend, a pair of jeans or a cotton dress. There was an additional concern that the plane would meet an horrific end in mid-flight, for Isabel worried excessively over the chances of mechanical failure in machines whose workings she could not understand.

We had been talking of gruesome aeronautical eventualities for some time when the name of an ocean made its first appearance.

'I'd prefer to crash on land than in the Atlantic,' said Isabel. 'You're more likely to survive on the ground.'

Focusing on the abstract issue, I rejoindered with bland reassurance, 'Don't be silly, plane travel is the safest way to get from A to B. They check these things very carefully. It really isn't in anyone's interest for a plane to fall out of the sky.'

'I know, but I hate flights over water, and I remember watching a nature programme on sharks in the Atlantic, and they're said to be a very hungry species, just waiting to tuck into passengers.'

'Isabel, there's no way you could crash into the Atlantic.'

'Well it's easy for you to say, you're just taking the Underground to an office in Holborn.'

'And you're not going to crash into the ocean.'

'You never know.'

'You know some things.'

'Not that. What if there was an accident?'

'Look, if the plane crashed, one thing you can be certain is that it's not going to do so in the Atlantic.'

'Why not? Don't be so sure.'

'Because, for God's sake, there's no way a plane from London to Athens is even going to be flying over the Atlantic.'

Whatever the capacity for a non-phobic flyer to empathize with a phobic one, it belatedly dawned on me that there might have been another issue at stake altogether, one requiring more an understanding of geography than psychology.

Because we inhabit the same material world and manoeuvre with languages tied to common definitions, we talk to others in the assumption that they largely share our images and conceptions. If you and I engage in a conversation about toothpaste, despite the wide variety of brands available and the different froths produced, we rely on a mutual understanding of the substance which renders it superfluous for me to take out my Crest and you your Colgate. Similar ideas operate in the geographical domain, for one assumes that if a flight from London to Athens is mentioned, something resembling the following geographical image will arise in the other's mind.

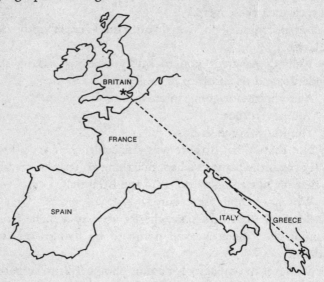

It therefore required a bewildering effort for me to step out of my own mindset for a moment, to grasp that Isabel's internal map might have been shaped very differently, that in the most literal sense, the world could have seemed a very different place through her eyes.

She had in the past alluded to geographical deficiency, she had spoken of a lack of a sense of direction which had meant losing her car near a cinema, she had even cited an argument over map-reading as a catalyst for the end of her relationship with Andrew. But I had apparently failed to grasp the importance of these elements, for only now did it become clear that Isabel's vision of the part of the globe in question showed no signs of matching any existing geographical conception.

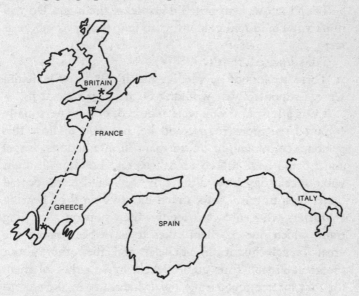

Like a throwback to some primal jigsaw, the landmasses had undergone a mutation from the ordinary understanding of the European continent. Greece had appropriated the position of the Iberian Peninsula, pushing it to where

Italy had been. The boot had drifted eastwards and Rome was now a short ferry ride from Barcelona. It seemed the rest of the world had suffered worse distortion, Australia floated somewhere near Japan, the Philippines were where Hawaii might have been, the ever troublesome Middle East had disappeared and Africa stood defiantly on its head.

'As for where India and Central Asia are, I really couldn't tell,' said Isabel.

'But if you had to make a guess, where would you put them?'

'I don't know, I suppose I'd just leave them out. Do you think you could make an effort to take that look off your face?'

'I'm surprised, that's all.'

'There are lots of people like me. It's to do with spatial sense. I suppose I just wouldn't be ideal for road trips.'

It was a lesson, if one were required, of how personally coloured the inner map could be, but also of how this personal colour might lie dormant in interactions. Isabel and I could have talked of Athens and London all night without realizing how differently we would have located the two cities on a map, much like two hard of hearing characters who enjoy a friendly discussion on a rattling train, which one of them takes to have been about the great French historian Michelet and the other about the great French tour guide, Michelin – neither of them for that matter registering any incongruity in their companion's responses which would have justified a sceptical enquiry.

But Isabel and I did not just perceive the landscape differently, we were also prone to using it in different ways. We were Londoners from birth, we could talk of parking in Russell Square, cycling to Waterloo or catching a play at the Barbican – and yet the associations and functions attached to these locations could not but reflect our contrasting histories. To go from Sarah's house in West Kensington to Swiss Cottage, Isabel had evolved a series of shortcuts which included leaving Park Lane at Brooke Gate, crossing Grosvenor Square, following on to Hanover Square, then taking the north exit up to Cavendish Square, through Portland Place, and then around Regent's Park. She was also an enthusiast of the A40 and argued for it as an alternative to negotiating the Bayswater Road when crossing from East to West. I would have argued against both choices, favouring the Edgware Road for the former trip, and a creative meander off Westbourne Grove for the latter. This was to make a point hovering precariously over the fault-line separating banality from profundity; that though there was materially speaking one London, there were as many Londons as Londoners.

'Stunning,' reacted Isabel, clear that the matter belonged to the former side of the above-mentioned fault-line.

Nevertheless, when she revealed that every time she drove past Big Ben, she could not help but think of Frank Whitford, a friend of her father's who had made a pass at her on a trip to the Houses of Parliament many years before, I realized that there was some validity to the idea of a profusion of personal and idiosyncratic Londons, one for each of its eight million inhabitants. The international symbol of the nation, herald of time to the adjacent chambers of government, phallic metonym which did for London what the Empire State building and the Eiffel Tower did for New York and Paris, Big Ben was Isabel's private symbol of a kiss with her father's friend at the age of seventeen.

Frank Whitford was a retired teacher who had helped Isabel with her English A-level, involving readings of *Pride and Prejudice, Middlemarch, Vanity Fair, Bleak House* and *Jude the Obscure*. It was not his looks which had drawn her, for his teeth did not promise to last a bite through the gentlest green apple and his skin had an ashen pallor more suitable for a figure of the underworld. But his conversation had been caustically witty, his understanding of human nature perceptive beside the stunted introspection of Isabel's peers and on a trip he had proposed to the seat of national government she had surrendered to his advances in an alcove off New Palace Yard.

Her feelings for Whitford had in part been founded on the idea that he shared her tastes in literature. The importance she attached to his literary responses reflected a prejudice that two people in love with *Vanity Fair* would stand a better chance of getting along than a Thackeray-ishly mismatched couple, that to experience the same emotions towards the same object was a sign of psychological compatibility, that to understand a book would mean in some way understanding its other readers.

It might explain the temptation to snoop around libraries in the lulls of parties, presuming an acquaintance with hospitable strangers through their reading matter, sipping their white wine and silently labelling them dark Conradians, effete Fitzgeralders or stark Carverites.

Though this method of discovering character no doubt has merits, the Athens–London flight was an indirect reminder that two people would be capable of loving the same book while the images filling their minds were at sharp variance. The issue was far from the chestnut addressed in literature courses, whether Holden Caulfield was a nice guy or Isabel Archer silly. The issue was not one of a book's meaning, but of the contrasting mental images, the mental film which a book could set off in its readers. It was a matter of asking, 'What do you actually *see* when you read *The Catcher in the Rye* or *The Portrait of a Lady*?' the equivalent of asking, 'But where exactly *is* Athens on your inner map?'

Isabel had recently finished Tolstoy's *Ivan Ilyich*, and we exchanged notes on how moving the masterpiece was. Though in sympathy with her opinion that no book had yet brought her so close to the reality of death, I wondered if I might ask the eccentric question of how she in fact *imagined* Ivan Ilyich, and the house he lived in and the faces of his wife and family. I wanted to go beyond generic literary discussions to a point where one was not simply talking of morality, symbolism and denouement, but how one *saw* landscapes, people and rooms, and where in a life these stage-props had originated.

Isabel had never travelled to Russia, and certainly not to nineteenth-century Russia, so her view of Ivan Ilyich's apartment turned out to have been fashioned from the memories of the Freud Museum in Vienna, which she had visited with her parents as a fifteen-year-old. It was an unprepossessing, bourgeois apartment, with dark wooden doors and worn Persian carpets. Not the whole Ilyich apartment was being played by this dwelling, for when it came to Ilyich's study, it gave way to Isabel's grandfather's study, which was packed with books on military topics, had a globe in one corner, heavy burgundy curtains, two corpulent armchairs against the wall and a set of feathers in a jar on the desk. She had often used this decor in Russian literature, and remembered resorting to it in sections of *Crime and Punishment*. As for the faces of Ilyich and his wife, they shared with characters in dreams the ability to contain comfortably more than one face. Ilyich was both her American cousin, who was stiff, punctilious and correct, and when Tolstoy revealed some of his humanity, Ilyich metamorphosed into Rembrandt as known from the later self-portrait hanging in the National Gallery. Meanwhile his wife had acquired the features of the middle-aged Queen Elizabeth II, as she appeared in a photograph which hung in the filing room of Isabel's office.

But my Ilyichian apartment had nothing to do with Freud's house, for me it was quite distinctly the apartment of the protagonist's wife in Bernardo Bertolucci's *The Conformist*, which I had seen some weeks before reading the book, and which had now become glued to it even though the course of the film had slipped my mind. And whereas Turgenev's *Fathers and Sons* was for Isabel set in a house stitched together from the front of the stables at Fontainebleau and the photographs of the inside of a Swedish hotel in a copy of *House and Garden*, my structure derived from a semi-detached near Brighton belonging to the parents of an old girlfriend who now worked as a travel agent in Bristol.

But the different images filling the inner eyes were not always haphazardly collected or value-free, for the sockets were connected to contrasting sensitivities, to the different things a person was attuned to or capable of registering in a given environment.

I never noticed flowers. They seemed useful to lend

colour to a garden, but were 'flowers' in the way an unknown race can be made up of 'Germans' or 'Americans'. Yet for Isabel, they were objects of a fascination I had previously associated with the contemplation of the eternal questions. When I asked her to describe her grandparents' house, she began with the garden, and ten minutes elapsed before I could interrupt and ask where exactly in Essex the dwelling was. I had understandably shocked her by describing Monet's garden at Giverny as quite colourful.

'In what way?' she had asked.

'Oh, I don't know, sort of lots of pinks and reds and blues.'

'Were there any rhododendrons?'

'Might have been, I don't really know. There were a horde of Japanese tourists, and a lot of them weren't using their eyes to look around, they were just filming everything with their videos, you know, the new ones with the view-finders in colour.'

What Isabel and I were sensitive to in other people was as divergent. Had she chosen to write a biography, it would have been dotted with descriptions of the contrasting moisture content of people's palms, something I never took note of. She remembered that her old head-teacher had been a man with sweaty palms, while her father's hands were always chapped. Paul frequently rubbed his hands in summer, a client from St Ives had been described as having a sense of humour as rough as his paws.

These might have been incidental points had they not been so symptomatic of the way people interpret situations in different ways, and then begin shouting at the situation rather than the interpretation. Take the word 'rational'.

In Isabel's dictionary, it meant one thing, in mine another, so that when I complimented her on how 'rational' she was, she suspected an insult, because her dictionary carried the following definition:

adjective
1. Denoting the faculty of being a bore and pedant.
2. Opposed to emotion, reminder of traditional family dualism: her sister as the emotional one, she the rational one.
3. Insult once thrown at her by Guy.

But what I had intended to suggest was the entry as defined in my dictionary:

adjective
1. A compliment owed to elevated minds.
2. George Eliot, Marie Curie and Virginia Woolf as rational.
3. Compatible with, and capable of enhancing, feeling.

The small conflict which resulted from the discrepancy showed the way a single incident could produce diverging accounts, and therefore a biographically alarming symbol of the capacity of a single life to spawn competing life stories.

During lunch at Isabel's flat, Mrs Rogers had ended the meal by recounting an anecdote which she had taken to be an illustration of her daughter's stubbornness, but which might have been read differently by a less partial observer.

Isabel had apparently loved baths as a child, and frequently pestered her busy mother to be allowed to have one. Mrs Rogers had on a given evening promised five-year-old Isabel that she would be able to run a bath at six o'clock, but six o'clock came, and Mrs Rogers turned out to have other things to do, as indeed she did when the same promise was made then broken the next day. On the third day, Isabel chose to act without her mother's permission and simply ran her own bath. Unfortunately, the hot water tank had just broken down, and the tub turned out to be glacial when Isabel dipped her toe in it. Nevertheless, determined to have the long-awaited bath, she simply sank into the freezing tub, to be found there by her mother who accused her of having lost what little mind she had.

Though at one level, this was a story about the blind wilfulness of a child, at another [and for Mrs Rogers, far less pleasant] level, it was the story of a child reacting against a permanently disappointing mother by taking charge of her own wishes, and having the boldness to carry them through, even when it might not seem logical to an adult for someone to spend the evening in a glacial tub.

Unfortunately, there was none of the certainty of the Athens confusion, where there was at least an atlas to resolve things on a factual basis, so Mrs Rogers left the flat dismissing her daughter's interpretation as 'pure nonsense' [while also advising her to 'do something about those frightening earrings'].

But one should not have assumed that Isabel was any more certain what events in her life meant. The more I knew her, the more I noticed her revising her stories. When she had had a good day, matters from her childhood onwards pointed in an optimistic direction, the day she fell out with her boss, she sat with her head in her hands, cried for a moment [she favoured rapid cathartic weeping] and concluded that she hadn't put a foot right since landing on earth.

Sitting side by side, there were therefore at least two childhood biographies.

Happy Childhood Biography	Sad Childhood Biography
1968: Missing sixties means avoiding naïvety of flower power, can spend adolescence thinking about boys not politics. Witnesses father in seventies purple jackets and orange ties.	**1968:** Born too late to experience sexual freedom and optimism of sixties, condemned to adolescence in the shadow of monetarism, Aids and the death of the LP record.
1970: Birth of sister Lucy, an ideal companion to avoid loneliness. Teaches her how to share toys, become more responsible, sociable and kind.	**1970:** Lucy denies her attention from parents, annoys her and fosters a competitive, cruel streak. Means she has problems being friends with women.
1974: Mother forces her to grow up and become a sensible adult. Harshness a good preparation for life's rigours.	**1974:** Mother throws away favourite toy blanket – destroys chances of evolving good relationships with men.
1976: Misses going to best primary school in the area, but learns to meet children from all backgrounds, makes her a rounded person.	**1976:** Refused entry into primary school of her choice, leads indirectly to a failure to get into Oxford or Cambridge.
1977: Birth of a baby brother: teaches her to be comfortable with boys, a nice toy to play with.	**1977:** Paul born: end of peace around the house, a brat, further prevents her getting attention from parents.
1978: Nice party to celebrate Dad's birthday.	**1978:** Realizes Dad prefers Mum to her.
1980: Start of turbulent but fruitful adolescence. Dr Ross lends her confidence. Boys who reject her give her valuable lessons. Judged acceptable looking, avoids problems of being too pretty.	**1980:** Start of nightmarish adolescence. Kiss from creepy Dr Ross dooms her to attract perverse men [Andrew, Guy, Michael]. Her face assumes ghastly dimensions – start of life-long envy of beautiful women.

1981: Meets her best friend Sarah and begins a hectic but enjoyable social life.	**1981:** Becomes friends with Sarah, led astray from naturally academic inclinations. Sacrifices worldly success for girlie chats.

Because the choice of biography depended on the vagaries of Isabel's moods, there could be no Archimedean point from which to settle the story once and for all – at least not until death had struck.

Attentive readers may have spotted a difference between this biographical venture and its more formal cousins, resting on a detail [mentioned with no morbid intentions] that Isabel was not yet dead.

Most biographies are about dead people. This has many attractions, including the ability to know the contents of any last-minute confessions, who got what in the will, whether the bad lung killed the old soldier or a stray golf ball did it. Death gives a life admirable completeness, the dead rarely stand up to refute an analysis and their departure from the land of the living provides a convenient point to draw a book to a close.

However, if the purpose of biographies is to understand how people experience their lives, the dead biography misses out on an important feature – that we rarely approach our story with the certainties so easily fastened to lives when they are over.

Standing at the graveside, we cannot help but think that Louis XVI was always heading for the block, that Mozart was going to die young and penniless, that Wilfred Owen was not going to survive the Great War and Sylvia Plath had to finish with her head in the oven.

Death is the enemy of latent alternatives. It makes us

forget how the purposefulness of a life viewed from outside lies at odds with the way things are witnessed from
within, how the possible plots will always outnumber the
actual adventures.

At the age of four, Isabel wanted to be a bricklayer.

'Did you?'

'Yeah, it was partly practical, partly aesthetic. You see,
I thought people who built houses would be the richest in
the country, because houses were so big and expensive.
There's child's logic for you. And then I was amazed by
how every brick in a building was carefully laid one
by one. I used to look at walls, and imagine how long it
had taken to finish them.'

But by eight, Isabel wanted to be a milkman.

'Or rather milkwoman. You see, I loved milk, and I
loved those electric buggies the milkman drove, so it
seemed a good way to combine the two. I'd also made
friends with our milkman, who was called Trevor and
came from Trinidad. He told me the milk he brought us
was from a cow named Daisy he kept in his garden,
and that's why it tasted better than milk from anywhere
else.'

But eventually, Isabel became neither a bricklayer nor a
milkwoman. No wonder she hated talking about her job
at parties. She didn't like the way her identity could reduce
itself to employment at Paperweight, when she had fallen
into the job by a network of chance. After graduating
from university, she had initially looked for work in a
radio station, but had been rejected for lacking the requisite experience. She had therefore decided to enrol on a
broadcasting course, and applied for government funding,
but the time required to secure this and her dire financial

position meant she had also begun applying for jobs. A mere day after she had sent the Paperweight application, her current boss had called and offered a reasonable post starting the following week, and Isabel had not felt confident enough to turn it down.

'I think in the end, I really wasn't cut out for radio. Other friends of mine work in it now, but they either had contacts or else had experience I never had,' justified Isabel, a trace of bitterness audible in her voice – a reminder that contingency might not always be pleasant, bringing with it the weight of individual responsibility. How much easier to suppose that the gods had decreed one would never have the chosen career, rather than that it depended on a little more tenacity and ingenuity.

'Radio was just the silly and over-ambitious dream of a sheltered girl,' she concluded, 'the kind of thing lots of people have after they leave university but before they learn what it's all about.'

It was in Isabel's nature to pour scorn on her younger selves and their opinions, drawing lines between herself and the past.

At fifteen, she told me she had been an obnoxious teenager who had believed in the following:

- that she was going to die before her twenty-fifth birthday
- that she would never forgive her parents for forcing her to be home by eleven when both Laura and Sarah were allowed to stay out until midnight
- that loving someone meant you would always want to live with them
- that those who made money were evil

- that you should pretend to be busy the first time a boy asked you out
- that marriage was reactionary, and children an unnecessary sacrifice
- that the purpose of a holiday lay in a suntan .
- that Marguerite Duras was a great novelist
- that she would never be as pretty as Grace Marsden.

'And those things seem totally ridiculous now,' she explained, 'I'd pay a hefty sum not to have to sit through dinner with the fifteen-year-old berk I was. Imagine those arguments one would have: 'No, dear, capitalism isn't always evil,' and, 'You know, Isabel, the Parthenon is a bit more interesting than the hotel pool . . .'

The brutal way the adult treated the teenager, a brutality made possible by a sense of radical separation, showed how a single person was really a succession of different people crowded within a deceptively continuous body. The shift from one person to another seemed akin to the hand-over of batons in a relay race, where members of the same team would run different laps of a circuit. The metaphor suggested both difference and continuity, the change in runners symbolizing the former, the permanence of the baton the latter.

I remembered a retrospective of the work of Picasso, which had showed breathtaking diversity over one life-time. There a baton had passed from a talented young man who painted blue pictures of gaunt figures to one who did softer, pink scenes, who had run with it a little before handing it to a painter who cut perspectives and called it Cubism. After a lap of this, the baton had gone to someone with *Guernica* in mind, and the process had continued ever more triumphantly I was told, for I had by then slipped off to the cafeteria.

Even from a hair-minded perspective, Picasso witnessed a radical succession of developments from 1881 to 1973. Pictures show him with short cropped hair at fifteen, a self-portrait done at eighteen has him wearing long hair parted in the middle accompanied by a moustache, at twenty he was sporting a full beard, in middle age he grew his hair long and had a parting on the right, a few strands often dropping into his left eye, at the liberation of Paris in 1944 his hair had thinned and greyed considerably, and by the time of the Peace Congress in 1949 he was bald. He also underwent important wardrobe changes – jackets in the early years, suits in the middle ones and blue and white striped T-shirts towards the end.

So where were the decisive shifts between one Isabel and another?

'I don't want to exaggerate, but I think I've become a lot more confident with others recently,' she cited as one example, 'Ever since I learnt to pass loo tests on people.'

'What's a loo test?'

'It's the best thing to combat shyness.'

Isabel had a tendency to take people she did not know well too seriously. As a child, she had alternated between precocious confidence in the company of friends, and crippling shyness when placed in a room full of strangers. Her first two weeks in kindergarten were spent not saying a word, until the teachers made an effort to introduce her to the other children – at which point, she was transformed into the life of the class, organizing a rebellious litany of tricks to torture her now-bemused guardians.

A trace of this childhood shyness had continued into adulthood, until she had discovered the loo test in a meeting shortly after starting work. She and her boss had been talking to a bank manager about a loan to acquire new warehouse space. Isabel had been asked to give a presentation outlining the company's strategy, using an overhead projector on which she had worked out, though her maths was notoriously shaky, figures from relevant balance sheets. She dreaded the task, but shortly before she was due to speak, the corpulent bank manager excused himself for a moment. The meeting was adjourned until he returned from the bathroom, but he had only been back ten minutes when, citing unfortunate shellfish the night before, he was forced to excuse himself again. Far from distracting Isabel from her presentation, his troubles filled her with curious confidence: suddenly the bank manager became a vulnerable human being, with an irritable stomach and bowels. His pin-striped suit seemed less daunting now she could picture him with his trousers around his ankles, the stripes melted into confused ripples, beads of sweat soaking over his brow while his insides contorted themselves in the tiled cage of a corporate cubicle.

'So I started doing this loo test on anyone who was scary. You know, policemen, waiters, academics, taxi drivers, people from the gas board . . . It makes them seem like they come from the same planet as me. It's changed my life.'

But however hard Isabel tried to separate her different selves and their lives, the demarcations had a disarming tendency to collapse. At the end of a busy day at work, she announced that she would from now on cease to be emotionally involved in the fate of her company. Lying on the grass near the Thames, watching the plume of a jet streaking its way across the sky, she remarked, 'I had a very cheerful thought today, just when everyone was shouting and the delivery hadn't come and the phones were ringing, I realized that everything was a bit "so what" in the end. I didn't finish what I had to do today; so what. My car's not running right; so what. I haven't got enough money; so what. My parents didn't love me enough; so what. See what I mean? It's very releasing, it's going to be my new way of looking at the world.'

But no sooner had this been announced than a yet larger office crisis developed, and the Buddhist wisdom disappeared as rapidly as it had arisen. Ways of looking at the world were in constant flux, relics of earlier selves intruded on the orderly assumptions of later ones. Isabel's decision to renounce self-pity could collapse after arguments where she would 'sob like a Sicilian widow' on her bed. She confessed to frequent desires to scream like a petulant baby, if it had not been so incongruous when people around her looked as though they had long escaped the play-pen. She had decided to explain herself when rejecting suitors, but when a Greek accountant by the name of Sotiris had begun pursuing her, she had reverted to old tricks, never calling back and pretending she had not received his letters.

Shifts in character were more gradual than Isabel wished to admit when she made bold pronouncements to the effect that she would 'never get involved with an emotionally repressed man again', or would from now on 'refuse to blame other people for my own mistakes' or would 'only eat healthy things for lunch and never drink white wine at dinner'.

The reason she now seemed to be entertaining a more adult relationship with her parents had little to do with growing wiser, and much to do with having her own flat and behaving with the civility owed to visiting friends rather than the bickering civil wars entertained by people under the same roof. But a Christmas weekend was a sobering reminder that nothing had altered deep down: she rowed with her mother with all the vehemence of the classic adolescent exchange, she squabbled with her brother over a roll of Sellotape as though they were both at primary school, and her father preached to her in a patronizing tone that suggested she would have had trouble buying her train fare home.

There was the temptation to declare certain dates turning points, like historians locating the decline of this or the rise of that to 1850, 1500 or 1066, whereas the truth was a far more muddled retreat or advance, when there would always be evidence of pre-industrial villages surviving into the so-called modern era or an empire showing remarkable resilience when it would have been more convenient for it to have died conclusively to make way for another fifty years before.

VIII

MEN AND WOMEN

Whatever care one might take to see the world through someone else's eyes, it was becoming clear that there would always be certain things one risked staying blind to, especially when one was in the unfortunate [though not unusual] position of having been born a man.

One Saturday morning, I arranged a meeting with Isabel outside Covent Garden station. She arrived a few minutes late, and after apologies and curses for the train, asked, 'Well, what do you think?'

'I don't know,' I replied, unsure as to the solicited opinion.

'Isn't it nice?'

'It's OK out today,' I said, for it had stopped raining for the first time in twelve days.

'No, not that.'

'What then?'

Isabel smiled, sighed with a dimple of humour in her cheeks, then said, 'Oh forget it, come on, let's get a drink.'

But we had only been sitting down for a moment when she resumed the pursuit of my opinion on the elusive topic.

'Do you really not notice anything?'

'I don't know,' I said, hesitantly turning around as if Louis Armstrong had occupied an adjacent table, 'I don't think so.'

'So you don't think anything has changed?'

'Changed? Eh, well, no, not really. I mean, it's the weekend, so you can tell everyone's a bit more relaxed. And I suppose the UN resolution is going to be good news in the long run, though . . .'

'God!' exclaimed Isabel, and buried her face in her hands, sighing what sounded like, 'Men' but could simply have been, 'Mpphhhm', a gesture of sorrow interrupted by the arrival of a waiter.

'Cappuccino?' he cried.

'That's for me,' I replied.

'So de orange is for madam,' he understood, displaying more sophisticated powers of deduction than I had yet mustered.

'Bon appetit,' he added, sarcastically smiling at the mournful couple.

'What's wrong, Isabel? Don't sulk. What am I suppose to see? I always had problems mind-reading.'

'I just thought it would be a bit obvious to anyone with half a brain cell or simply half an eye that I'm looking a little different today than I did yesterday on account of the fact I've just spent two hours and twenty-five quid at the hairdresser and now have hair that's about two and a half inches shorter than it was, which I'm sure is not world-shaking news and the UN is of course always a worthy topic, but I might have expected you to notice that *something* had changed.'

Sighing again and removing a purple straw from its wrapper with a rapid pull, Isabel concluded, 'But I suppose you're a man, so I really shouldn't be surprised.'

Now that I looked at Isabel properly, that is, with an awareness of possible difference, everything had changed. Her chestnut hair which had previously reached comfortably below her shoulders now reached only the top of the blades. It had altered the shape of her face, accentuating her cheek-bones and making her seem more mature.

'I look younger, don't you think?' asked Isabel.

'Ehm.'

'It's the more girlish look that's in at the moment. It was Dave's idea. We talked about it a lot, you know, because I wanted to change something, and he was first thinking of putting in some streaks, but I think in the end he did the right thing.'

It was a depressing reminder that, unless work in the haircutting trade offers us incentives to do otherwise, our sensitivity to the appearance of others remains inferior to that of our own. While aware of days in which our hair falls appealingly over our brow and days in which, quite mysteriously, it falls over the same brow but reduces us to tears, we are unable to follow the similarly complex but always unique pathways of sensitivity which govern others' relations to their outward selves. They only have to retain the essentials for us to overlook the incidental problem of puffy cheeks, lined foreheads or a swollen stomach which may have driven these unfortunates to heights of self-loathing.

'Oh, I'm sorry, I'm not quite ready,' said Isabel at seven forty-five on a Tuesday evening, the time we had agreed to set off from her flat for an award ceremony at the annual Amateur Gardeners' Association meeting in Kilburn, where Isabel stood to win a prize for something green she had planted on her balcony.

'Do you think this is too smart?' she asked.

'No, it's fine, let's just go, otherwise we'll be late,' I answered.

'Hang on, look, why don't I change really quickly, and you tell me what you think?'

She went into the bedroom, changed languorously, then came out looking much the same.

'Do you prefer the shorter skirt or the longer skirt?'

'Ehm.'

'I think the longer one, don't you?'

'Either one,' I prophesied, from the vantage point of a man whose leisure hours were spent in cotton trousers and denim shirts and was hence hampered in his understanding of the nuances separating one black skirt from another.

'And do you think this blouse goes?'

'Goes?'

'With the skirt.'

'Of course.'

'I was hesitating between a beige one and a light blue one. Do you want to have a look at them?'

'Quickly.'

'OK.'

I followed Isabel into her bedroom, where the drawers were extended, the cupboard doors swung open and it seemed as if a careless burglar had been rifling in a frantic search for a gold ingot or handgun.

I was struck by the self-consciousness the wardrobe implied, the physical awareness to which it catered. It allowed Isabel to distinguish between casual-casual and casual-chic, a difference resting on the apparently superficial detail of the colour of a pair of jeans or the bagginess of a sweater. There were skirts, jackets, blouses, trousers and jumpers, all of which had a specific role to play in matching the expectations of a given occasion. The

Gardeners' Association meeting demanded one thing, a friend's birthday quite another.

'The blouse you have on is fine,' I lied, a colour-blind character bluffing through an opinion on Matisse's use of red.

The decision-making process seemed to have drawn to its close, and so we made our way to the door. Unfortunately, a mirror hung to one side of the hall, and Isabel caught sight of something which made her run back into the living-room with the explanation, 'There's a bloody volcano on my temple.'

I searched for evidence of this Vesuvius, but an examination revealed only a tiny spot, one of the smaller in dermatological history, lurking on her left temple.

'It's nothing,' I reassured her.

'I wish you wouldn't lie for your convenience,' she said and headed for the bathroom.

'Isabel, don't be silly.'

'It's easy for you to call me silly,' she replied with sudden bitterness.

Was Isabel not being silly? But then again, what could it matter what I thought when from the inside, the spot was deemed a monstrous volcano? What could another's judgement do when confronted with the rigours of self-perception?

The disparity was the symbol of yet another challenge to the notion of biographical objectivity. If one was trying to understand Isabel, whatever an assembled panel of volcanologists might say, could one really have dismissed as irrelevant her own sense of the spot's Vesuvian size? Or did one not have to take it into account as an objectively ridiculous, and yet subjectively authentic belief?

Many such tensions between self-perception and outside judgement were pleasant ones, in the sense that the correction demanded by the discrepancy ran in a favourable direction: the lasagne was excellent, even if the cook had thought it terrible, the after-dinner speech was a comic triumph, even if the speaker had judged it a damp squib. But other misperceptions were not so harmless. It was no wonder biographers so often offended relatives and admirers as they adjusted in a negative direction the self-image of their subjects, just as frowns could be expected when telling Isabel that she was not quite the dancer she imagined, that her French accent was not as fluent as she had announced or that she could afford a little more humility concerning her computing skills.

'I need some time in the bathroom to set things right,' Isabel called out. 'It'll just take a moment or two. There's wine and beer in the fridge if you want.'

'Why don't we just go now? You look fine.'

'Give me a little time. Please?'

'OK, we'll just arrive when it's over,' I answered gruffly.

I waited in the living-room in front of a game show on television, glancing occasionally at my watch and over at the closed bathroom door with the self-righteous indignation of a Swiss citizen awaiting the 8.02 train at 8.03. Moreover, I sighed the way Isabel had done a few weeks before, a quiet but emphatic 'Women' escaping my lips, but drowning in the guffaws of the game show audience, one of whose members had just won a holiday to Hawaii as a reward for consuming a jar of worms.

Biographies are traditionally written without hesitation

in crossing lines of age, class, profession and gender. An urban aristocrat captures the life of a rural pauper, a fifty-year-old follows the experience of youthful Rimbaud, a timorous academic allies himself to Lawrence of Arabia. An enviable faith lies behind these enterprises, the idea that men and women remain essentially comprehensible to each other despite a ripple of surface difference.

Dr Johnson thought so: 'We are all prompted by the same motives, all deceived by the same fallacies, all animated by hope, obstructed by danger, entangled by desire and seduced by pleasure.' People belonged to the same disparate but unitary family, suggested Johnson, and could therefore understand one another on the basis of their passport to the human community. I could understand your motive, because I would find much the same if I looked under my pillow. I could understand a fragment of your experience by finding the same experience within myself. I would know how love had made you suffer, because I had also endured evenings by a phone which had not rung. I would recognize your envy, because I too had known the pain engendered by my insufficiencies.

But there were darker implications to this pillow model of understanding. What if little lay beneath the pillow? Adam Smith had unwittingly articulated the dilemma in his *Theory of Moral Sentiments*. 'As we have no immediate experience of what other men feel, we can form no idea of the manner in which they are affected but by conceiving what we ourselves should feel in the like situation. Though our brother is upon the rack, as long as we ourselves are at our ease, our *senses* will never inform us of what he suffers. It is by the *imagination* only that we can form any conception of what are his sensations. By the imagination we place ourselves in his situation and conceive ourselves enduring all the same torments.'

Despite the virtue of suffering with others, the sombre consequence of the pillow theory lies in the need for a sufficient stock of experience genuinely to imagine the experience of others – depressing because our stock can never adequately answer the emotions we encounter beyond ourselves.

What if I had never been on a rack before? What would I then feel for my brother condemned to this fate of unimaginable agony? Would I imagine the last time I had been on a crowded Underground train and then extend the experience a hundredfold, perhaps mixing with it the recollection of a painful tooth extraction or lanced boil? In other words, how can we understand experiences of which we have no experience?

We may suppose that no experience is so unique as to be incomparable. There are always adjacent experiences to which we can appeal to inform us of the original, we proceed with metaphors when our images run dry. I had never eaten shark, but when Isabel informed me that it tasted half like cod and half like tuna, both of which I had bought on occasion, the mystery of the fish receded. When we say that a book has transported us to a foreign land we have never travelled to, we are paradoxically also saying that it has succeeded in reminding us of places that we knew, but had never yet combined.

But there are situations in which we may be granted neither cod nor tuna. Others may resist suggesting the nature of their experience out of an assumption that we should know what these are without requiring to have them spelt out. The sulker's fantasy is to be understood without needing to speak, metaphorize or explain, because words embody a defeat of a prior and more intimate level of communication. It is when intuition breaks down that we have to clear our throat, and our voice risks reminding us of our loneliness. We research only what we have not felt.

'I can't imagine what she's doing in there with that spot,' I asked myself, looking once more towards the bathroom door and at my watch with the self-righteous irritation of a Swiss citizen still awaiting the 8.02 train at 16.45. 'She's been in there about two hours.'

As I continued to tap my fingers on the glass coffee-table and the television game-show gave way to a more subdued survey of the nesting pattern of the swallow, I reflected on my ill-tempered inability to understand Isabel's bathroom delay. What in Adam Smith's name did women in fact do in bathrooms? Why did I assume that a person who did not wear make-up could understand someone who did? Why would someone who felt no qualms about a four-day shadow grasp the meaning of a spot on another's temple? How would a man who had not yet tried on a skirt empathize with a woman whose cupboard contained half a dozen?

'What are you actually doing in there?' I therefore asked Isabel in a voice far removed from the irritation of earlier enquiries.

'Just hang on will you. Stop bothering me, or it'll take even longer. I told you, I'll be out as soon as I can,' she replied, clearly not detecting a change of tone from harassment to philosophical research.

'I don't mean to hurry you. Forget the damn gardeners, I'm just interested in what you do in the bathroom when you put on your make-up and things.'

'Oh, cut the sarcasm, I said I'd be ready in a minute.'

'I'm not being sarcastic. I'd like to know.'

'Know what?'

'Well, what you spend ages doing in front of the mirror.'

'I'm not taking as long as all that.'

'I know you're not, I'd still like to understand though.'

'You're joking.'

'I'm not.

'You really want me to explain?' asked Isabel, opening the bathroom door with a quixotic smile.

'Sure.'

So explain she did. We missed the gardening meeting altogether, but in return I was taken into a realm of Isabel's life whose difference from my own I could not have deduced from the Smithian imagination. I had known other women's bathrooms, yet the issue of facial preparation had been overlooked, I had taken it for granted that their owners had different lotions in their washbags and that there were things called mascara, eyeliner and moisturizer – but I had no idea what a facial routine might be, and what difference it could make to the experience of the two genders.

Isabel's day began with a cleanser. It was manufactured by Clarins, it was a white liquid and came in a blue bottle. She removed it with a pad of cotton wool, which she ran under the hot tap, then squeezed to expel the water. It prevented the fibres from moulting on her face as she rubbed, the heat opening the pores of the skin. Then it was the turn of the toner, a clear liquid substance which removed the residue of the cleanser and any remaining make-up. It had the added advantage of closing pores. Moisturizer was applied afterwards from a Nivea tub, Isabel remembered to put some on her neck, which her mother had suggested so as to avoid the later perils of a crow's neck. Once a week, after the bath, Isabel would apply a different moisturizer [this time it came in a larger pink bottle] over her legs, and still another kind [in a light green tube] would go onto her hands.

'Now the concealer, which covers up red blotches or spots. Then some foundation cream, which is skin coloured and . . . Do you really want me to go on?'

'Yes, of course.'

'So I dab on bronzing powder which is a bit darker than natural skin colour. It takes away the shine and you put it on with a large brush, first wiping off the excess on the back of your hand. If I can be bothered, I might also put on blusher to highlight the cheek-bones.'

Then it was the turn of the eyes: a rub of mascara against her lashes, a brush of shadow on the upper lid [brown to match the colour of her eyes], followed by a gentle combing of the brows to assure their symmetry. The odd hair might at this point be plucked, a process which remained incomprehensibly painful.

The banality of such a ritual to anyone of the female species did not obscure its significance. What is most banal for one person strikes another as exotic precisely on the basis of this banality – the thing that one believes unworthy of interest sparks exceptional curiosity if one happens to be surprised.

The ritual lay at a crossroads of difference between us. It accounted for Isabel's sensitivity to the fact that the heroine of a Hollywood weepie had not taken off her make-up before she retired to bed, or that at the funeral none of the women's copious mascara had run – details which my equally damning verdict of the verisimilitude of the film had ignored with masculine blindness.

One could conclude that the competent male biographer would need a trace of the transvestite in him to appreciate female experience. Stories of Henry James dressing up in a wig now seemed explicable more as an ingredient of cod and tuna research than as something belonging to a branch of psychopathology. It could have been as important for Virginia Woolf's male biographer to hunt down her letters as to spend a day circumnavigating Bedford Square in a pair of Edwardian stockings.

IX

PSYCHOLOGY

Everyone has something to hide, because everyone suspects that if others knew certain things about them they would no longer be loved. Behind our need for privacy lies a fear that we are unacceptable when everything about us is known. It is no wonder the subterfuge breeds an occasional dread of spilling the beans, a dream that we find ourselves naked in the street or our suitcase opens at the carousel of a crowded airport.

Something of this night-time horror returns us to a sense of childhood nudity. Children are bad at keeping secrets and grown-ups clever at unearthing them, so the sensation of having one's secrets revealed echoes the superiority of the parent before the child. But the fear of transparency, the fear that another person may find our secrets without giving us a choice, is gradually tamed through the assumption that we are the masters of our own disclosure, that we know ourselves better than others do.

Nevertheless, in the presence of psychologists, the assumption may break down, and the feeling of transparency return. What we imagine the psychologist knowing without asking is of course our most dangerous [for our chances of being loved] secrets. It is not the knowledge of the psychologist we fear, so much as the judgement which will follow, and the judgement cannot be good as we are all somewhere attached to the notion of original sin. We thereby relive a scenario of a child who has furtively stolen a favoured sweet, only to cross his mother in the corridor and realize that she has understood everything he should not have done.

It might have explained the discomfort I felt at the sight of Isabel writing in her diary, for the diarist shares the symbolic position of the psychologist, someone who knows more than they say, and whose knowledge is dangerous enough to be classified as secret.

'It's amazing how you get into a bad mood every time I do this,' she remarked, having taken out a pen and the burgundy volume in a coffee shop near her house.

'I don't get in a bad mood.'

'So why are you suggesting I stop?'

'It's just not very good manners.'

'But it's all right for you to read the paper?'

'So why can't you explain what you're writing about?'

'Because it's private. And it's not about you.'

'I'm sure it's not. I don't care, write what you want,' I replied with enviable maturity before turning back to global infamies.

The diary is an alarming item because it threatens to be a repository of another's most unlovable thoughts. When Virginia Woolf went to hear Ethel Smyth rehearse in one of the elegant houses in Portland Place, one can imagine her to have been full of civility towards her hosts, sipping tea and nibbling at the raisin cakes on offer. Imagine then the surprise of Ethel Smyth, Lady L. and her friend Mrs Hunter, had they had the misfortune to stumble upon Virginia's diary of February 4th, 1931, describing her visit to them that day:

A vast Portland Place house with the cold wedding-cake Adams plaster: shabby red carpets; flat surfaces washed with dull greens . . . There was a roaring fire in the Adams grate. Lady L. a now shapeless sausage, and Mrs Hunter, a swathed satin sausage, sat side by side on the sofa. Ethel stood at the piano in the window, in her battered felt, in her jersey and short skirt conducting with a pencil. There was a drop at the end of her nose.

It is a feeling of dread that someone will notice the drop at the end of our nose, metaphorical or real, which fuels the boundless suspicion directed at those unfortunate enough to look closely at others.

But however much diaries may alarm, our worry is perhaps only saving us from the greater panic that judgement spreads beyond their pages, and that in the course of our conversations, our good-humoured neighbours are often in the process of appraisals which stretch beyond the cosy confines of what they are telling us – a thought which would not evade us if we believed of others what we know of ourselves [but which might at the same time render us mad].

'Derek, I've called up Bretherton, and the boxes will be here on Thursday.'

'That's great, Malcolm. And I've received notice from York that they're shipping two thousand next week.'

'That's more than they expected.'

'No, it's always been two thousand.'

'Oh, all right. Will you let Jenny know before the deadline?'

'Of course.'

Another fragment of nine-to-five dialogue as I overheard

it across the open-plan office, my colleague Malcolm standing by the photocopier, his hunched frame carrying a few too many layers of fat, his rapid dialogue muffled by the salivous interior of his cheeks, his breath smelling like an unaerated bathroom in autumn. And Derek with his brittle hands, unwieldy nose, giant pair of creaking shoes and remaining hairs grown to their tethers and combed back with maniacal care. Two more characters in the human comedy, and yet how unmentionable their eccentricities were. Derek and Malcolm might have recognized each other's clownish aspects, but the thought that these could have formed the inner gossip of the other would no doubt have struck them both as unexpected and offensive.

Un-self-conscious dialogue is possible only thanks to the assumption that the other person is taking our words at face value rather than jotting things in the margin of the conversation. No wonder we grow immeasurably upset when we hear that someone has spoken disparagingly of us: the real offence is not so much *what* has been said [yes, all right, we are hairless, ill tempered, too pushy, too shy, too rich, too poor . . .], but the idea that someone we thought was simply imparting office news was simultaneously storing judgements to share with others at a later date.

It begins to explain how the word psychology may in certain circles send shivers down spines, provoking anxiety that the soft-spoken psychologist standing in line for rum punch at the wedding reception in fact has no interest in your polite patter about loft insulation, but is instead performing an unobtrusive X-ray of your psyche while pretending to straighten his bow-tie.

178

Yet viewed without melodrama, psychology is merely the name for a myriad of incompatible theories of the antics of the human mind. We are all psychologists in interpreting the behaviour of others, coming to conclusions as to what could explain their everyday abnormalities.

Isabel had a friend called Jerome who had walked out of his legal practice and his marriage and moved to a village in Yorkshire, where he had found work as a baker. When his name came up in conversation, everyone was ready with an explanation for his actions. To some he was afraid of intimacy, to others, he was dogged by a fear of failure – though some argued it was a fear of success. Others thought he had a father complex, Isabel suspected latent homosexuality, Sarah manic depression.

Psychological clichés could be found in every analysis, brandished without care for clinical accuracy or the threat of libel. Loose theories propounded links between being fat and being funny, between having an absent father and being ambitious, between being clever and being unhappy, between being nervous and developing cancer.

Nevertheless, there was an awareness that even if Isabel and her friends were unsure what had happened to Jerome, more sophisticated accounts of his troubles were available. The age of modern psychological science had instituted a hierarchy in an area where anyone could previously have had their say, forging a difference between the knowledge of mental processes available to experts and lay folk.

The problems created by this discrepancy must in part have belonged to biography. If one was trying to understand someone's life according to old-fashioned intuition, and yet was aware of experts wielding more powerful tools in a building across town, it would throw the claim to be writing a complete life of Alexander the Great or Dante Alighieri into doubt. Did biographies not have to keep up with the developments of science if they wished to be arenas where the complexity of human nature could be explored?

But the problem was compounded by a fundamental insight of psychology; that whatever our deficiencies in understanding our friends and colleagues, the person we are fated to understand least is ourselves. What we recall of our childhood is not the significant portion, but memories designed to shield us from difficult truths. We remember a yellow sofa in a room, but cannot remember the couple whom we glimpsed making love on it. A rivalry within the family torments us in our sleep, but the plot we recall the next morning is so disguised that we cannot see, because we should not see, what we are in fact anxious about. Strangers to ourselves, we are unreliable autobiographers – and hence render almost impossible the task of our biographers. They are left with the choice of either believing and reporting what their subjects suggest, thereby falling prey to the subjects' fantasies, or doubting and interpreting, thereby risking the addition of their own fantasies to an already muddied picture.

'I had such a strange dream last night,' reported Isabel one bleary-eyed morning.

'What happened?' I asked, stirring sugar in my coffee and hoping the answer would be brief or might include me, for there is flattery in being assigned a role in the night-time fantasies of others.

'Do you really want to know?' asked Isabel.

'Of course.'

'Well, it was weird. I was in a forest with a guy from school who I haven't seen in ten years, he was called Adam Fontana, and was quite odd. Dad was there and he told me Adam and he had become best friends and he'd be part of the family from now on. Then we were on an inflatable boat, actually it was a kind of sausage-shaped hovercraft. It was being dragged across the Channel by an enormous propeller, and we were lying down and trying not to get blown off because there were sharks in the sea. I was gripping on to the material for dear life but Adam Fontana started playing the violin on one side of the boat and wasn't getting blown off. Eventually we arrived on a desert island, and there was Tim Jenkins, my boss, who it turned out owned the whole thing and had a coal mine employing hundreds of natives. A funeral was going on for one worker who had eaten too many mangoes, and Tim said it proved how well he treated people. Are you following me?'

'Yeah.'

'So then I realized the worker had been you.'

'Me?'

'That's right, but that wasn't important, because Tim then took us down a long underground tunnel and it turned out there wasn't a coal mine there, but a museum full of Old Master paintings. The thing is, they weren't real paintings so much as cut-outs from newspapers. Everyone started looking at them reverentially and I couldn't understand why no one was complaining, because I knew the real paintings had been sold to my mother to pay for the island, and then I woke up with a splitting headache. What do you think?'

I knew this dream was central to an understanding of

Isabel's character, but it made little sense beyond leaving me aggrieved that I had died in such an incidental role. It might have explained the analysis.

'Well, clearly it's about us, and your feelings of jealousy about some of the women I meet at the office.'

'What?' exclaimed Isabel incredulously.

'If you ask me what I think your dream means, you could at least be polite about the answer.'

'I would be, if it wasn't so unlikely.'

'It's far more likely than anything you'd come up with.'

'How do you know? You haven't even asked me.'

'No, that's because I've spent the whole of breakfast listening to you.'

'God, I've never heard anyone row like you about a dream.'

Despite the obstacles, attempts to apply the insights of psychology to everyday life should not have been avoided, in the cowardly manner of biographers who continued to write as though dreams did not rock our relationships and self-understanding. The indiscretion of applying scientific theories non-scientifically might have been overridden by the challenge of discovering what someone with their own breakfast weariness could discern of another. As ever, the question was not: 'What can we conceivably know of someone?' but rather, 'What do we in fact grasp before the phone rings?'

The great biographers had always made use of psychological ideas. They had once looked to humoral theories formulated by Hippocrates, who had identified four elements whose relative strengths would influence character. Blood meant one would be sanguine, black bile melancholic, yellow bile choleric and phlegm phlegmatic.

When the seventeenth-century biographer John Aubrey wrote the life of Hobbes, he reported that the man was 'sanguineo-melancholius; which physiologers say is the most ingenious complexion'. As for the wisdom of astrology, Aubrey decided of the unfortunate William Marshall that the 'conjunction of Mercury and Leo had made him stutter'.

There seemed no reason to avoid such precedents, especially when Divina, who had once accused me of self-absorption, asked if I might continue to hold on to two crates of books she had been storing in my house. They were a treasure trove of orthodox and a little less orthodox psychological theories.

A volume which seized my eye was bound in purple and entitled *What You Can Tell About Someone From Their Handwriting*.

I could tell that Isabel was visiting Dorset with friends, that the bed and breakfast had geraniums growing in window pots, that the weather was warm, that they had rented bicycles and that she wanted to go on a diet when she returned. The postcard ended with 'love' and a hope we would see one another soon. It was no substantial communication, particularly when Isabel later flippantly admitted that she had 'written the same postcard to everyone'. But whatever the banality of the message, according to the author of *What You Can Tell About Someone From Their Handwriting*, the card could hold nothing less than the clue to human personality.

The science of graphology argued that a person's traits were manifest in the way they crossed *t*s and hooked or, more significantly, did not hook, *r*s. Forward-sloping script would suggest an interest in other people, upright handwriting was practised by hermits, writing that sloped upwards signalled optimism, writing that sloped downwards indicated depression or physical weariness. Tight letter formation was a sign of pragmatism and logical thinking, decorated letters hinted at showiness and theatricality.

After a Sunday morning with the book and Isabel's Dorset postcard, the science was yielding the first of its truths. It taught me to note that Isabel looped *l*s, leaving a hole between the upward and the downward stroke, revealing the setting on which her emotional thermostat had been adjusted. To those who might frown, *What You Can Tell About Someone From Their Handwriting* was uncannily right – Isabel *was* a very warm person.

I had last noticed this over two salads we had ordered which, in Anglo-Saxon style, had been presented with a dearth of dressing. But Isabel's had been doused with more than mine, which, in response to her dining companion's mournful face, led her to suggest: 'Why don't we swap? I don't mind if I take one with less dressing. I've done nothing but eat all day anyway.'

'No, no, I'm OK,' I replied grimly, as though refusing a place on the *Titanic*'s last lifeboat.

'Go on, I don't mind, really. Take it.'

'No, no.'

'Don't be silly. You should have it, it's good for you, you don't eat enough fresh vegetables.'

This last sentence, with its concern for my dietary requirements and its impulse towards vegetable self-sacrifice, signalled the strength of Isabel's ministering quality which some would have labelled her maternal instinct, and which one could detect in the way she said goodbye to friends or her tone when asking her father if he needed another cushion to be more comfortable in front of the television.

'Rubbish, I'm just asking you if you want my salad, I'm not mistaking you for my baby. God, men will jump to regressive conclusions if given half a chance!' she replied at the suggestion. And yet, with all the presumption entailed, I stuck to the original analysis.

If one needed more evidence, one only needed to look at the following letter of the alphabet, because her *m*s were not the well-formed alpine *m*s of cold spirits, whereby the curves would rise sharply then fall back into a narrow valley then climb steeply again, but rather they were the wavelike undulations of warm-hearted souls. They were the *m*s of someone who gave Christmas presents to her postman, who had once accused relatives of frigidity for sending their son to boarding school and who was unusually affected by films, emerging tearful and unable to speak when she had been moved [those which made her cry most contained scenes of reconciliation between erstwhile enemies].

Yet there was in her *r*s a clue as to why this warmth was not openly admitted. Indeed, one could have suggested a conflict between *r* and *m*, the uprightness and structure of the former standing for an externally imposed history of restraint over the wavy latter. Her mother's buried resentment at having had Isabel at the particular time and with the particular man God had inflicted had led to a firmness and lack of indulgence during her childhood. The mother had the particular form of harshness common amongst those who have been spoilt and led to expect much only to see their life take a turn for the worse, and who hence resent the bruised feelings of others [even a five-year-old child] in relation to how sorry they feel for their neglected selves.

To skip further through the alphabet, Isabel's gs were a sign of humour [they curved backwards], which came as news to her, for she always chided herself for taking life too seriously. For a start, she claimed not to remember more than three jokes.

'Only three?' I queried one night when she was standing on her head, which she claimed was excellent for the brain.

'And even that's good going. I forget them as soon as I've heard them. I once thought I should make a note and learn them by heart, but it seems to defeat the point.'

'Why don't you remember more?'

'I don't know, and it's arbitrary why I remember the ones I do. I think they stuck in my mind because I heard them in a memorable situation, or else they were appreciated when I told them. Pure narcissism, you see.'

'So what are they?'

'Oh, don't make me tell them.'

'Go on.'

'They're hard to remember.'

'Give it a try.'

'OK. Why do the Irish sleep with two glasses by the bed, one full of water and one empty?'

'I don't know.'

'One for if they're thirsty, and one for if they're not. See, I'm pathetic at this. Then there's another. There was an astronomer who was coming to the end of a lecture about the stars, and explained that the sun was going to die out in four to five billion years. "*How* many years did you say?" a woman stood up to ask him from the back of the room. "Four or five billion," replied the scientist. "Phew," said the woman, "I thought you said *million*." '

'That's funny.'

'You sound convinced. Then there's a dirty one, I've just got to try to remember it. OK. Don't be shocked, it's really rude. There's this man who walks down the road and sees a sign saying fifty pounds for a pint of sperm. He thinks, "Oh, that's a good deal," and goes in and gives a pint of sperm. Then he walks further down the road, and sees another sign, saying a hundred pounds for a pint of sperm, so he decides to go in there too, and comes out with a hundred quid. Then he walks further on and he sees a sign saying ten thousand pounds for a pint of sperm. So then, he thinks, oh God, I forget how it goes. I can never remember how to tell jokes. It'll come back to me. Let's just talk about something else for a while.'

The problem with discussing a sense of humour is the ease with which everyone claims to have one, requiring a distinction between those who only laugh at what has been placed in the parameters of a joke and those with a facility to unearth the comic side of an apparently stern situation. The distinction came to mind when Isabel recounted an incident with a set of Canadian immigration officials. Having flown to the country for a holiday a few years before, she had been stopped at passport control and interrogated under suspicion of trying to gain illegal entry as a worker rather than a tourist. She was kept in a bare room for an hour, and asked a range of inane questions. In despair at this treatment, Isabel finally said half-jokingly, 'I know you're only doing your job, but why haven't you stopped to ask yourselves one obvious thing, which is why would anyone *want* to live in a place like

Canada?' Needless to say, the humour was missed and earned her another hour in the bare room.

'Oh, actually I do remember the rest of the joke, it slipped my mind for a second. OK, so this man has given two pints of sperm and he sees a sign advertising ten thousand pounds for a pint of sperm. By this stage he's very tired, but he decides to go in anyway, although there's an enormous queue stretching around the block. Nevertheless he waits patiently, and while he's waiting, he sees a woman ahead of him. He's very surprised to see a woman in such a queue, so thinking she's been caught up in the wrong place, he pats her on the shoulder and says, "Excuse me, but aren't you in the wrong queue?" And she replies [Isabel imitating a woman shaking her head, her cheeks puffed], "Nnnehh." '

'I told you it was disgusting. What's even worse, I must have learnt that joke when I was about fourteen or so.'

If its claims were not momentous enough, *What You Can Tell About Someone From Their Handwriting* devoted a chapter to the way people signed their name. A signature betrayed self-concept: a bold, expansive one would signal confidence and gregariousness, small signatures to the left of a page indicated reclusiveness and introversion.

By this reading, Isabel suffered from a problem of identity, for not only did her signature keep changing, but its change meant she was often interrogated in restaurants and garages when the signature on her cheque showed few signs of resembling that on her card. At a service station on the Queenstown Road, she fell into an argument with an Indian attendant from whom she was trying to buy several litres of unleaded petrol.

'Do you really think I'm a forger?' she exclaimed.

'Why not? They come in all shapes and sizes,' replied Mr Aulak, for that was the name on the plastic badge.

'But then why would I forge it so badly?'

'Maybe you're a bad forger.'

'Look, if I was a forger I would never do such a stupid fake. I agree that the one here looks nothing like the one on the card, but I just have a signature that changes.'

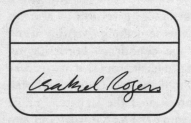

Signature on card	Signature on checque

'Have another go here,' ordered Mr Aulak more charitably.

'Would you mind not looking at me while I imitate it? I get self-conscious.'

'Imitate, madam? Do you want me to call the police? Why don't you pay me cash and stop wasting my time.'

Isabel's problems with her signature had begun in early adolescence, when she had decided that the childish letters she had until then used to signal her written presence were no longer appropriate for someone who had inhaled marijuana and taken the Underground without paying. Her mother's signature had struck her as the essence of what it meant to be grown up, it had been a visible sign of her mother's control over the adult environment. It was impatient and full of brusque forms, the Rogers identifiable only by the first and last letter – something which *What You Can Tell About Someone From Their Handwriting* suggested to be a sign of marital dissatisfaction expressed in the deformation of the male surname. When Lavinia went into a department store to buy a new cooker and brandished her chequebook the signature operated like a final flourish of a magic wand which would miraculously set in motion the energies of half a dozen workmen. For a girl who wrote out her name with the painstaking precision of a scribe preparing a wax seal, there was something daunting about a mother who signed with a confidence bordering on insouciance, while managing to elicit from this act a flurry of goodies from gas cookers to nights in a Cotswolds hotel.

Isabel had therefore appropriated the signature's tone when placing the earnings from her first Saturday job into a bank account, but did so without assuring the power to reproduce the proof of this adult identity at will. Awkward incidents resulted from the ensuing confusion; having to borrow money from a neighbour to pay her share of a mid-teenage dinner and having to spend a week in Portugal at the mercy of friends because her traveller's cheques were refused by banks unable to see a connection between the two signatures needed for the vital escudos. By the time she was mature enough not to require a mature signature, her cards were inscribed, and she could not gather the energy to tell her bank to reissue virgin copies on which to reinvent herself.

The problem was aggravated by Isabel's tendency toward self-consciousness, for when she imagined someone imagining her to be a criminal she began acting according to the presumption. Rather than maintaining faith that she had no interest in robbing a tankful of petrol, the suspicious glance of the garage attendant would throw her signature off course. She recalled incidents at school where the teachers lined up the class to extract a confession for some misdeed, and while everyone would stare blankly and guiltlessly at the wall opposite Isabel would blush as though she had been the central plotter in a scheme to steal a Bunsen burner or paint a moustache on the portrait of the headmistress. It had happened so frequently, Isabel eventually became as much of an offender as her teachers suggested, for the least she could do if regularly punished was to enjoy the deed she would in any case be paying for.

What You Can Tell About Someone From Their Handwriting had yielded a host of insights, but it seemed helpless to explain one aspect of Isabel's writing which would soon have struck a lexically minded observer, namely, the spirit of invention with which the spelling of certain words was approached. The two-wheeled steel contraption operated by a chain and a set of pedals which Isabel and her friends had rented in Dorset had been ingeniously transformed into a *bycicle*, while the way she had chosen not to share accommodation meant she had been assigned a *seperate* room. And whenever she had a thought to ponder, Isabel would wander around the subject instead of settling for a more sedentary wondering option. There had always been a set of words with which she had had a problematic relationship; *definetely, dilemna, succesful* [or sometimes *successfull* or indeed *sucessfull*], *concurrently, bizzare* and *dissapointed* all remained tinged with the particular vision of their author. Isabel was ready with an appropriately psychological explanation.

'I think I have a part of my brain missing. It's why I can't do maths and play cards and stuff.'

'What part of the brain is that?'

'You know, the mechanical computer side that women sometimes don't have because they're so good at sewing and cooking. I don't know. Maybe it's to do with my father, he's a big spelling pedant, always theorizing about why the Americans spell theatre one way and the English another and the relationship with the French, etc. Perhaps spelling badly is a rebellion against him. I remember writing to him when I went on holiday as a child, and he thanked me for the card, but in the politest way possible, pointed out that I'd signed off with lots of "kises". For some reason the mistake made me very ashamed – you'd probably say it was because I wanted to secretly kiss him.'

'Did you?'

'What girl wouldn't?'

Isabel's approach to numbers was equally fraught. 7 × 4 and 6 × 8 left her stranded and long division and multiplication were best abandoned to a calculator. She confessed to an additional problem with historical dates, for if asked what century 1836 was in, her impulse was to say the eighteenth.

Despite the richness of *What You Can Tell About Someone From Their Handwriting*, the ease with which it reached its conclusions could have alarmed anyone trusting in the greater complexity of the human mind. Was it not important to consult Isabel rather than read the world into her squiggles?

Once one is attuned to their presence, psychological tests and questionnaires manifest themselves everywhere, inviting us to share our motives when choosing a kettle, cruise ship or husband. Their frankness can be welcome. If a single woman has endured a number of dinners with men falsely described as eligible, she may be grateful for a glance at a Dateline questionnaire. Without shuffling towards melancholy acquaintance while a candidate picks at his shrimp and she stares at what Caesar would not have called his salad, a questionnaire would reveal everything about what, for instance, was in the man's record collection:

1. classical
2. opera
3. pop
4. jazz
5. folk
6. country and western
7. rock

or what he liked to do at home:

1. listening to music
2. reading
3. watching television
4. watching televised sport
5. listening to the radio
6. being with the children
7. cooking/entertaining
8. DIY/crafts
9. gardening

[one wonders at the subtle psychological difference illuminated by the distinction between 'watching television' and its more sinister counterpart, 'televised sport'].

Think of the heartache Anna and Vronsky could have skirted by completing a section entitled 'Your Relationships':

1. Are you looking for one special relationship?
2. Is romantic love necessary for a successful marriage?
3. Should divorce be made more difficult?
4. Have you just finished a serious relationship and wish to meet someone new?
5. Should sex be reserved for special relationships?
6. Are you primarily looking for emotional support in your relationships?
7. Is it advisable to live together before marriage?

For those ready to admit to the worth of questionnaires, but snobbishly worried at their lack of pedigree, it should be pointed out that Marcel Proust had once filled one in.

At the age of twenty-one, he had replied as follows to a sheet of questions doing the rounds of fashionable Parisian salons [Isabel's responses following those of the master].

My main character trait:
PROUST: *The need to be loved; more precisely, a need to be petted and spoilt more than a need to be admired.*
ISABEL: Shit, I don't know. I suppose an inability to make a decision and to stick to it, or perhaps being too nice to people when I don't want to be.

The qualities I want to see in a man:

PROUST: Feminine charm.

ISABEL: The usual, you know, bright, funny, sexy, but in someone who doesn't know they have them. I'm fed up with peacocks.

My favourite quality in a woman:
PROUST: *The virtues of a man, and openness in friendship.*
ISABEL: Self-confidence. I should really drop into the chemist today.

What I most appreciate in my friends:
PROUST: *Their feelings of tenderness towards me, if they are beautiful enough to set a high value on that tenderness.*
ISABEL: I like having a shared history with them, being able to look back on good and bad times. And I love talking to them on the phone. Did Proust have a phone?

My greatest fault:
PROUST: *Not knowing, not being able to 'want'.*
ISABEL: Same here. There's hope.

My favourite occupation:
PROUST: Loving.
ISABEL: Lying in the bath comes way before loving – it's predictably good.

My dream of happiness:
PROUST: *I'm afraid it wouldn't be sufficiently elevated: I daren't express it, and I'm afraid of destroying it by expressing it.*
ISABEL: God, no, I'd want to have a house in a sunny climate, maybe the south-west of France, where I could have

all my friends living, and interesting people coming to visit. The house would be huge, so you could both be with people and yet retreat to your separate apartment when you wanted to be alone. There'd be no financial worries, and I'd look after the garden. I'd have a most amazing garden built, I won't go into it, present company considered, but to give you an idea, it would be a couple of acres at least, with lots of Mediterranean plants, and things would be growing all year around. Then everyone I was with would be honest as well as kind, no one would play games, or be sulky and insensitive. Are you still awake?

What my greatest unhappiness would be:
PROUST: *Not to have known my mother or my grandmother.*
ISABEL: If I had a child that died.

What I would like to be:
PROUST: *Myself, as the people I admire would like me to be.*
ISABEL: Myself in my good moods.

The country I would like to live in:
PROUST: *A place where certain things I want would come about, and where feelings of tenderness would always be shared.*
ISABEL: This one, but only after it had been miraculously dragged by a million ships to a spot where the weather was better.

My favourite colour:
PROUST: *Beauty doesn't reside in colours, but in the harmony between them.*

ISABEL: Rubbish. Green.

The flower I like best:
PROUST: *The flower of one's self – beside that, all of them.*
ISABEL: This is difficult. Maybe sidalceas or delphiniums.
Or perhaps campanulas or digitalises.

My favourite bird:
PROUST: *The swallow.*
ISABEL: I'm not really into birds. The parrot perhaps, but
I don't care so much. After all, why not a pigeon?

My favourite prose writers:
PROUST: *Today they are Anatole France and Pierre Loti.*
ISABEL: I hate this sort of question. The last two writers I
really enjoyed were George Eliot and A. S. Byatt, but there
are loads more.

My favourite poets:
PROUST: *Baudelaire and Alfred de Vigny.*
ISABEL: E. E. Cummings and Emily Dickinson.

My favourite fictional heroes:
PROUST: *Hamlet.*
ISABEL: Heathcliff.

My favourite fictional heroines:
PROUST: *Bérénice [he had crossed out Phèdre].*
ISABEL: Lady Macbeth, but I might quite fancy Bérénice if
I knew who she was.

My favourite names:
PROUST: *I only have one at a time.*

ISABEL: Rachel, Alice, Saul, can't think of any more.

How I would like to die:
PROUST: *Better – and well loved.*
ISABEL: In my sleep suddenly, with no one around me minding too much about it.

My present state of mind:
PROUST: *Bored of thinking about myself in order to answer all these questions.*
ISABEL: I'd die for a cheese sandwich.

Within the eclectic range of the Proust questionnaire, one could detect both curiosity and confusion as to what was required in order to know someone. Why were favourite birds important? And why heroines, or names? Perhaps there should have been space to reveal a choice of writing implement or cold remedy? The possible questions were infinite; if the ones included hinted at the character of their recipients, they did so more by chance than design. They were like a guest who fires a battery of enquiries at a dinner party companion, and is surprised by how meaningfully Camilla responds to a remark on the seating arrangement, when there had been only fruitless answers to questions of God, literature or ambition.

Isabel loved responding to the enquiries of market researchers. She was unable to pass a questionnaire without reaching for a pen, a habit acquired as the result of her work in retailing. Shortly after her trip to Athens, I found her concentrated over a form investigating the service aboard Olympic flights:

Please tick to indicate how you rate each of the following criteria when you fly	Very Important	Important	Unimportant
1. I have a choice of classes	x		
2. I have an opportunity on board to place international inflight telephone calls			x
3. I can await my flight in a designated lounge			x
4. I can participate in a frequent flyer programme and collect miles on every flight	x		
5. I can travel aboard a nonsmoker aircraft			x
6. My seat offers ample leg room	x		
7. My seat offers ample elbow room	x		
8. I have a choice of inflight meals	x		
9. I am served a hot meal on board		x	
10. I can choose from a broad selection of magazines		x	
11. The flight attendants respond to my individual wishes			x
12. The flight attendants speak my language	x		
13. There are separate check-in counters at the airport for Business Class travellers			x
14. I can hire a mobile telephone or mobile telefax at the airport upon arrival			x
15. I can book a hotel or rental car together with my flight			x
16. There is a separate passport and customs control for Business Class travellers			x
17. I can book a limousine service to take me to the airport or to pick me up			x
18. There is chauffeur-driven parking service at the airport			x

Despite the economically valuable role of such questionnaires, whatever Isabel's responses it would have been impossible to detect anything specifically Isabelish within them. Had Henry VIII been granted a spare moment with an Olympic sheet, it would not have been on the basis of his taste in in-flight meals, magazine selections or frequent-flyer programmes that we would have learnt much about what made him particularly Henry VIII rather than Edward VII, Charles II or Doris Day.

What questions therefore detected a person's significant psychological traits if they had so little to do with cabin attendants and hot towels in business class? It was the dilemma at the heart of dinner party talk and political interviews, police profiles and Dateline questionnaires. Some enquiries were more effective than others. 'What would you do if the world was about to come to an end?' seemed to outclass 'Do you have a push-button phone?'; 'Do you seek to avoid or create collisions when in bumper cars?' had an edge over 'What's in your handbag?' The Proust questionnaire had stumbled upon fertile soil, but lacked a coherent vision of human personality which could explain how someone who loved Bérénice in fact differed from a fan of Lady Macbeth. The vision had to wait for the work of modern psychologists, for only they could provide the rigour to interpret personality out of what would merely have been judged quirks.

'Are you a talkative person who enjoys opportunities for verbal expression?' I might have asked Camilla at a dinner party.

'Oh, yes,' she might have replied, 'I'm dying to propose a toast to the guest of honour,' but unless I had read the work of the psychologist R. B. Cattell, I could not have made sense of this wish.

The enquiry had been part of a questionnaire prepared by Dr Cattell, which had as its aim the discovery of one's relation to some sixteen factors which separated human beings from each other. Factor A considered whether someone was introverted or extroverted, Factor B whether they were stupid or intelligent, Factor C whether they were neurotic and Factor D insecure. Other letters measured tender-mindedness, suspicion, jealousy and liberality – words as likely to crop up loosely in analyses of friends, colleagues and the cross-eyed commuter nibbling the stem of his umbrella at the end of the station platform.

The question to Camilla had come from a section investigating Factor H, indicating gregariousness, and Cattell would probably have decided that Camilla's love of toast-making betrayed an H+. So what was Isabel? I had fallen upon the range of Cattell's questions, and decided to put them to her after a tasty salmon dinner one Sunday evening.

'Wait, let's do the washing up first,' she protested.

'It'll only take a minute.'

'All right, hurry, or it'll get congealed.'

'OK. "When coming to a new place, are you painfully slow at making new friendships?" '

'A bit slow, not painfully slow. Can I pile these plates?'

'Yeah, thanks. "Are you relatively free from self-conscious shyness?" '

'You know I'm not.'

"Are you a talkative person who enjoys opportunities for verbal expression?"

'Remember how I was when I met those Dutch friends of yours?'

'You can only answer yes or no.'

'That's silly.'

'Perhaps. "Do you find it difficult to get up and address or recite before a large group?" '

'Sort of. I mean yes.'

' "In conversation do you find it difficult to jump from topic to topic as some people do?" '

'I don't understand.'

'Nor do I. "Do you occasionally have the uncomfortable feeling that people in the street are watching you?" '

'Definitely. In fact, I didn't tell you, I got accosted on the Underground home on Friday. This man told me I reminded him of his sister who had committed suicide. He was rather spooky, so I got out at the next stop and waited for the train behind.'

Without Dr Cattell's experience, I couldn't gain a scientific measure of Isabel's H trait, but it seemed she was averagely H– and above average at attracting men on public transport, for only a week before, a passenger had asked if he might sculpt her in ice, a craft he claimed to practise in a studio in Fulham. Isabel had politely declined, citing work commitments and the onset of a cold.

When I read Isabel a list of other traits investigated by Dr Cattell, she was intrigued by a Factor M, though she had by now begun soaking the dish in which the salmon had roasted. The factor indicated whether someone was bohemian or conventionally practical.

1. Which would you rather do on a fine afternoon?
   (a) Enjoy the beauty of an art gallery or some fine scenery.

(b) Enjoy a social meeting or a game of cards.   *(b)*

2. Do you generally succeed in keeping your emotions, of whatever kind, under very good control?   *No*

3. Do you tend to dislike being waited on in personal matters, i.e., by personal servants?

What's an impersonal servant?

4. Do you think that racial characteristics have more real influence in shaping the individual and the nation than most people believe?   *No*

5. Do you ever have a fit of dread or anxiety for no ascertainable reason?   *Yes*

6. Do you ever try to bluff your way past a guard or doorman?

'God, this is meaningless,' interrupted Isabel, 'they'd never catch the difference between Jim Morrison and an accountant.'

The issue of whether someone was bohemian may have interested her, but Isabel had little faith that Dr Cattell's questionnaire could be of use in finding out.

'What would you ask, then?' I queried.

'I don't know, I'm not a psychologist,' she replied, and handed me a towel to start drying the cutlery.

Dr Cattell had isolated a set of important psychological traits, but he seemed hampered by an inability to investigate them with requisite subtlety. Wanting to know whether someone was gregarious or not, he would ask them whether they liked public speaking, without taking into account the nuances by which the shy may at times be confident, and the confident shy. He resembled a bad novelist who, wishing to show us a character's grief at his mother's death, would describe a pale young man weeping copious tears at a wind-swept funeral, rather than a character feeling no emotion at the graveside nor for several weeks afterwards, coming out of a cinema one evening and seeing in the street a woman whose umbrella resembled that of his mother's, and only then collapsing into tears in the middle of a crowded thoroughfare, struck by a sorrow which had proved too great to be tangible, guilty at the days in which he had been numb to his loss.

Isabel's distinction between straight and bohemian went beyond R. B. Cattell's understanding of the term.

'I think I'm pretty conventional, but I was once weird enough to call a phone chatline, and had a conversation with a guy in Hull about this and that at one in the morning,' she revealed.

'What did you find out?'

'Oh, he was very nice, but a bit sad. He was thirty-three and still a virgin. He was thinking of becoming a Christian, not because he believed in God but because it made his virginity more respectable. I said not to worry, that some women stayed virgins quite late too.'

Isabel's disregard for convention was perhaps nowhere more evident than in her reluctance to follow the rules governing Dr Cattell's test. She had glided over a pertinent issue in Factor M, the attitude towards what the questionnaire called 'being waited on in personal matters, i.e., by personal servants'.

Dr Johnson had realized the value of this trait long

before Dr Cattell, remarking that 'More knowledge may be gained of a man's real character by a short conversation with one of his servants, than from a formal narrative, begun with his pedigree and ended with his funeral.' Later biographers have taken note, apparent in Richard Ellmann's gratitude to 'Professor Thomas Staley, for interviewing Mrs Maria Eccel, once the Joyces' maid in Trieste'.

Because Isabel could not afford a proper vacuum cleaner let alone a cleaning lady, the question seemed somewhat outmoded. Nevertheless, she did confess to cleaning up before the maid came whenever she stayed in a hotel, an attitude perhaps engendered by her close relationship with the one person who had waited on her in personal matters in her youth.

Flo Youngman had been helping to clean the Rogers' household for two decades; she was now eighty-three, had five grandchildren, a flat in Hounslow and had recently lost her husband. A pretence had been maintained that she still came to help with the Rogers' housework, but her weekly calls were nothing more than social visits. When Isabel's parents went on holiday, they asked if Isabel could drop by to check the house, and it was then we bumped into Flo lighting a cigarette in the kitchen. Isabel had clothes to sort through in the attic, so while she rummaged upstairs, I stayed in the kitchen with Flo and thoughts of Johnson, imagining a fountain of stories with which to enrich my portrait.

'A lovely girl, as I say, a lovely girl. Known her since she was this size, pretty as a doll. Now my granddaughter, you should have seen her when she was born, she had hair as blond as the sun, and now she's a brunette. Before the war, Bill and I used to live in Leytonstone, a little house, we called it paradise. There was a neighbour who painted birds as a hobby. You know, as a hobby. He'd sit in the garden when the weather was nice and spend all day doing it. His wife worked at the newsagent, a lovely woman with a son who joined the navy. People don't do that these days. My grandson, the older one, Jimmy, he wants to be a mechanic, he loves cars. He gets all dirty from them, but he's no trouble really. Apart from for the girls, that is. He gives them a run for their money, loves 'em and leaves 'em, that's what I always say.'

'Oh, don't be nasty,' protested Isabel as we made our way home, 'she may be a windbag but she's the sweetest woman you could meet. She's a truly nice person, even if she sent you out to buy her cigarettes. And it probably did you good to take out the rubbish bags as well. Flo would stick by you in any crisis, say you lost your money or your job or family. She's a sweetheart because one couldn't imagine her thinking anything bad of anyone. She gives people every benefit of the doubt, she'll say that the guy who snatched her handbag in the supermarket must have needed the money more than she did or that the Yorkshire Ripper probably had a bad day.'

The fact that Isabel was devoting such attention to Flo's niceness rather than her gregariousness or intelligence, her bohemianism or liberality revealed the general truth that what we first need to know of a stranger, in daily life as much as in cowboy films, is their status as a goody or baddy. Our simplistic need for moral orientation assumes precedence over other traits, a relic of the primitive hunter's need to separate friend from foe. It was a pity that Dr Cattell had omitted to formulate a niceness test.

Was Isabel nice? The question sounded banal. She didn't think so.

'It's just a front, you've got to dig down to get to the nasty bits,' she declared as though by way of challenge.

She suggested a need to distinguish between a nice person and someone who behaved nicely, and wondered how her agreeable friends would fare on the raft of the *Medusa*.

'The what?'

'You know, the David painting, where those sailors were on a raft out at sea and some began eating the others for food.'

'So?'

'Well, if you imagine yourself on the raft with someone, it's a way of trying to tell what they would do when push came to shove. Who would be the diner and who the dinner? Take my friend Chris, I know he'd make sure he was the diner.'

'How can you tell?'

'Oh, just something about the way he reaches for the vegetables when we're in a restaurant. He'd fight tooth and nail for the last parachute on a crashing plane.'

'You pick your friends well. And your metaphors.'

'Listen, if I had to choose my friends because of who they are deep down, I'd probably be eating a lot of dinners alone,' she snapped, casting sinister aspersions on the pleasant meal we had just shared.

'But I'm easy to flatter, so if someone's nice to me, whatever they're really like, I'm probably going to like them back,' she added with ambiguous reassurance. 'Come to think of it, the raft picture is actually by Géricault, but that doesn't change the point, just the painter.'

Depending on one's attachment to the virtues of the human race, one might have called Isabel's views cynical, but then, they were so cheerfully and artistically outlined, one almost didn't notice. She wore her cynicism lightly: if someone paid her a compliment on a pretty dress she had on, she would reply with a smile, 'All right, let's have it out, what do you want from me this time?'

Nor did Isabel limit her harsh verdict to others. She judged herself to have been 'a dreadful bitch' from the age of ten to fifteen and 'an intermittent bitch' from fifteen to eighteen. She had teased twelve-year-old Louise Stobbs to tears about her braces, she had spread the rumour that Jane McDonald liked being slapped by her boyfriend and nicknamed her 'Pain Jane', she had led a boy into the bathroom at Laura's house as if for a kiss then escaped and locked him inside, she hadn't let a day go by without reminding Julie Gibson of the dimensions of her nose, she had misinformed one of Lucy's suitors that he was wasting his time chasing her, she had been nice to her grandmother only when money might result from the action and she had told her eight-year-old brother that his penis was the smallest, when in fact it had been the only one she'd ever seen.

'But in what way are you still nasty?' I persevered.

'Well, I lie quite often.'

'About what?'

'Elizabeth rang me the other day as I was leaving to go to her house for dinner, and asked if I could bring over some chairs. I couldn't be bothered, so I said my kitchen chairs didn't fold up and couldn't go in the car. Or take this grapefruit on the table. Just before you came, I had a swig of it directly from the bottle. I'd hate it if anyone presented me with a bottle like that, but I was too selfish to get a glass, and too dishonest to warn you.'

'That's not criminal,' I replied [though I did stop drinking].

'No, but that's how it starts. I'm just a coward about robbing banks, but I wouldn't mind, particularly my branch. I hate my manager, I'd like to tie him up and force-feed him bank statements.'

Isabel also confessed to jealousy. It was ignited not by the larger discrepancies between her current state and its ideal, but by attainable and hence frequently trivial details. When Sarah was given her own office with a door that closed, Isabel sulked because she was still working in an open-plan space where there was no privacy and constant interruptions. Jealousy was a form of annoyance with herself for not having attained what she felt she deserved, and in its productive dimension, was a guide to unconscious ambition.

In so far as psychologists had touched on the question of niceness, they had concentrated their research on how aggressive a person was. I discovered a lyrically-titled 'Ascendance-Submission' study, which aimed to determine the forcefulness with which someone might point out to an imposing neighbour that they were unfortunately standing on their foot, or how readily they might overlook the matter for fear of making trouble.

Some of the questions ran as follows:

1. Someone tries to push ahead of you in line. You have
   been waiting for some time, and can't wait much
   longer. Suppose the intruder is the same sex as
   yourself, do you usually:
   a) remonstrate with the intruder

b) 'look daggers' at the intruder or make clearly
audible comments to your neighbour
c) decide not to wait and go away
d) do nothing

2. Do you feel self-conscious in the presence of superiors
in the academic or business world?
a) markedly
b) somewhat
c) not at all

3. Some possession of yours is being worked upon at a
repair shop. You call for it at the time appointed, but
the repair man informs you that he has 'only just
begun to work on it.' Is your customary reaction
a) to upbraid him
b) to express dissatisfaction mildly
c) to smother your feelings entirely

Isabel laughed and admitted to being a poisonous
example of someone whose aggression was neither effectively expressed nor repressed, but seeped out in the pass-
ive hostility typical of the second answer. She was an
enthusiast of 'looking daggers' at enemies, and swore by
this method in London traffic. If a taxi driver wished to
cut across her path, she adopted a world-weary expression
designed to take the fun out of the scheme. She trusted
this look as a method of distracting muggers when walking
home, the idea being to demonstrate a blasé annoyance
which could rival and hence neutralize that of the most
brutalized misfit.

Her alternative response was excessive politeness, in

which an observer keen on cultural stereotypes could have detected a national trait. Chris had related an anecdote from their visit to Portugal, when they had been forced to eat in the only restaurant open late in a small town, an upmarket tourist-trap. Early on in a meal which demanded to be forgotten, a waiter came forward with an earthenware jug to pour Isabel a glass of water, a jug from whose spout there flowed not simply the desired liquid, but also a large and only partially incapacitated cockroach. Some might have refused to pay the bill, cried or threatened to have the restaurant closed, but Isabel merely remarked, 'It seems we've brought someone in from the kitchen.'

This testified to a quaint and somewhat obsolete belief in shaming others into apology, as opposed to more contemporary ideas based on the ability to sue or sack the offending party.

Needless to say, the Portuguese waiter, despite his country's historic links with Isabel's, proved unable to detect the nuance of his customer's complaint, and replied with admirable frankness and concern for animal rights:

'He's not from the kitchen. He must be from the pantry. He'll be OK.'

Isabel's problem with complaint reached its climax the summer day when I saw her trying to read a newspaper despite a fly's best efforts to circle noisily around her head. After several attempts to shoo the insistent creature, she slammed down the paper and, addressing the fly as if it might experience guilt for ruining her weekend, asked with metaphysical weariness, 'Why can't you just leave me alone?'

A more artistic way of measuring aggression had been devised by a Dr Rosenzweig, who had designed a test made up of a group of line drawings showing two people in frustrating situations, where one was the frustrator and the other fuming. A speech bubble hovered over both, with the bubble over the latter left blank so that the person taking the test could fill in their reaction to their toe being stepped on or wife slept with. Some people showed tendencies to blame themselves and grow ulcers, others shouted at opponents with throaty rage, a few would appeal to reason and wise bits of the Bible.

Flipping through the choice of pictures, I asked Isabel how she would have reacted to a couple of oafs who had splashed her with their car.

'Why are you asking me if it's a man being splashed?' she replied.

'It's not the point. You're just supposed to imagine how you'd reply.'

'God, well, let's see. I think I'd be perverse and say something like, "Oh, that's all right, don't worry," but in such a bitter way, they'd know full well it wasn't. Something like that happened last week, a woman poured a glass of wine down my dress. She looked like a Rottweiler and I wanted to give her a hard time for it, but I couldn't, because she was something to do with work, one of Tim's clients. So I just said everything was fine, but made a face as if she'd destroyed all my plants.'

But Isabel's annoyance was not always so muted, as she

213

showed when confronted by another Rosenzweig picture.

'Oh, I'd definitely get angry here.'

'Why?'

'Because these sticks look like a couple, and I'm far less inhibited about raising my voice with people I'm close to. I mean, if you can't get angry with them, you're really in trouble.'

'So what would you say?'

'I don't know, maybe, "I haven't lost them, moron, they'll turn up in a minute, so keep your hair on." But look, I don't really see what all this is telling us. It's ridiculous, no doubt you'll soon have taken up palm reading.'

It was not an inappropriate suggestion, because according to the science of palmistry, a life mapped itself out in astonishing detail in the lines imprinted on the palm, each one standing for a particular trait: the life-line predicted how long one would live, the line of fate spoke of the chances of success while the head-line revealed degrees of intelligence.

A drawing from a volume entitled *Palmistry Revealed*

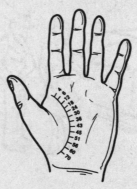

illustrated a way to read the number of years left in store.

'Oh dear, I think you're going to die before you're fifty-six,' I informed Isabel.

'You'd make a terrible palm-reader. You're supposed to flatter your clients, not tell them they're going to kick the bucket before they're eligible for a cheap bus pass. And what about my fate line?'

'Just a second. Ehmm, I think you're going to be very successful, but quite late on.'

'If you look at the line, it seems it'll happen after I'm dead,' spotted Isabel.

'You're right,' I puzzled and turned to the back of the book for help.

'Well, that doesn't matter,' answered Isabel cheerfully, 'some of the most successful people have reached their peak after their life-line ran out.'

Isabel's respect for the art of palm-reading had its bounds, for she was soon inventing subversive theories as to the meaning of a strange squiggle on her life-line.

'Look, here the line suddenly becomes double, it forks for a while, like I'm going to have two lives for a few years, and then there's a bit when I'm dead and then come back to life, around my forties. That would be rather good, spending time in hell, with a lunch or two in heaven for all the years I sent Gran Christmas cards.'

Isabel may have scoffed at superstition in its formal, palm-reading sense, but it did not prevent a superstitious frame of mind, notable when she said of an Underground train which she had just missed, 'It left because I didn't give that beggar some money outside. And now I'm going to be late.'

'How do you mean?' I enquired, confused as to what a Piccadilly Line train could have to do with refusing the solicitations of a beggar at the station entrance.

'Well, if I'd been nice to the beggar, the train would have been nice to me.'

'Why?'

'I don't know, it just makes sense.'

Though she adhered to no faith, Isabel trusted in a religious distribution of good and evil. If something bad happened to her, she held that it was because she was paying for something evil done in the past, while suffering would prepare the way for an upturn in her fortunes. A happy phase when she was awarded a raise at work, went to three enjoyable parties, bought a nice dress and saw a good film would lead to a necessary downfall, a way of explaining the onset of a terrible cold which would leave her bed-ridden for a week. Having atoned for the arrogance of the happy phase with a runny nose, she would then be ready to see fortune smile once more, which it might in the shape of a tax rebate or letter from a friend.

There were attendant superstitions: whenever Isabel had a decision to make, she would look for signs of what Fate [a thing she never admitted to when it was a question of a line on her palm] had in mind. When she had been choosing between two flats which both had advantages, she eventually settled on one for the simple reason that a taxi she had ordered to go and visit the other had failed to arrive on time – which she took to be a sign from Fate to steer clear of the basement in Stockwell.

Of course, the interpretation of the direction of Fate was always in some doubt: should she have seen her repeated difficulties in booking a holiday as a hint to give up on the idea or as a challenge to persevere and be rewarded for it? Was the long cinema queue a warning not to join it, or an entreaty to be patient and be thanked with a moving performance? Were difficulties with a boyfriend to be taken as signs to break off, or the clearest evidence yet of essential, though problematic, compatibility?

Whatever the answers, there was an optimism in Isabel's belief that Fate was a benevolent creature. Though not anthropomorphic enough to be called God, it would look after her if only she accurately read the obscure sign-language it used.

X

IN SEARCH OF AN ENDING

The art of writing a good biography might be defined as knowing when to stop. 'A biography should either be as long as Boswell's or as short as Aubrey's,' declared Lytton Strachey, distinguishing between James Boswell's 1,492-page monster on Johnson, and John Aubrey's diet-conscious page-length sketches of seventeenth-century worthies. 'The method of enormous and elaborate accretion which produced the *Life of Johnson* is excellent, no doubt,' conceded Strachey, 'but, failing that, let us have no half-measures; let us have the pure essentials – a vivid image, on a page or two, without explanations, transitions, commentaries, or padding.'

He had a point. There is something appealing about fitting a whole life into a space no larger than a piece of toast. Here is Aubrey at work on a certain Richard Stokes MD:

> His father was fellow of Eton college. He was bred there and at King's college. Scholar to Mr Oughtred for mathematics (algebra). He made himself mad with it, but became sober again, but I fear like a cracked-glass. Became a Roman-catholic: married unhappily at Liege, dog and cat etc. Became a Scot. Died in Newgate, prisoner for debt, April 1681.

Here is a piece of toast:

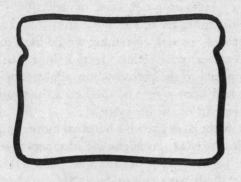

Whatever concessions he made to the *Life of Johnson*, one senses Strachey's preference for Aubrey's concision over more bloated Boswellian efforts. He ridiculed his contemporaries for their production of 'fat volumes... with their ill-digested masses of material, their slipshod style, their tone of tedious panegyric, their lamentable lack of selection, of detachment, of design'.

Unfortunately for him, the ridicule had no discernible effect, and biographical size continued to suffer relentless aggrandizement. Whereas in 1918, the average length of a biography was 453 pages, by the last decade of the century, it had risen to 875, an increase of 93.2% – far exceeding any gains in life expectancy over the period.

What could account for such expansion? Why did Aubrey's brief and brilliant portraits slide for ever out of fashion? Where did the machismo of length originate, the belief that more was necessarily better?

It may in part have emerged from a crisis of uncertainty, uncertainty as to *what* it was important to know when knowing someone, and the conclusion, in the absence of any clear answers, that *everything* was important. Abandoning the arrogant prerogative of selection [for how could a biographer play God in judging what to include and what to leave out?], everything would have to be kept in, not because anyone claimed it had value, but because it had happened to the person whose life was being written. As it had been a part of the life, so it should quite naturally be part of the life story.

Aubrey might have known a hundred more things about Richard Stokes MD, he might for instance have known how often Richard went out for a walk, whether or not his handkerchiefs were embroidered, if he preferred mustard to horseradish, what the name of his horse was and what passages of the Bible he recalled by heart. However, though a part of his existence, Aubrey must have judged these details to be subsidiary to the task at hand, namely, to reduce a life to its fundamental traits, adding as little superfluous material as was compatible with the desire to bring the dead man back to life within the parameters of a piece of toast.

This was far removed from John Keats's view of the matter. In a letter to his brother George, the poet expressed a touching desire to know every aspect of the lives of the great. He informed George that he was writing to him with his back to the fire, 'with one foot rather askew upon the rug and the other with the heel a little elevated from the carpet . . . These are trifles – but could I feel the same thing done of any great man long since dead it would be a great delight: as to know in what position Shakespeare sat when he began "To be or not to be." '

The position in which he sat? Was Keats being serious?

Could this really be of concern to anyone interested in Hamlet's anguish, let alone to a great Romantic poet, author of 'Hither Hither Love', 'What the Thrush Said' and 'Ode to a Nightingale'? But imagine Shakespeare had written the line on a chair at a desk, with both feet on the ground, both hands on the table and no fire in the grate for it was a spring morning, warm enough to leave the window open. Could we claim a genuine enrichment of our understanding of the Bard, or indeed of any of his plays [the puzzling bits of *The Tempest*, the symbolism of *King Lear*, the moral of *The Taming of the Shrew* . . .]? Or lest the example be too undramatic, imagine that Shakespeare had been at the Globe, watching a performance of *Julius Caesar*, when he had been struck by how few people were in the audience, how difficult it was to pay his actors, how competitive the theatrical world was and how ill the actor playing Brutus looked, and this had led to a sigh and the question of whether or not the whole thing was worth it. He might then have thought of putting much the same ideas into the mouth of the hero of the play he was writing, and so run backstage, seized a pen and a few sheets, and sat down to write on a pile of purple curtains, using his right knee to support the paper, crossing his left under it and leaning on one hand for balance.

One might not wish to swap two balcony tickets for *Hamlet* in order to learn this, but Keats does seem to have raised an important point. Not least, in the act of wondering about Shakespeare's seating position, he revealed much about his own, enabling posterity to imagine him with his foot askew on a rug and his heel a little elevated from the carpet – information which might have been lost had Keats simply told his brother George what Fanny Brawne made of Shelley's 'Stanzas Written in Dejection, near Naples'.

Keats's letter leads one to the thorny question of whether the way people sit is interesting *per se*, or if it is interesting only or primarily when they've written *The Merchant of Venice* or 'Sonnet on the Sea'.

Certain things are important whoever does them. If a woman kills her boyfriend while he sits in the bath, this is a noteworthy event, even if the woman is not Charlotte Corday and the boyfriend not a French revolutionary by the name of Marat. Though one death would shock the neighbours and the other changed history, the act itself is significant enough to surmount the question of who it is being done to or by.

However, the same might not be said of writing positions. Who cares how the traffic warden goes about it or whether the accounts manager prefers a leather swivel-chair or a stool? Many who would willingly grant a paragraph on the topic in a biography of Lenin or Montesquieu would shudder to mention it of more humble characters even in the longer conversational pauses.

The attraction of Shakespeare's seating arrangement and other small things besides seems founded on a central, and in some ways complex premiss of large Boswellian biographies: the idea that what in normal life might be considered trivial becomes fascinating when great people get involved – and therefore deserves to be recorded in painstaking [embittered critics might say long-winded] detail. Techniques of sitting on chairs are not usually of much interest, in fact the subject seems downright trivial, but the combination of having written several masterpieces of Western literature *and* reporting a habit of slouching on top of velour-covered benches seems truly fantastic.

The grander a person's actions, the more their trivia is imbued with interest. No one gives a damn what time you like to go to sleep if you clear drains for a living, interest will be universal if you wrote *Great Expectations* and like to be in bed by eleven. To be fair, if you clear drains *and* happen to kill your wife, then your face will no doubt feature in the papers. Clearing drains and polishing the car on Sunday mornings is the true promise of oblivion, a combination with none of the requisite discrepancy between stature and action.

Humanity can be said to divide itself into three biographical categories, listed in descending order of importance:

   [i] To be extraordinary and yet do ordinary things [sit on chairs, procreate]
   [ii] To be ordinary and yet do extraordinary things [murder, win the lottery]
   [iii] To be ordinary and do ordinary things [eat crisps, buy stamps].

Boswell was acting according to the premiss of the first category when he jotted down the following on Dr Johnson: 'While talking or even musing as he sat in his chair, he commonly held his head to one side towards his right shoulder, and shook it in a tremulous manner, moving his body backwards and forwards, and rubbing his left knee in the same direction, with the palm of his hand. In the intervals of articulating he made various sounds with his mouth, sometimes as if ruminating, or what is called chewing the cud, sometimes giving a half whistle, sometimes making his tongue play backwards from the roof of his mouth, as if clucking like a hen, and sometimes protruding it against his upper gums in front, as if pronouncing quickly under his breath, *too, too, too*: all this accompanied sometimes with a thoughtful look, but more frequently with a smile.'

And to return to his defence, Boswell knew precisely why he was telling us this: 'I remain firm and confident in my opinion that minute particulars are frequently characteristic, and always amusing, when they relate to a distinguished man.'

But I had learnt a slightly different lesson: that 'minute particulars' were just as likely to be of interest when they related to a more undistinguished woman. One such 'particular' lay in Isabel's way of looking at paintings in a museum. Responding to his three young children's boredom at being dragged around museums with no purpose beside the disinterested contemplation of beauty, Mr Rogers had long ago come up with an ingenious plan to keep their attention: he had told them to look as though they would be able to choose any two paintings to take home and decorate their room with. At once, every painting assumed the status of a potential possession, and was hence scrutinized with enthusiasm. Would Isabel take the Degas or the Delacroix? Why not the Ingres or Monet? A relic of this habit continued into adulthood, where Isabel always emerged from a museum with the names of two paintings she would want to take away with her.

Finding space for such trivia meant implicitly following Rousseau's approach to biography. His *Confessions* began with the famous declaration: 'I am like no one else in the world. I may be no better, but at least I am different.' In the space of 'at least I am . . .', substitute the words 'at least I look at paintings differently . . .' and you have something approaching a new biographical manifesto.

But this does not solve the original problem brought up by Lytton Strachey, which is one of space. Isabel faced it whenever she went on a trip, for her impulse was to take the wardrobe rather than narrow matters to five items which could comfortably fit in a bag. She did not trust her judgement, and so preferred to take three suitcases rather than be stranded on an unexpectedly cold day without a duffel coat or on a warm one without a bikini – even if the destination was unambiguous in its climatic disposition [Bali, Helsinki].

Much the same packing problem was present in fat biographies. At the risk of slightly boring the reader around the half-thousand page mark, they could at least be sure of having left nothing out. A lack of imagination could have been detected in this [the same could have been said of Isabel's packing], but then biographers may have little time for the imagination, a tool used by children, liars and novelists.

Yet however hard one tries, imagination [and hence choice] cannot wholly be avoided, because it is impossible to imagine a book exactly as long as the life it describes. Scales must be reduced. Much as Isabel eventually had to choose which of her six jumpers to pack for her trip to Athens, so too biographers would have to identify which one of the thirty-three anecdotes about Albert Camus and the waiter at the Deux Magots would best illustrate his character.

Choosing the wrong thing, or not enough things, could lead to an unwelcome accusation of caricature or premature foreclosure.

'You're always doing it to me,' said Isabel when we were planning a holiday to France, and I had joked we could rent a separate ferry for her luggage.

'I'm not caricaturing you, don't be ridiculous.'

'Yes, you are. You're making me into this neurotic traveller, who can't fly or pack a suitcase. I'm a real scatter-brained eccentric for you, aren't I? Someone who it's fun to tickle and who has strange parents, who can't get organized and everything.'

'No, you're not. It's just . . .'

'Well, it seems that way to me, so I'd appreciate it if you saw things in a slightly more complex light.'

'That's what I do.'

'I'm not going to argue, you don't, OK, so please shut up or change the subject.'

Isabel did have a packing problem. On a spectrum of difficult packers, she came firmly at the six-trunks-with-porter end. Nevertheless, mentioned on a bad day, it was clear why she flew off the handle at a churl who pointed it out, for it threatened to become a symbol of a host of attributes, a metaphor for her character. To be called a neurotic packer could suggest one had a problem not simply with suitcases, but with overlooking half the ingredients on the shopping list, leaving one's purse at the counter, forgetting the children at the bus stop and needing six goes at parking in a tight spot.

So if there were problems with saying too much, there were also dangers with saying too little – for the absence of information could engage the imagination in a host of devious ways. Had I not spared a few words to tell you how Isabel drove [skilfully, she could fit into a confined space in one go, impressive gear change from third to fourth], you too might have presumed her problem with packing implied a problem with parking.

If a range of characteristics is not outlined, a person may swiftly disappear behind a dominant trait or habit which seems to entail all others, he or she may become simply a divorcee, an anorexic, a fisherman or stutterer. If someone is captured by their inclination towards the music of Barry Manilow, reductive associations may arise, suggesting:

[i] The fan is a woman
[ii] A pair of white stilettos resides in her cupboard
[iii] Aristotle's *Nicomachean Ethics* is not on the bookshelf
[iv] She loves strawberry daiquiris shaded by miniature paper parasols.

To those familiar with British press and society, to describe someone by reference to a subscription to the *Guardian* might be a derogatory way of pointing to their:

[i] Envy of Rolls-Royce owners
[ii] Misunderstanding of macro-economics
[iii] Espousal of fashionable ecology
[iv] Grating sincerity.

Would any of this be true? Certainly not in this schematic form, which is what makes caricature a somewhat dangerous sport – manifest whenever an entire group decides they'd like to play and announces that people called Goldberg should be shot and worshippers of the Dalai Lama buried alive in concrete.

Yet the game has its charms. The less we know of someone, the more they strike us as distinct and knowable. The memorable, colourful characters of fiction are predominantly two-dimensional: we know far more about Proust's narrator than the Princess of Parma, and yet the Princess succeeds far better as a character. We remember her because she has just one trait; that she wishes to be thought the epitome of kindness, and all her behaviour and its consequences flow from this ridiculous injunction. The narrator on the other hand, who magisterially guides us through the range of perceptions and thoughts he has had over a lifetime, remains maddeningly opaque. The story of his life is too rich for us happily to imagine, too rich in contradiction and absence of causal connection.

The most sensitive, intelligent biographies may therefore often be judged the weakest, because they are unable to leave us [at the end of 600 pages] with a seductive, Princess-of-Parma-ish sense of who exactly the Duke of Windsor, Rainer Maria Rilke or Man Ray actually were.

Squeezed awkwardly between the biographical risks of over-inclusion and under-inclusion, a delicate path would have to be negotiated between saying too much in order to provide a clear picture, and too little to do anything but stereotype. Not a million miles separated crude caricature from a process which would have to go on if the Amazonian rainforests were not to be swallowed by the voracious appetites of the fattest biographies, or if one wished to describe one friend to another without making them miss the last train home.

One might have thought John Aubrey had a hard task fitting a life into a space smaller than a piece of toast, but nothing could compare with the breathtaking challenge of having to fit a life into a space smaller than a half-eaten cheese biscuit.

Quite aside from the burden of having no one to cuddle in the evening, such was the task befalling every author of a lonely hearts box. Isabel had a particular fondness for them, and had been sent a copy of the *New York Review of Books* by an American friend simply to look at the 'Personals' section, rumoured to be the best in the world.

INTELLECTUALLY CURIOUS BOSTON MAN, athletic and adventurous. I have a passion for stories: reading them, writing them, watching them, listening to yours and telling mine. A little dreamy but successful. Looking for a pretty woman with a playful spirit.

WIFE WANTED, I divorced a year ago and seek a normal level-headed woman interested in marriage and family. In my 30s, I'm tall, handsome and in great shape. I'm a millionaire, have many interests. I seek an attractive woman, 20s or 30s with a great body. Snobby types will prefer someone else. Please send picture.

GLAMOUROUS, CHEERFUL AND WARM-HEARTED WOMAN, accomplished but enjoys simple pleasures like music, reading (novels and histories), outdoor sports, travel and adventure. I am looking for a flexible man of integrity aged 37–47 who enjoys a thoughtful woman and is interested in love, marriage and family.

SAN FRANCISCO WARM WOMAN, professional writer and workshop leader. Enjoys travelling and still looking for love of her life.

PETITE, RADICAL, COSMOPOLITAN WOMAN wants a very sharp, liberated, funny, healthy guy, 45–58. I enjoy cultural activities, golf and liberal politics. Ithaca area.

'What a bunch of weirdos,' said Isabel, looking down one column. 'You wouldn't want to meet any of those in a dark alley. Check out the man who "wants" a wife. That's a bit brutal, like "wanting" a second-hand encyclopaedia. He has his eye on a "normal and level-headed" woman; he probably had the last one locked up because she wouldn't iron his shirts. You can just imagine their arguments in one of those American kitchens with food blenders and waste crushers. The wife would be a hyperpolite, well-bred, passive-aggressive type, who one day lost her cool with this monkey and lunged at him with a large kitchen knife after he'd said something like, "Is that a crumb on the kitchen table, darling?" And he's in "great shape". What does that mean, "great shape"? Maybe he'd arrive at a meeting with a health certificate. He just wants to shag someone.'

'Don't be unfair, Isabel. Perhaps he's all right, on the lonely side, but . . .'

'I can tell he's a psycho. Normal people don't write in with requests for women with "great bodies".'

'Well, maybe he missed out on women's lib.'

'Maybe that's why women have missed out on him and he's reduced to writing to the *New York Review of Books*, which it doesn't look like he reads much. Look at the way he adds, "Snobby types will prefer someone else." Horrible.'

Whatever his flaws, the handsome, great-shaped millionaire had adequately suggested a strong character within the cramped confines of a lonely hearts box. The sheer blandness of many of the personals indicated how hard it was to flesh oneself out for Romeo or Juliet. The women in the third and fourth boxes had been so desperate for material, they had resorted to an old stalwart of the genre – a declaration of a love of travel.

Love of travel? What did this hope to tell us about them? Doesn't everyone love travel if it's to a nice destination, the plane lands on time, the suitcases don't get lost and the exchange rate is favourable? But on the other hand, who doesn't hate travel when it involves a forced march across enemy territory, arrival coincides with a general strike, the *moules marinières* at the harbour restaurant breed food poisoning and the credit cards are stolen in a carpet stall at the crowded souk?

The differing success of lonely hearts indicates how some words and phrases denote character more effectively than others. Some are *characteristically weak*, others *characteristically strong*. If I told you Isabel cooked lasagne in a Pyrex dish, you would learn next to nothing about her other than that her lasagne was cooked in a Pyrex dish. The information would go no distance beyond the facts. However, the particular way she answered the telephone hinted at more fertile soil.

'Why do you always wait so long?' I asked her, when she was sitting beside her ringing receiver, and yet was waiting for a certain number of rings to pass before picking up.

'I don't know,' she answered. 'I wouldn't want them to think I was too keen, would I?'

To identify someone as an artificially slow phone answerer was to suggest a belief that popular people sat far from their phones [mixing Martinis in the kitchen], a fear of displaying too great an enthusiasm for others, social anxiety, a streak of coyness or a belief in the respect generated by keeping someone waiting.

Had it not been insulting, it could have been a suitably rich trait to put in a lonely hearts about Isabel [then again, to answer the fear of bitchiness, Boswell had written, 'I well remember that Dr Johnson maintained, that "If a man is to write *A Panegyric*, he may keep vices out of sight; but if he professes to write *A Life*, he must represent it as it was." '].

'How would you write your lonely hearts?' I asked Isabel.

'God, I hope I wouldn't ever have to.'

'Let's say you did.'

'I did think about it once. There was a period after Guy when I was very lonely.'

'So how would you do it?'

'Oh, don't.'

'Come on.'

'I don't know, something like, "Seeking bright, funny, good-looking guy for good chats, sex and Sunday afternoons. No men with commitment problems please. Send photo and penis size." '

'Seriously.'

'That is serious.'

'It isn't.'

'Because of the last bit?'

'Among other things.'

'It *is* important for lots of women, despite our comforting noises about performance not size. All right, why don't you try and write mine, for a challenge?'

'Fine, give me a moment.'

Isabel turned to a crossword, I picked up a pencil and faced the problem. It wasn't easy. There were obvious points to make: she was a woman, lived in London, was in her twenties. But how could one handily suggest a character? An image came to mind, of her eating a carrot at a bus stop near the supermarket, waiting for a bus home. What did this imply? I couldn't tell exactly, a certain impatience, frankness, perhaps humour. Should one mention her hobbies? Her attitudes to men? Her very reluctance to fill in such a box?

I wondered how the great biographers would have fared at this game. How would Proust scholars have completed one?

> **GAY WRITER PARIS AREA,** close to mother, asthmatic, keen on socialising, Vermeer, long sentences, Anatole France, chauffeurs, men if bearing women's names, Venice. Problems with travel, being brief, getting to bed without a kiss. At work on a big project. Send photo.

Long acquaintance with Isabel didn't help me come up with anything much more inspired:

> **YOUNG, BEAUTIFUL BUT DOESN'T USUALLY THINK SO WOMAN,** not used to filling in such boxes and thinks people who do should make friends with their neighbours, eats carrots at bus-stops, tired of having maso-chistic relationships, loves gardening, good driver, bad at programming videos, prefers margarine to butter, flirts with the idea of throwing in her job every Monday (dull job, doesn't wish to be judged on it, so won't mention it, avoids the subject at parties, and suspicious of those who don't), quite tidy apart from the kitchen. Hates gherkins, gangster films, Milton, the Rolling Stones, putting out the rubbish bins on a Tuesday, too many bones in fish, getting to bed past midnight during the week. Sometimes loves her parents, swimming, gossip, picking something big out of her nose, Bob Dylan, orange juice, Václav Havel, reading in the bath.

233

'Oh, that's awful,' said Isabel, 'you wouldn't get any idea of who this person was. She sounds idiotic.'

'Does she?'

'What's more, it's far too long, I could never afford to put that in the paper, it's almost treble the length of any other. And you should ask them to send a photo, I'm still choosy in that area. If you're going to go for a stranger, might as well get a pretty one.'

Evidence of the correct moment to call a halt to the biography eventually came from another quarter. I had been riding on the Underground, eavesdropping on a conversation between two old ladies who seemed to be searching for a birthday present for one of their husbands.

'What are you going to get Larry, then?'

'Don't know, I haven't got any ideas this year.'

'Why don't you get him a book?'

'No, dear, he's already got one of those.'

'How about a bottle of whisky, then?'

'I know exactly what he'll say to that.'

'What will he say?'

'He'll say, "I may be blind and deaf, but you don't need to make me drunk as well." '

To know exactly how a person would respond to something, without them needing to be there to prove it. Was this not the perfect symbol of knowing someone sufficiently well? Though sometimes judged a depressing feature of marathon marriages or the prelude to affairs and enrolment on pottery courses, great wisdom lay in the rare skill of correctly finishing another's sentences.

Could I claim such a thing with Isabel?

I imagined a rigorous examination:

IN SEARCH OF AN ENDING

In the time allotted, circle the correct ends of the following Isabel-sentences and dialogues:

1. Isabel: 'It's great you can come for dinner at my place on Friday, oh, and please remember to . . .'
   a) Bring a bottle of white wine
   b) Come at around eight
   c) Ring the bell twice
   d) Eat beforehand as the food will be foul
   e) Park on a meter

2. 'You're very beautiful.'
   a) I know
   b) Thanks
   c) Is someone paying you for this?
   d) You are too

3. 'Aren't men trustworthy?'
   a) No
   b) Yes
   c) I prefer women
   d) And they promise not to come in your mouth

4. 'Your parents are really great people.'
   a) Nice of you to say so
   b) I'd think so too if they weren't my parents
   c) I want to spend more time with them
   d) I prefer yours

5. 'I'm feeling a bit down today.'
   a) Don't worry, all will be well
   b) So am I

c) At least the weather's sunny

d) Think that it's worse than it is and it'll get better

For a while, I thought that I had scored an A grade:

1. (d)
2. (c)
3. (d)
4. (b)
5. (d)

XI

AFTERWORD

Biographers rarely have the courage to conclude their works with a confession of partial puzzlement as to the behaviour of their subjects, a confession that these great figures have symbolically rejected them. It would not look good to throw one's hands in the air after eight hundred pages on Dostoyevski and announce one had never really grasped what drove a man to write a book as strange as *The Brothers Karamazov* or arrive at the conclusion of Kennedy's life and confess bewilderment as to the rationale behind the Bay of Pigs. If there are gaps in knowledge or understanding, the biographer moves swiftly on: not knowing the colour of Napoleon's horse, he will at once tell us what he does know, namely the chestnut sheen of his donkey Ferdinand.

'What's wrong?' I asked Isabel.

'Nothing.'

'So why are you making that face?'

'If you want someone with another face, go and find one.'

'I'm not referring to the face, I'm referring to the expression on the face,' I outlined with greater precision.

'*I'm not referring to the face, I'm referring to the expression on the face,*' repeated Isabel in the accent of an asphyxiated academic.

'Why are you in that mood?'

'I'm not in a mood. This is the way I am.'

'Something's wrong.'

'Nothing is wrong.'

'So you're always like this?'

'Yes.'

'And I'm dreaming?'

'Yes.'

There were obvious but irredeemable explanations. There was someone else she would rather have been sharing a mood with this Sunday afternoon, she had grown bored of humanity, her star sign was in the wrong phase, something chemical had gone wrong. And then there were reasons closer to home. Somewhere along the path from morning sunshine to afternoon gloom, I had said something offensive and, moreover, in the careless way hikers murder colonies of ants with their walking shoes and then consider themselves blameless people fit to enter churches and receive honours.

My mind raced back to a history of the morning. We had arisen, gone to buy papers, Isabel had read each section first and reacted calmly to my demands that she hand over a favoured supplement. She had been the first to use the bathroom, I hadn't left a mess either there or in the kitchen, I had made the bed and remembered to arrange the cushions in the right order [she wanted the larger paisley ones at the back, and the smaller blue ones at the front], she had been on the phone to three people who had elicited several apparently sincere ' "That's so funny"'s'.

'You only ever think of yourself,' snapped Isabel by way of explanation for not being in any sort of mood.

My immediate temptation, comparable to a man pulling out his gun when fired at across a saloon bar, was to reply that only that morning the fate of eight hundred and forty million people had been my concern, via an article on social changes in the Indian subcontinent. Having missed out on the foreign news, Isabel might have been impressed by this curiosity, or by a long daydream during her phone calls as to what happened to leaves when they fell off trees in autumn, as they were doing in profusion outside Isabel's living-room window, gathering in a damp carpet along the pavements and matting car windscreens. Did they dissolve or were they primarily swept away by the old man employed by the local authority to make stabs at the profusion of litter with a green plastic broom [but whose real interest lay in sitting on a low stone wall a couple of houses down smoking cigarettes]? No conclusions were reached, and little achieved other than a series of *faux-profond* reflections on the role of nature in cities and the ability of the earth to recycle its own waste.

'I don't always think of myself,' I therefore answered at once.

'Why be so sure?'

I wasn't sure, I was simply being shot at.

'I think of you sometimes,' I said sentimentally.

'Oh, come off it,' she replied, in a tone I imagined to have been that of the sports teacher when falsely told it was Isabel's time of the month.

'Why can you never guess what someone means? Why do I have to spell everything out?' continued Isabel.

'Perhaps because I'm not too bright?'

'Don't try and be cute. It makes me sick.'

'So what is it?'

'It's nothing big, that's why I said it was nothing when you asked, I'm just frustrated.'

Despite my willingness to search the past for the offensive detonator, I need not have strained memory further back than the perimeters of the previous ten minutes.

'Do you want to go for a walk?' Isabel had asked me, in her last question addressed in a language we both professed to speak.

'No,' I had replied and cleared an obstruction in my throat.

There had been a silence, the birds had continued to chirrup in the garden, an Underground train had been heard distantly shuddering into Hammersmith station, a certain number of leaves [perhaps ten to twenty in the five trees surrounding the house] must have drifted to the ground, shaken loose from their shrivelled moorings by the whips of a damp westerly wind.

And then? And then I had said nothing, I had foolishly presumed this to be the end of the particular clause of the conversation, a conversation I had hoped we might take up again with similar geniality and good humour were something as pressing to drift through either of our consciousnesses in minutes or weeks to come.

I had made a mistake. Like a blundering policeman walking past the cadaver of a suspect, I had overlooked a part of Isabel's psychology which I should have recognized had I derived the moral of the way she had ended her relationship with Andrew O'Sullivan or indeed her behaviour with a cockroach stranded in her water glass in the Portuguese restaurant.

Isabel had not asked if I wanted to go for a walk, she had requested I do so.

How had this been fitted into a sentence as compact as, 'Do you want to go for a walk?'?

By the operation whereby an enquiry into another's intent could stand for a declaration of her own.

Isabel often spoke in condensed prose which needed to be unfolded and inflated like a balloon before its meaning emerged. She felt a curious reserve about asking for things directly [curious because she preferred a comparatively more demanding argument], and hence performed oblique requests concealed beneath a range of questions, general reflections on the topic at hand [i.e. 'Walking is a fine pastime'] and enquiries with a third person about what she wished to ask the second [i.e. 'Sarah, are you going to go for a walk this afternoon?'].

The following weekend, my workload meant I had to cancel an arrangement to meet her.

'So I won't see you all weekend,' she said in answer to my announcement that I wouldn't be able to make it for lunch on Saturday.

Had it not been for the previous lesson, I might have ignored the condensed request for me to say, 'Yes of course you will. We can try and fix something else at once,' and might simply have answered, 'All right, then' – in the idiotic manner of a man who takes matters at face value when his beloved declares a desire to sleep with another.

'You want to sleep with Malcolm?' I asked with surprise when Isabel suggested the plan. 'He's not that good looking.'

'Doesn't matter. I want to anyway. It doesn't look like his wife really satisfies him.'

'I think she probably does,' I replied thoughtfully, an image briefly springing to mind.

Isabel sighed in the manner I had learnt to recognize as

a symbol for an impasse in human understanding. Again I had not translated the message. She had only wanted to elicit a jealous declaration of my desire, not suggest a target for infidelity.

In short, there was much to interpret, what Isabel said was not necessarily what she felt or believed. She might say 'sorry' when one had blithely stepped on her shoes, she might say, 'Isn't the table crowded?' when the man beside her was digging his elbow into her ribs. If things were not decoded, they could build a head of steam and erupt unexpectedly. I had been whistling a tune in Isabel's presence [a rendition of 'Ave Maria'] for ten minutes when she slammed the book she was reading and exclaimed,

'Can't you stop that bloody, goddamn, silly . . .'

Her fury was such, the torrent of words seemed stuck in her palate.

'Yes?' I enquired.

'The whistling.'

'I'm sorry. Did it bother you?'

Spending time with Isabel meant encountering a succession of hidden tripwires, wires of tension strung across issues I had taken to be beyond contention, and hence strayed into ignorant of the reactions they could elicit. How might one have predicted a wire being strung across some glasses and a dishwasher?

I saw dishwashers as machines which had freed mankind from the chore of scrubbing cutlery and crockery, machines which could joyfully and guiltlessly be used. But the same tool had a quite different meaning for Isabel. She had one in her flat, bolted to the floor by the previous occupant, and felt ambivalent about ownership, fearing the laziness it implied, its consumption of electricity and its pollution of rural rivers and lakes. The machine was in regular, but psychologically complicated, use.

Each time I had a drink in the kitchen, I had the habit of using a new glass rather than wash out an old one, then placed it on the upper level of the dishwasher. I had been doing this for some months [long enough for the leaves to shake loose off the trees] when Isabel said to me, 'You haven't understood any of the hints I've been leaving, have you?'

'About what?'

'The glasses, it's maddening the way you always take a new glass when you get a drink. It's such a waste.'

'But you'll use the machine anyway, so what's the problem?'

'It seems unnecessary.'

'What does it matter as the machine will soon be on?'

'There's no reason. Just don't insist, it's my hang-up, I'm sorry, but then again, it's my kitchen as well.'

There were areas of Isabel's mental functioning I had to give up on understanding in an empathetic sense, settling instead for the sad decision to respect our differences. Why sad? Because when one smugly speaks of respecting the differences, one speaks of respecting things one cannot understand – and therefore, if one is to be honest, cannot logically respect, for how can one respect the value of something which one fails to fathom?

And aside from such psychological incomprehension, there were a medley of factual things I never learnt: what Isabel wrote in her diary, where her nickname 'Skate' [used by Chris] had come from, why she was in a bad mood every Tuesday, what her sister's boyfriend was called, where in Arizona her uncle came from, how her Magimix had broken, what she thought of *Jane Eyre*, whether she had eaten cod roe, what she thought of people who used thesauruses, when she had stopped writing with a fountain pen, whether she had had sex on a train, if she had been attracted to Eastern religions during adolescence, what she thought of prostitution, what domestic animal she preferred, who her favourite primary school teacher was, whether she thought service should be included in restaurant bills, how she judged foldaway umbrellas, what her favourite car was, whether she had been to Africa, what it was she most respected about her mother and a few matters besides.

The ignorance was partly the result of an unfortunate but perhaps natural slope of the learning curve. When first meeting someone, the amount of information we seek and derive from them is at its peak. Over lunches and dinners, we survey the topics of family, colleagues, job, childhood, philosophy of life and romantic history. But once acquaintance is more advanced, an unhappy development sets in: far from intimacy being a catalyst for longer conversations on ever more profound topics, it initiates an opposite scenario. Lunch time with a silver jubilee couple is enlivened with remarks on the texture of the lamb, the inclinations of the weather, the state of the tulips in the vase on the sideboard, and the question of whether to change the sheets today or tomorrow – this in a couple whose start in life might have been promising, who would have asked each other incisive questions about painting, books, music and the role of a welfare state.

What could account for the change? The paradox that the more one has the chance to talk to someone, the less one in fact will. Presuming there to be a limitless expanse of time in which to discuss matters, there seems no point heading for the great topics until the apple crumble and dripping tap have been covered. By virtue of sharing a life, the upheaval of a grand enquiry may be avoided. Knowledge implies a degree of possession, and the fact that others are within grasp eschews a need to gain a sense of them through something as comparatively cumbersome as their view of Kierkegaard's theory of irony.

Moreover, the longer one has known someone, the more shameful it is not to have grasped things about them. There is only a finite period before ignoring the name of their dog, their child, father or job becomes an offensive reminder of a foreignness which now seems out of context.

But though I felt that there were gaps in my understanding of Isabel, I never suspected their dimension.

Despite protestations to the contrary, despite cherished beliefs as to the wisdom of learning and the virtue of empathy, despite my good faith in acting on Divina's suggestion that I develop more interest in people around me, Isabel woke up one morning and got bored of being understood.

I had asked her why she never wore her hair up, she said nothing for a minute, then provided me with a concluding and conclusive answer:

'I don't know why I don't wear my hair up. Perhaps I should, perhaps it would be better, but I don't, and I don't know why, much as I don't have any clue why I cut cheese up into cubes, what the last bit of my postcode is, where I bought this wooden comb, exactly how long my journey to work is, what kind of batteries my alarm clock takes and why I can't read on the loo. There's lots about me I don't understand, and quite frankly, don't want to understand. I don't know why everything should be so clear for you, as though people's lives could be summed up like in those daft biographies. I'm full of weird things that make no sense to me and nor should they to you. I know I should read more, but TV is easier. I should love people who are nice to me, but grumps are more of a challenge. I want to be compassionate, but I don't like people enough. I want to be happy, but I know happiness makes you stupid. I want to use public transport, but a car is more convenient. I want to have babies, but I'm frightened of becoming my mother. I know I should do something worthwhile with my life, but it's past eight fifteen and I'd be late for the train.'

There was a pause.

'And I think we should stop seeing one another as well.'

There was a longer pause. The sink burped in the kitchen next door.

'But unfortunately I can't be sure about that either. I don't know any more, all right? God, I'm going to be so late. Where's my coat?'

Humbled, I fell silent.

INDEX

Abba, 101–2
Alexandria, 5
Algarve, 101–2
Amateur Gardeners'
    Association, 165, 166–7
anchovy paste, 82
Aristotle 31, 227
Armatrading, Joan, 99
Ascendance-Submission
    study, 209–10
astrology, 183
Athens, 142–3, 146, 148,
    199, 225
aubergines, 78
Aubrey, John, 183, 218–20,
    229
Auden, W. H., 8, 61
Aulak, Mr, 189
Austen, Jane, 34
Austerlitz, 9
Australian anteaters, 32

Balzac, Honoré de, 8
banal advice, 139

Barbican, London, 49, 51–4,
    55–6
bathroom, activities in, 171–2
Beckett, Samuel, 39, 91
Belgian confectionery, 77
Bellow, Saul, 123
Belsize Park, 28
Berlin, 105
Bertolucci, Bernardo, 150
Bertrand, 119–21
Big Ben, 147–8
biography:
    categories, 223
    of dead, 155–6
    details given in, 41, 225–7,
        228
    discrepancies between
        author and subject,
        168–9
    eating habits in, 77–8, 88
    ending, 128, 218, 233–7
    family research, 46, 48–51
    ghost-written, 25
    impulse to write, 43

247

lack of understanding of
  subject, 237–46
length, 218–20, 225–7,
  228–9
men writing about women,
  163–74
private life in, 106–41
psychology in, 163–74
relationship between
  author and subject,
  43–4
writing, 3–10, 18–22, 23–5
birthday present, 233–4
blanket, teddy bear's, 69
Blondie, 102–3
blushing, 119–20
Boswell, James, 25, 26, 41,
  43, 79, 218, 219, 222,
  223–4, 232
Brawne, Fanny, 222
bricklayer, desire to be, 156
Brighton, 150
Brint, Charlie, 138–9
Brithton, Mrs, 15
Brontë, Emily, 138
Brookner, Anita, 95, 96
bubble baths, 98–9

Caesar, Julius, 8, 36, 79, 81,
  193
Cambridge, University of, 12
camomile tea, 97

Camus, Albert, 39, 225–6
Canadian immigration,
  187–8
car park tickets, losing, 52, 54
caricatures, 226–8
Carter, Jimmy, 32
Cattell, Dr R. B., 201–5,
  207
Catten, Michael, 134–5
chatlines, 204
child-raising, rules for, 70–74
chocolate raisins, 78, 134
Chris, 89–90, 101–2, 207,
  243
Churchill, Winston Spencer,
  8, 106
Cinderella, 121
Cioran, E. M. 7
Clapham, 18, 19, 20
cockroach, in water glass,
  211, 240
coffee drinking, 20, 97–8
Cohen, Leonard, 103
Coleridge, Samuel Taylor, 43,
  78
communication, 96
Confessions (Rousseau),
  224–5
Continental Selection, 75–7,
  79
Copernican revolution, 10
Corday, Charlotte, 222

Cornwall, 119
cuddles, 12, 229
curriculum vitae, 9

Dave, 165
death, convenience to
    biographers, 155–6
Deauville, 105
dental care, 33, 37, 116–17
diaries, 176–7, 243
directory enquiries, 22
dishwashers, 242–3
Divina, 3, 183, 245
Dordogne, 119–20
Dorset, 183, 191
Dostoyevski, Fedor
    Mikhailovich, 237
Doudan, Ximenes, 79, 81
Dowler, Yvonne, 129
dreams, 17, 36, 175, 180–82
Duras, Marguerite, 158
Dylan, Bob, 103–4

Eccel, Mrs Maria, 205
Edwardian stockings, 174
Einstein, Albert, 106
Elf, 119
Elizabeth II, 150
Ellmann, Mary, 22–3
Ellmann, Richard, 21, 22–3,
    49, 50, 205
Emma (Austen), 34–5

empathy, 103, 142
Enfield, 104

facial routines, 172–4
family trees, 46–51, 57–8, 67
Fate, 214–17
father fixation, 62, 98, 133,
    137, 192
favouritism, 72
Finchley, 48
fire-screens, 58
flying, phobia for, 142–3
Fontainebleau, 150
Fontana, Adam, 181
food consumption, 77–9,
    81–4
Footsteps (Holmes), 44
forgery, 189
Forster, E. M., 78
Fort William, 100
France, 226
Freud, Sigmund, 7, 43–4
Freud Museum, Vienna, 149
friendship, after sex, 129,
    133–4

Gabriella see Graziella
Gallic passions, 12
gardens, 150–51
geographical deficiency,
    143–7
Gibson, Julie, 208

ginger biscuits, 98
Ginsberg, Alan, 48
Giverny, 151
Gladstone, William Ewart, 25
Glasgow, 100
Goethe, Johann Wolfgang
    von, 8
Gorbachev, Mikhail, 32
grandfather, recounting life
    story, 5–6
graphology, 183–91
Graziella, 108–9
Greece, 142, 145
Gripper, 75, 76, 80
Grosvenor family, 46
Guardian readers, 227
Guy, 128, 130–32, 133–4,
    232

Hammersmith, 35, 37, 39,
    103
Hammersmith Grove, 37
hands, taking notice of, 151
Hardy, Thomas, 108
Hausmann, Baron, 78
Havel, Vaclav, 140
Haworth Parsonage, 138
heaven, 15
Heisenberg's Uncertainty
    principle, 24, 25, 26–7
Hendrix, Jimi, 28
Henry IV, 95

Henry VIII, 199
Heskett, Mr, 139–40
Hippocrates, 182
Hitler, Adolf, 8
Hobbes, Thomas, 183
Holly, Buddy, 8
Holmes, Richard, 43, 44
Hotel du Lac (Brookner), 95
House of Bernarda Alba
    (Lorca), 51
HP sauce, 82
Hudson, Mrs, 16
humour, sense of, 186–8
humours, 182–3
Hunter, Mrs, 176–7

illness, 87–8
imagination, 169–71, 225
incest, 114
insults, self-inflicted, 1–2
interpretation, personal,
    149–56
intimacy, 108–12, 244
Invalides, Paris, 8

Jacques, 12, 58, 119
James, Henry, 174
Janet, 101
Jencks, Tim, 138–9
Jenkins, Tim, 181
Jerome, 179
Jesus Christ, 8

John, Elton, 1–2
Johnson, Dr Samuel, 2, 9–10, 25, 26, 41, 43, 61, 79, 169, 205, 218, 223–4, 232
jokes, 186–7, 188
Joyce, James, 21, 22–3, 49, 50, 95–6, 205
Jung, Carl Gustav, 95

Keats, George, 220, 222
Keats, John, 220–22
Kennedy, John F., 237
ketchup, 83
Kierkegaard, Søren Aabye, 245
Kingston, 39, 58
Kingston Secondary School, 137
kissing:
    attempt at, 44
    first, 114–15

lamps, flower-shaped, 58
Larkin, Philip, 107–8
Laura, 101, 102, 157, 208
Lausanne, 91
Leeds, 47
Leman, Lac, 92
Lenin, Nikolai, 222
lesbianism, 114
Lincoln, Abraham, 78

literary interpretation, 148–50
London:
    finding way round, 147
    views of living in, 40–41
London University, 39, 105, 123
lonely hearts columns, 229–33
loo tests, 159–60
Lorca, Federico Garcia, 51
Los Angeles, 28
louche males, 29
Loughborough, Lady Clarissa, 135–6
Louis XVI, 155
lovers, choosing, 122–3, 125–6, 127–8, 133
Luke, 14

McDonald, Jane, 208
Madingley, 12
make-up, secrets of, 172–4
Manhattan, 98–9
Manilow, Barry, 227
Marat, Jean Paul, 222
Marie-Claire, 20
Marie-Laure, 119
Marsden, Grace, 101, 158
Marshall, William, 183
mascara, 174
Mediterranean, 5

Medusa (Géricault), 207–8
memory, 89–105
men, differences between
    women and, 163–74
Milan, 105
milkman, desire to be, 156
mini skirts, 102
moisturizers, 173
Monet, Claude, 151
Monroe, Marilyn, 8
Montesquieu, Charles de
    Secondat, Baron de,
    222
Mountbatten, Lord Louis,
    128
Mozart, Wolfgang Amadeus,
    3, 104–5, 155
music, memories evoked by,
    99–105

Nabokov, Vladimir, 95
Napoleon Bonaparte, 8–9,
    61, 237
Natalie, 36
Nelson, Admiral Lord, 133
New York, 98–9, 147
New York Review of Books,
    229–31
Nietzsche, Friedrich Wilhelm,
    79, 93–4
Nightingale, Florence, 95
Norfolk, 5

North Africa campaign, 5
Notting Hill, 102
novels, 33–4

Oedipal fixation, 98
Oedipus, 132–3
Olympic Airways, 199–200
O'Sullivan, Andrew, 123–30,
    145, 240
Owen, Wilfred, 155

Painter, George 21–2
Painter, Joan, 21–2
paintings, method of looking
    at, 224
palmistry, 213–16
Palmistry Revealed, 214
pantomime, 138–9
Paperweight, 32, 156, 157
Paris, 22, 104–5, 147
party, 28–35
pasta, 84, 231
Pepys, Samuel, 61
'Personals' ads, 229–31
Perugino, 19
phobia, of flying, 142–3
Picasso, Pablo, 19, 158–9
pizzas, 84
plane crashes, 142–3
Plath, Sylvia, 155
Poland, 47
Poppy, 14

Portugal, 101–2, 190, 211, 240
Proust, Marcel, 21–2, 79, 89, 91, 194–8, 200
Proustian moments, 89, 91, 93, 97, 98–105
psychoanalysis, 25
psychology, 29, 86, 125, 175–217
Punjab, 48

Queen Mary College, London, 39
questionnaires, 193–203, 209–10

radio, 157
radishes, 81
'rational', interpretations of, 151–2
Reitzman, great-grandfather, 48
Rembrandt, 150
Rogers, Christopher (father):
  behaviour in restaurants, 55
  birth of child, 11
  dental work, 116
  family background, 47–9, 62
  interest in technology, 53, 54

  with Isabel as child, 14, 15
  Isabel's opinion of, 40, 47, 54–5, 56, 60–61, 62, 97–8
  lack of jealousy, 59
  losing car park tickets, 52, 54
  making friends with everyone, 55
  marriage, 13
  mildness, 58
  move to London, 13
  plan for looking at paintings, 224
  seeing Isabel at Barbican, 51–6
  sex with Lavinia Rogers, 11–13
  singing, 97
  spelling pedantry, 192
  work, 11, 13, 20
Rogers, Isabel Jane:
  aggression, 36–7, 210–13
  anxieties, 85
  appearance, 31
  arrival of siblings, 13
  behaviour alone, 24
  beliefs at fifteen, 157–8
  biographer's meeting with, 28–35
  birth, 11
  books, 13–14

character, 32, 35, 36–7

childhood, 13–19, 90–91, 92, 97, 153–5, 185

childhood ambitions, 156–7

conception, 11–13

confidence, 159–60

cynicism, 208

dental work on, 116–17

dislike of sports, 38–9

disregard for convention, 204–5

drinks preferred, 17–18, 20, 23

driving ability, 227

eating habits, 77–8, 80\84, 85–7

education 15, 39, 71–2, 98

family background, 46–9, 57–9, 67–74

finding diving impossible, 38

first impressions of, 28–9, 32

first kiss, 114

at grandparents', 13

half-losing virginity, 119–21

handwriting, 183–4, 185–6, 188–91

inability to distinguish right from left, 38

inventing language with sister, 16

inviting biographer home, 26

jealousy, 209

jobs, 32, 39–40

losing virginity, 121

love of ironing, 68, 70

loving baths, 153

lying, 208–9

meeting parents at Barbican 51–6

mother's derision for, 70

nicknamed Skate, 243

new hairstyle, 163–5

not forgiving mother for childhood incident, 69

opinion of father, 40, 54–5, 56, 60–61, 62, 97–8

opinion of mother, 37–8, 40, 54–5, 59–60

packing problems, 225, 226–7

playing with sister, 16

problems with numbers, 192

Proustian memories, 90–91, 92, 96–105

reaction to flattery, 207–8

rejecting kiss, 44–5

relationship with sister, 40, 64–6, 72

religious ideas, 216
resemblance to older
    family members, 11
respect for louche males,
    29
scorning younger selves,
    157–8, 208
self-consciousness, 36,
    189, 190–91
sense of humour, 186–8
shifts in character, 159–62
shyness, 159–60
sister's opinion of, 62
sleeping habits, 113–14
spelling problems, 191–2
stomach flu, 87
superstitions, 216–17
sweet purchases, 16–17
toys, 14
unanswered questions,
    245–6
unrequited loves, 137–41
use of language, 62–3
vulnerability, 70
warm personality, 184–5
Rogers, Janice (aunt), 48–9
Rogers, Lavinia (mother):
    affairs, 59, 124
    attitude to children, 56
    birth of children, 11,
        15–16
    collections and hobbies, 58

comments on clothes, 53,
    59–60, 102, 153
complaints about husband,
    73–4
confiding in children,
    73–4
considering Isabel
    stubborn, 152–3
dental work, 116
education, 12
emotional balance, 56–8
family background, 47, 48,
    57–8
fighting spirit, 103
harshness, 185–6
with Isabel as child, 14, 15
Isabel's opinion of, 37–8,
    40, 54–5, 59–60
language studies, 13
liberal attitude to sex, 72
love for French artist, 11,
    12
marriage, 13
move to London, 13
pretensions, 60
provoking guilty feelings
    55–6, 72–3
reaction to others'
    emotional sensitivities,
    57
resentment at having
    Isabel, 185–6

seeing Isabel at Barbican,
  51–6
self-criticism, 73
sex with CR, 11–13
signature, 189–90
type of men preferred,
  57–8
Rogers, Lucy Emma (sister):
birth, 15–16
chatting in bed, 114
dental work, 116
inventing language with
  Isabel, 16
lack of confidence, 64–5
masochism, 65
meeting sister's biographer,
  63–6
neurotic traits, 64
opinion of sister, 62
ordering in restaurants, 55
relationship with brother,
  72
relationship with sister, 40,
  64–6
studying fashion, 64
taking over sister's
  boyfriends, 65
Rogers, Paul David (brother),
  40, 66, 71, 72, 151, 208
Rogers, Tony (uncle), 48
Rommel, Erwin, 5
Rosenzweig, Dr, 212–13

Ross, Dr, 116–17
Rousseau, Jean-Jacques, 79,
  225
Russell, Bertrand, 106
Russia 8

Sadat, Mohammed Anwar
  el-, 32
Sade, Marquis de, 79
St Colman's College, 49, 50
Salome, Lou Andreas, 93, 94
sandwich problem, 64
sandwiches, 40, 42
Sarah, 99, 101, 138, 147,
  157, 179, 209
Sartre, Jean-Paul, 79
secrets, 114–22, 175–6
servants, 203, 205
sex:
continuing friendship after,
  129, 133–4
embarrassment of, 119–20
first experience, 114
liberal attitude to, 72
manual of, 121
substitutes for, 59
as symbol of intimacy,
  108–10
tastes in, 9
Shakespeare, William, 32,
  221, 222
shark, 170

Shelley, Percy Bysshe, 43
Shifton, Valerie, 138
shipwreck, usefulness in, 124
shyness, combating with loo
     test, 159–60
signatures, 188–91
Singh, Mr, 16
sitting positions, 220–24
Smith, Adam, 169, 171
smutty, silly stuff, 114
Smyth, Ethel, 176
snogging, 114–15, 117
snoring, over telephone, 74
snot, 111–12
snuggles, 108
'so what' attitude, 161
Sontag, Susan, 110–11
Sotiris, 161
spelling mistakes, 191–2
spotted dick, 78
Staley, Professor Thomas, 205
Stalin, Joseph, 8, 32, 106
staplers, 48
steam engines, 8
Stendhal (Marie Henri Beyle),
     8, 12
Stobbs, Louise, 208
Stokes, Richard, MD, 218,
     220
Strachey, Lytton, 218, 219,
     225
supermarket trolley test, 82

superstitions, 216–17
suspense, 120–21
swimming, 37–8, 40, 42, 92
Swiss citizens, 168, 171
Swiss confectionery, 77

Tammy, 101
teapot collection, 58
teeth cleaning, 33
telephone answering, 231
telephone operator, 22
television, 75–6, 171, 193,
     194
   child's interest in, 15
   watching during meals, 83
Tennyson, Alfred, Lord, 25
Theory of Moral Sentiments
     (Smith), 169
toast, 218–19
toenails, 109–10, 141
Tokyo, 28
Tolstoy, Leo, 56, 95, 149–50
toothpaste, 144
tourists, 37
Tractatus (Wittgenstein), 4
travel, attitudes to, 86,
     230–31
Traviata, La (Verdi), 8
Trevor (milkman), 156
Troilus and Cressida
     (Shakespeare), 120–21
Tucson, Arizona, 48

Turgenev, Ivan, 150

Ulysses (Joyce), 95–6
understanding someone else,
    difficulties of, 237–46
University College Hospital,
    London, 11
unrequited love, 137–41

Vauvenargues, Luc de
    Clapiers, Marquis de,
    106–7
Verdi, Giuseppe, 8, 61, 116
Vienna, 149
Vikings, 16
violence, 131–2
voyeurism, 9, 24

Wales, 19, 48
walnut oil, 82
Warhol, Andy, 6, 8

watch, as symbol, 124–5
Waterloo, 9
Welch, Sally, 102
Welles, Orson, 36
*What You Can Tell About
    Someone From Their
    Handwriting*, 183–91,
    192
Whitford, Frank, 147–8
whole hog, going, 119, 121
Wilson, Stuart, 103–4, 121
Wisden, 39
Wittgenstein, Ludwig, 3–4
Wolfgang, 102
women, differences between
    men and, 163–74
Woolf, Virginia, 25, 174, 176
woolly mammoth ribs, 120

Youngman, Flo, 205–6

Zurich Delights, 79